Crushing It

Lucky in Love Book 1

Jen Desmarais

Renaissance
Diverse Canadian Voices

PressesRenaissancePress.ca

First edition 2023

Cover art by pinkpiggy93/flowerraven93.
Cover design by Diana Galván Mejía and Nathan Frechette.
Interior design by Éric Desmarais.
Edited by Mackenzie Emberley, Joel Balkovec, Allyson Throp, Anne Coderre and Molly Dessen.

Legal deposit, Library and Archives Canada, September 2023.

Paperback ISBN: 978-1-990086-44-1
Ebook ISBN: 978-1-990086-56-4

Renaissance Press - pressesrenaissancepress.ca

Renaissance acknowledges that it is hosted on the traditional, unceded land of the Anishinabek, the Kanien'kehá:ka, and the Omàmìwininìwag. We acknowledge the privileges and comforts that colonialism has granted us and vow to use this privilege to disrupt colonialism by lifting up the voices of marginalized humans who continue to suffer the effects of ongoing colonialism.

Find our cover artist :
Instagram: http://www.instagram.com/flowerraven93
Tumblr: https://pinkpiggy93.tumblr.com
Patreon: http://www.Patreon.com/pinkpiggy93

*Printed in Gatineau at
Imprimerie Gauvin
Depuis 1892
gauvin.ca*

For Adrien:
I wrote this book one-handed on my phone while nursing you to sleep. This book would not be what it is without you, even if you weren't aware of it at the time.

Note To Reader

I would like to note that although this is a low-stakes romance, there are still some heavy themes, such as alcohol, sickness, and bullying. There are also sexual situations (kissing, grinding over clothing) between consenting and enthusiastic minors.

Please note that there is no homophobia in this book. This was not the reality in 2003 (or today), but it is not my story to tell. My story is about a boy, who just happens to be gay.

Prologue - A Favour

♥

Carter focussed on his student as she threw her first knife at the target. It landed in the snow. "What do you think you did wrong that time?" he asked.

The tall blonde huffed, her breath clouding the air in front of her face. "I know, I know. I flicked my wrist."

"Good. Next." He watched her pick up the second knife and focus on the target, her brow furrowed.

She made the same mistake.

Carter wrinkled his cold-reddened nose. "Alright. What's wrong?"

"Nothing's wrong," she replied quickly.

"Kennedy, we've known each other for almost four years. Give me some credit." Carter gave her a *look;* one he'd seen on her face when he hadn't been concentrating properly on her math tutoring. "You made the same mistake twice in a row."

Kennedy scuffed the toe of her boot in a pile of snow like a child who had been caught with one hand in the cookie jar.

"What did you do?" he asked, smirking. "How do you need me to cover for you?"

"Now, see, you are jumping to entirely the wrong conclusion," Kennedy said, shaking a finger at him.

Carter shrugged. "Then tell me what's distracting you. You need a clear mind to throw knives properly."

Kennedy picked up her third knife and played with the handle. "You know Door Tech's camp you're going to for March Break?"

"Yeah, course. I'm super excited about it! A little nervous, to be honest, but mostly excited." Carter scratched his fingers through his brown curls. "What about it?"

"Well, Veronica sponsored someone else as well."

"Yeah, a girl in my math class. Her name's Elyse." Carter frowned. "What about her?"

"No, someone else. My brother."

Carter's eyes widened. "Really? He's coming here?"

"Yeah." Kennedy took a deep breath and focussed on the target again, throwing the knife. She only over-rotated a little bit, and she nodded in satisfaction as it hit the target. "I was wondering... I was hoping..." she trailed off.

"Are you worried about him making friends?" Carter asked. "If he's anything like you, he shouldn't have a problem."

"No! I mean, if you want to be friends with him, I'm not going to stop you. I encourage you, mostly because you're awesome and he couldn't have a better friend than you—"

"Kennedy, spit it out." Carter interrupted her rambling with a chuckle.

"Would you be willing to walk with him to and from camp? He doesn't know the city and I'm worried he'll get lost, and I know you can take care of yourself and him if you run into trouble and—"

"Of course." Carter had to cut her off again. "I would be happy to walk with him."

Kennedy smiled with relief. "Oh, thank you. I knew you would, but I was nervous to ask you. I don't want to force a friendship, even by proximity." She picked up her fourth knife and sent it spinning solidly into the centre of the target. "Hey look, you were right! A clear mind really does help!"

"That's why I'm the teacher," Carter said with a smirk. "What's he like?"

"Tommy? I... I don't really know him." Kennedy flushed and

looked away. "When I left for university, he was ten. People change a lot between ten and almost fifteen."

"Did I?" Carter hadn't really thought about it, but Kennedy had been tutoring him in math since he was twelve. If anyone knew whether he'd changed, it would be her.

"Of course!" Kennedy looked surprised that he'd asked. "You're more focussed now, more mature. Just look at your progress in Kung Fu since September! I also really enjoy spending time with you now, something that, no offence, I wouldn't have said when you were twelve."

"I guess my conversation topics have broadened," Carter said sheepishly, rubbing the back of his neck. "You haven't spent much time with Tommy. What do you know about him?"

"He's eight years younger than me, the same age as you. We got along well as kids. He likes books and music. He looks a lot like me, even more so now that he's older, and we both look like Mom. Our older siblings have brown hair like Dad, but we look kinda like the twins." Kennedy thought for a moment while she threw the fifth, and last, knife. It hit the target beside the fourth one, perfectly straight. "According to Mom, he's brilliant. He doesn't need to try to get good grades, in math in particular."

"Another math genius." Carter worried at his bottom lip. "You don't think he'll laugh at me?"

Kennedy shook her head. "Carter, I don't think you've realized, but you haven't been needing my help as much as you think you do. Once you understand the concepts, you have no trouble with the homework. You have difficulty on tests because you get so anxious about them that you freeze." She turned to face him, expression serious. "You were picked by Veronica for this camp for a reason, and it certainly wasn't because of anything Jason or I said. It was because of your abilities." Kennedy smiled. "In other words, no, Tommy won't laugh at you. Not that he would even if you were as bad as you seem to think you are." She rolled her eyes.

"Thanks," Carter said, blushing at her evaluation of him. "Does he know about Aetherborn?"

"No, he doesn't." Kennedy frowned. "I don't think Jason will tell him while he's here over the break. I doubt it'll be important. Probably before the wedding, though. We'll have a better sense of his character and how he'll take it by then."

"Yeah, I can see how Jason telling him 'there's a race of people that came into existence thanks to the power of human imagination, oh and I and your sister's best friend are two of them' could be a little much, especially in such a short visit," Carter teased. "Don't worry, I'll let Elyse know so she won't let anything slip."

"Thanks." Kennedy smirked. "You think you're my best friend?"

Carter grinned. "I was talking about Rachel, but if you thought it, I won't disagree." He headed over to the target to collect the knives. *Tommy looks like her, eh? I'll have to be careful not to develop a crush on him. It's bad enough to have had an unrequited crush on* one *unattainable Fairfield; I don't know if I'd survive a second!*

Chapter 1

♥

FRIDAY THE 7TH OF MARCH, 2003 - WESTMEATH, ONTARIO

Tommy stared out the side window of his mom's car, not watching the snowy roads or trees, but avoiding conversation with her the same way he had been the majority of the four-hour drive. He'd answered her questions with as few words as possible, not giving her any openings to talk about his friends back home or why she thought they were a bad influence on him.

He sighed and ran a pale hand through his blond hair. So what if he'd skipped a couple classes? It's not like he'd missed anything important. So what if he'd wanted to try cigarettes? He'd decided he didn't like them, and he wasn't going to touch them again. The alcohol wasn't so bad, not that she knew about that. He liked the way it made him feel; looser, like he was cool enough to be friends with the cool kids. The taste left a lot to be desired, though. Especially how it lingered in the back of his mouth afterward.

Westmeath was visible in the dim evening light now; shining towers of steel, the technology centres, interspersed with muted greys and creams of condo buildings, all shining with lights. Tommy's heart sped up. He was excited to be here, even though he was trying not to show it. There was a buzz of energy here that he didn't feel back home.

He'd been worried when the school called his parents the week before to tell them he'd been skipping class. He'd thought his forged notes would be sufficient. And then his mom had found the pack of cigarettes that Cindy Lou had given him in his coat pocket. Never mind that only one had been used, he'd been grounded on the spot. He'd been sure that his plans for March Break would be cancelled as well.

Apparently not.

He'd overheard his mom on the phone with Kennedy, saying that getting him away from home might help him get his head on straight.

Tommy fought back a groan of frustration. His head was fine. He was fine.

Sitting up, Tommy watched as the rolling fields gave way to apartment buildings and houses, and the road widened from a two-lane cross-province road to a busy, well-lit four-lane, and then six-lane, highway.

It wasn't long before his mom took an exit, and they were travelling down a street flanked by tall apartments. They passed a bus with dark windows letting people off on a corner. "Isn't that Kennedy's work?" he asked, reading the side of the bus. "Westmeath ARC?"

"Yes, that's right." His mother turned onto another street, one that had little shops with apartments over them. "Your sister said she takes the shuttle to and from work. That must have been it."

"Cool."

"We're almost there." She turned onto a side street.

There were small bungalows on either side of the street, and Tommy wrinkled his nose. "Do they live in one of these? They're so... *little!*"

"They do, and you'll be polite and grateful to them for taking you in," his mother snapped.

"I don't want to hear them having sex." Tommy shuddered.

"I told you to bring earplugs."

"You won't be here all week watching them be all... lovey-dovey with each other."

"Maybe you could learn a thing or two about communication,

love, and respect from them." She parked in a shovelled driveway and turned off the car. "Thomas, look at me."

Tommy rolled his eyes but turned to his mother. He looked a lot like her; both the blond hair and similar bone structure had strangers often mistaking them for siblings. *It's annoying and weird,* he thought. *She doesn't look* that *young.*

"Kennedy and Jason are doing us a huge favour, taking you in while you're attending Door Technology's camp. *And* they got you a sponsor. In short, the only reason you're here at all is because of them. I will be calling daily, and I want to hear glowing reports about your behaviour and your attitude, otherwise I *will* get back in this car and come get you, even if I have to drive all night! No cigarettes, no drugs, no alcohol, no skipping! Do I make myself clear?" She glared at him.

"I've never done drugs," Tommy muttered.

"And I hope you never will." His mom huffed impatiently. "There's so much ahead of you..." she trailed off. "Get your things."

Tommy sighed again. The speechifying was getting old. It looked like he was going to be in for a lot more throughout the week, and from his sister and her fiancé no less! Suddenly, he wasn't sure this week was going to be much fun at all.

SATURDAY THE 8TH OF MARCH, 2003 - WESTMEATH, ONTARIO

The early morning sunlight streamed in through the window, and Tommy groaned. At home, his curtains were never open, so it hadn't occurred to him to close them before he'd fallen asleep. He buried his face into the pillow and tried to fall back to sleep.

But the noises of an unfamiliar house crept into his consciousness and made him more alert. He groaned again and threw off the covers, rolling to a sitting position, head in his hands. His mother's voice pierced through the door, followed by laughter, low and rumbling from Jason and cheerful rippling from Kennedy.

Tommy sighed and got to his feet, grabbing clothes from his suitcase and pulling them on over his boxers from the night before. He hesitated before opening the door, steeling himself to deal with his mother. She'd be leaving shortly after breakfast, and she'd demand a hug from him before she left. It always felt like she was trying to show dominance or ownership over him, not love, when she forced a hug.

The door opened soundlessly, but the creaking hallway floor announced his approach to those in the kitchen.

"Morning!" Kennedy greeted him cheerfully. "You sleep alright?"

"Yeah," he grunted. "Forgot to close the curtains, though."

Jason, Kennedy's fiancé, chuckled. "The sunrise must have been a rude awakening."

"A bit, yeah." Tommy offered a small smile to the giant man.

"It was about time for you to get up anyways. I'm leaving shortly," his mother said and took a last sip of coffee.

Tommy's smile vanished, and he slouched into his seat, choosing eggs and bacon from the platters in the centre of the table and placing them on his plate. He caught the tail end of a glance between the couple and frowned at his food. He didn't like that people were talking about him, whether he was present or not.

His mom got to her feet and brought her dishes to the sink. "Thank you for breakfast, and for looking after Tommy this week. I hope he *behaves himself*," that last was said directly to him, and he cringed at being chastised so publicly, "and I'll be in touch daily to ensure he is."

"We are very happy to have him," Jason said, and Tommy glanced up at the older man, surprised to see his smile looked authentic.

"We're going to have a lot of fun this week," Kennedy added, and she, too, was genuine.

Tommy relaxed a fraction.

"Give me a hug goodbye," his mother said, arms open toward him.

After a moment, Kennedy stepped in for the hug. "Drive safely. Call when you get in, please. I'll probably be in class, but I'll get your message afterward."

"Bye, Mom," Tommy said, not getting up from his chair.

His mother sighed and moved toward him. Jason intercepted her with a hug. "Is there anything you need at home that we can get for you?"

Tommy tuned out her answer, eyes wide as Jason led her over to the door. He picked up her overnight bag and walked her out to the car, leaving the siblings alone in the kitchen.

"How... Why did you do that?" he asked.

"Do what?" Kennedy took a sip of her coffee. It smelled like the coconut coffee that his parents sometimes bought from up north. Her green eyes, identical to his own, blinked at him over her mug.

"Stop Mom from hugging me," he whispered.

She frowned and flipped her long blonde hair over her shoulder. "You looked uncomfortable with the idea. Nobody should have to do something they don't fully consent to, and that includes getting hugs from family."

Tommy stared at her. He didn't know what to say to that. When Kennedy didn't say anything else, he silently returned to his food.

Jason came back in. "I'm going to work out in the basement before class." He turned to Tommy. "You're welcome to join me. Have you been able to keep up with the routine I showed you?"

Flushing, Tommy shook his head.

"Hey, no problem." Jason smiled and headed down the stairs off the kitchen. Halfway down, he turned around and came back up, dropped a kiss on Kennedy's head, and returned to the basement.

Kennedy smiled shyly into her coffee mug.

"Is he mad that I didn't do his routine?" Tommy asked anxiously.

"Jason is very direct, and he doesn't get mad easily. He also knows that it's not easy to do a full workout the way he does it, especially if you're on your own." Kennedy drained her coffee. "Have you had a chance to unpack yet?"

"What's the point?" Tommy couldn't keep the bitterness out of his tone. He pushed a piece of egg around his plate with his fork.

"Tommy, we do actually want you here," Kennedy said seriously. "We weren't just saying platitudes to make Mom go away."

"Sure you do," Tommy muttered under his breath.

"Did you want help unpacking? The drawers and closet should all be empty. Jason's sister Zoe cleaned everything out when she, her wife Gabrielle, and their daughter Brooke moved from Vancouver in December."

"No, I got it, thanks." He wasn't going to bother unpacking. There really wasn't a point; they'd send him home by the end of the weekend. He finished his breakfast, put his dishes in the dishwasher, and went back to his temporary room.

It was a nice room, although a bit smaller compared to his own back at home. The double bed covered most of the floor space. Other than that, there was a desk and a dresser, and a short three-shelf bookcase at the foot of the bed. All were empty. The closet had hangers, but nothing else.

He considered putting his things away just to tempt fate.

In the living room, Kennedy put on music and started singing along with it. Tommy walked over to the doorway to listen, and recognized P!nk's powerful vocals. *Kennedy isn't bad,* he thought, then winced when she went flat on a high note.

He scowled at his suitcase. *Sure. Why not?* He lifted his suitcase onto the bed and opened a drawer, transferring his socks and boxers into it. Pants went into the drawer below that. Then he grabbed hangers and unrolled his shirts, hanging them back in the closet when he was finished. Luggage empty, he zipped it up and placed it in the bottom of the closet.

Next, he turned to his backpack, pulling out textbooks and placing them on the desk. Beside them, he put the binders with his notes and homework. His agenda and pencil case went on top. The camp said it would be providing everything they'd need, including lunches, so he tucked his backpack into the closet as well after pulling out his sheet music.

He leaned his guitar case against the bookcase and placed the music on a shelf.

The room didn't look much different, but he felt a tiny bit more like he belonged there.

Tommy sighed and sat down at the desk, pulling his agenda toward him. He flipped to the appropriate week and stared at the list of homework the teachers had assigned for the break. "Might as well get started," he said to himself and grabbed his science textbook.

He lost track of time as he worked through the assigned reading. The unit on electricity wasn't as bad as he'd thought it was going to be. The problems were straightforward, and he got them all right on the first try. He was about to start on his English homework, reading chapters from *To Kill A Mockingbird*, when tapping on his open door got his attention.

"Hey, I've got a lesson in twenty minutes. Did you want to come with or are you good here?" Kennedy asked.

Tommy noticed she was dressed for a workout. "What kind of lesson?"

"My private lesson with my Sifu. Judy teaches me Kung Fu."

"I didn't know you were learning Kung Fu." Tommy was surprised. "You sure I'm allowed to stay here alone?"

Kennedy frowned. "Of course. I'm asking because I'll be gone for a couple of hours. After my private lesson, Judy trains Jason and I to fight together."

"I thought engaged couples took ballroom classes, not martial arts," Tommy snarked.

"We're not like most couples," Kennedy said with a laugh. "You want to come or not? You can bring your book."

Tommy got to his feet and stretched. "Sure, why not. A change of scenery could be good." He grabbed his book and found Kennedy getting dressed for winter by the door. "We're walking?"

"It's ten minutes. You'll be walking further than that during the week. Mom told you that we wouldn't be able to drive you, right?"

"Yeah, she mentioned it. Don't worry, I brought the appropriate winter gear. I just wasn't expecting to walk right now."

"Both Jason and I prefer walking to driving when we can. Judy's dojo is super close. She teaches multiple martial art disciplines."

Once Tommy was dressed, Kennedy set the house alarm to *away* and they left, locking the door behind them.

"We'll get you a key and get your biometrics set up for the alarm system later today or tomorrow." She started off down the sidewalk at a brisk pace that had Tommy struggling to keep up.

"Biometrics?" he gasped and noticed that she slowed her pace to match his.

"Yeah. Your fingerprint will be enough. No eyeball scanning or blood samples needed."

Tommy wasn't sure if she was joking or not. "That's pretty high tech for a house."

"We've got a friend in a high-tech place," Kennedy said with a chuckle. "Veronica designed it. Jason had it installed after—" Kennedy cut herself off. "It was installed after we met in the fall."

"Veronica, the person who sponsored me?" Tommy asked, interested despite himself.

"The very same."

They crossed the street and Kennedy gestured at a bakery that read *Oven Baked* in bright lettering. "My favourite bakery. Judy's is just up here."

"This is a butcher shop," Tommy said when they reached it, sure he was being pranked.

"Very observant," Kennedy said with a giggle. "I didn't realize there was a dojo here for years. It's on the third floor. We've got some climbing to do." She opened the glass door beside the butchery, unwrapping her scarf and taking off her jacket before climbing the stairs.

Tommy copied and hurried after her. On the third floor, immediately inside the door, there was a room filled with coats and boots. Kennedy hung hers next to what was obviously Jason's and tucked her boots under the bench. She gestured to Tommy to do the same.

"You can take a peek through the glass if you like." Kennedy gestured at the door. "There's only five minutes left, but I don't want to bother them, even if we're unlikely to distract the advanced black belt class. They're more disciplined than I am."

Curious to see what a class might be like, Tommy approached the door and watched the young adults inside. He spotted Jason easily. He was paired with a lanky boy who looked a lot younger than the rest of the class but was keeping up with the pace of the choreographed punches, kicks, and blocks with ease. The boy was, in a word, beautiful, and Tommy wasn't sure what to make of the fact that his mind went there first. His chestnut brown curls were damp with sweat, and his light bronze skin glistened. He didn't even flinch at Jason's strikes, who looked like he wasn't pulling his punches. Tommy winced as a kick knocked the boy backward a step, but he came right back with a kick of his own that had Jason grinning his approval.

"Who are you watching?" Kennedy asked, approaching him.

Tommy jumped, having forgotten she was there. "The boy with Jason. He's keeping up with him, but he looks like he's my age."

"He is. That's Carter. He'll be at camp with you. Veronica sponsored him as well."

Narrowing his eyes, Tommy said, "Carter, the one you asked to be in the wedding party?"

"Yes, that's right. He's a good friend. He's teaching me how to throw knives," Kennedy added absentmindedly.

All thoughts of jealousy fled his mind at her admission. "You're learning how to *throw knives*?" he hissed. "Does Mom know?"

Kennedy scoffed. "As if I'd tell her *that*! She doesn't even fully approve of—" Kennedy cut herself off. "No, she doesn't know, and I don't plan on telling her."

Tommy turned back to the door, where the students were bowing to their Sifu, a tall, powerful Black woman who must be Judy.

"Great, we can go in. I can't wait to introduce you to Carter!"

"Awesome." Tommy flipped his book back and forth between his hands, anxious about meeting someone who was so close to his sister that she asked him to be in her *wedding party.*

"Hey, Kennedy!" Carter broke into a wide grin. "Hi," he said to Tommy, giving him a once over. Tommy felt his face heat up and got an inexplicable urge to hide behind Kennedy.

"Tommy," he said, sticking his hand out.

"Hi, Tommy." The boys shook hands. "Nice to finally meet you."

"Don't believe anything Kennedy's said about me."

"Oh?" Carter's eyebrows rose. "You're not a math whiz?"

"I wouldn't say that," mumbled Tommy, caught off guard by the easy compliment.

"Ah, so you're not the youngest of the family." Carter's grey eyes were twinkling with mischief.

"I'm not." Tommy lowered his voice to a whisper as if telling a secret. "My nephew Arthur's the youngest."

Carter chuckled. "You're funny, too. See you Monday for the walk in?"

"Uh..." Tommy glanced around for Kennedy, but she'd already started her stretches on the mat in the centre of the room. "Are you on the way?"

"Yeah, I live above Oven Baked. It's my dads' business." Carter smiled. "Kennedy asked me last week if I'd be willing to walk with you. Guess she didn't let you in on the plan."

Tommy returned the smile. "We didn't really talk much about it this morning, just that I would have to walk. It'll be nice to walk with someone rather than by myself in a strange city."

"Shoo, Carter," said the woman that Tommy assumed was Judy. "I've got a lesson to start." To Tommy, she added, "You may sit *quietly* in the corner." She pointed. "Nice to meet you, young Master Fairfield."

Appropriately cowed, Tommy waved goodbye to Carter and curled up with his book. After a few minutes of pretending to read, he gave up and watched Kennedy's lesson. As it was a private lesson, she moved through the choreography on her own, with Judy correcting her positioning occasionally. Halfway through the lesson, she squared off against her Sifu for increasingly complicated punches, kicks, and blocks.

By the end of the hour, Kennedy was sweating but grinning. "I feel like I'm improving," she said happily.

"Stop fishing for compliments, child," Judy told her with a chuckle. "I will admit, I'm impressed that you didn't try to show off in front of your brother."

Kennedy flushed, to Tommy's surprise. "I did consider it."

"Get some water. Now that Jason has returned, we'll start again in five minutes."

Tommy hadn't noticed the big man enter.

Judy left the room, and Kennedy walked over to Jason, who handed her a water bottle. "Thanks." She guzzled half of it before handing it back, taking a towel from him and wiping her face. "Ugh, we need to wash that with the extra-strength detergent this afternoon."

Jason chuckled. "Noted." He tucked the towel back inside his bag and led her onto the mat again.

Out of the corner of his eye, Tommy watched them stretch together. Although they were focussed on what they were doing, there were flirtatious glances and smiles that made him blush and feel like he was intruding on a private moment.

Judy returned, and the couple stood up, prepared for their lesson. "Let's get to work."

If Tommy had found Kennedy's solo work interesting, watching them together was riveting. His book lay forgotten at his side throughout the lesson as they came up with different methods of working together to fight. He was impressed at how well they complemented each other and had a tough time keeping his eyes off Jason; his strength and dexterity were mesmerizing. It was difficult to reconcile his fierceness now with the gentleness shown when interacting with Tommy's nephew Arthur over the holidays.

The second hour passed even faster than the first, and Tommy was surprised when Judy called an end to the lesson.

"You two are doing well. Why don't you take a break until next Saturday?" Judy told them.

Kennedy laughed. "Our next lesson isn't until Saturday."

"You're already following orders. Good." Judy cracked a smile.

Scooping up the sweatshirt that she'd thrown off the mat partway into the first hour, Kennedy walked over to Tommy, offering him a hand up. He took it, feeling the strength in her grip despite having worked hard for two hours, and allowed himself to be pulled to his feet.

"Take a break from following us around on patrol, too," he overheard Judy tell Jason.

"Come meet our Sifu properly," Kennedy said excitedly, towing him over.

Tommy looked up at the stern woman and performed an awkward bow. "Nice to meet you."

Judy relaxed into a smile. "A pleasure to meet Kennedy's younger brother. She's been so excited for you to get here, I think she's even managed to stop talking about the wedding."

Smirking, Tommy glanced at his sister, who looked sheepish. "I'm honoured. The wedding is only three months away."

"It's kinda consuming my thoughts, between making decisions and fending off Mom," Kennedy sighed.

Tommy felt for her. Their mom had become obsessed with the wedding and was constantly on the phone with either Kennedy or a supplier. He didn't know if Kennedy had approved the changes their mom made, or if she even knew about them. He made a mental note to ask.

"Shall we head home?" Jason asked. "I, for one, could really use a shower."

"Mmmm, me too," Kennedy said, eyeing her fiancé hungrily.

Tommy looked away, embarrassed.

Judy chuckled. "Hope your bathroom has soundproofing."

"I think I might go to the other side of the house," Tommy said, making a face, "doing something that completely absorbs my attention so that I don't notice the passage of time."

"Great idea," Kennedy said eagerly, and Tommy rolled his eyes at Judy, who seemed sympathetic.

On the way home, Jason fell back to walk with Tommy. "Sorry if we made you uncomfortable back there." He looked awkward.

"I've known about the birds and the bees for a while." Tommy made a face. "I'm just not used to people talking about it so openly in front of me, especially my sister."

"If it makes you feel any better, we would have had the exact same conversation with Judy had you not been there." Jason shrugged. "The Community here is pretty laid-back about sex. We'll try to tone it down around you if it makes you uncomfortable."

"I... I don't know." Tommy squirmed under Jason's intense gaze. "I might be able to get used to it. I don't want you to change for me."

"Not change, just be sneakier." Jason grinned. "At least this way, you know to put on loud music."

Tommy groaned. "Yeah, okay, I can see how that's mildly better." He tried not to think about it too hard, with mixed results.

"Did you get any reading done this morning?" Jason asked, pointing at the book.

Glancing down at his book, having almost forgotten it was there, Tommy shook his head. "I was too interested in the lessons. You two work well together."

Jason puffed up with pride. "Kennedy's working hard to catch up. I'm proud of her. She should be able to join the black belt class by the fall, if not sooner, if she keeps up this pace."

"Why is it so urgent that she catch up?" Tommy asked, curious.

Jason hesitated. "Westmeath isn't necessarily the safest city. There are gangs and other... unsavoury characters. Kennedy was attacked right before our first official date."

Tommy's jaw dropped. "She never said!"

"No, we didn't want to worry your parents. But I think it's important for you to understand why she's working so hard. I'm not around her twenty-four seven, and neither of us would want that. Her being able to protect herself is important to both of us."

Jason glanced ahead at Kennedy, who was waving cheerfully at someone on the other side of the street. "It's given her the confidence to become more herself, and the Community loves her for it."

"You're both really involved in the community here, aren't you?" Tommy asked. "Is it a tight-knit one like back home in Parry Sound?"

Jason hummed thoughtfully. "I'm incredibly involved. I'm co-head of the Oldtown Council. Kennedy is still considered a bit of an outsider, but most people love her. Parry Sound gets a lot more tourists than we do down here in Oldtown, so your community is quite different. We've also got a more... diverse population." Jason glanced at him. "Nationality, ethnicity, physical appearance, bodymind diversity, and sexuality."

"Yeah, back home is pretty homogenous," Tommy agreed. "That doesn't mean they aren't accepting of outsiders."

"That's not what I'm saying." Jason shook his head. "Prejudice is everywhere. I've been racially profiled more often than I care to remember. But there are also some amazing and supportive people, too. Find those, and it doesn't matter what you look like or who you love, because you've got someone who'll be there for you through anything."

"Like Kennedy for you." It wasn't a question.

"She supports a lot more people than just me."

Tommy digested that information silently.

"When we get in, I'm going to put your biometrics into the alarm system. Then you won't have to wait for one of us when you want to come or go. Just make sure you set it." Jason's jaw clenched. "My house was broken into back in September. We were home, and they had knives—"

"Wait, wait..." Tommy stopped walking. "Are you saying that Kennedy was attacked *twice* in the fall, and she didn't tell us?"

Jason winced. "There were extenuating circumstances."

Tommy whistled and kept walking. "You sure keep a lot of secrets."

"To keep others safe," Jason muttered. They walked in silence for a minute or two before he spoke up again. "There's a dance tonight. Mostly high school kids, as it's a special occasion."

"Special occasion?"

"First Saturday of March Break." Jason gave him a crooked smile. "My restaurant usually only hosts dances on weeknights, and it's open to all teenagers and young adults."

"That sounds like a great way to keep kids out of trouble."

"You'd know a bit about trouble."

Tommy looked sharply at the older man, but he was smiling slightly.

"Your sister might be a saint in general, really, except... Sorry, you probably don't want to hear that." Jason smirked. "Did you know I used to smoke?"

"Really?" Tommy found it hard to believe.

"Yeah, in grade ten I thought it was a cool thing to do. Felt like everyone smoked; Walt Disney, Kurt Cobain." At Tommy's confusion, Jason added, "Nirvana? I forget how young you are."

"Why'd you stop?" Tommy asked. Jason seemed like a 'go big and *then* go home' sort of guy.

"My little sister kicked my ass." He smirked. "Not to teach me a lesson, but because I couldn't keep up. Lung capacity and wasting so much time looking cool."

"Your sister does martial arts too? Does everyone here do that?"

"No, but my dad insisted we do it."

"Was she in your class just now?"

"No. Thankfully. She's the best fighter I've ever seen. She and her wife teach the kids classes. But back to cigarettes. I had trouble breathing, I stank, and it made it hard to think when

I hadn't had one in a while. But from your smirk I'm guessing you've already come to this conclusion."

Tommy nodded.

"Well, here I was being all big brotherly. Alright, fine, but one more thing." The full weight of his gaze fell on Tommy as he continued, "Veronica is my best friend. She sponsored you for this camp and what you do reflects on her. Please don't do anything that will get her fired. No skipping. Got it?"

Tommy's heart hammered in his chest, and he swallowed hard. "Sir, yes, sir. I understand."

Jason smiled. "Smartass, just like your sister. Good." They started walking again, now on Jason's street. "A little bit of harmless mischief, though… If you pass it by Veronica and get her in on it, that should be alright."

Tommy glanced up at Jason to see that he was smiling. "I'll keep that in mind."

"Oh, and a little tip. You want to get out of class without your parents flipping out, join a sport or club. Newspaper and Yearbook will get you out for almost anything." Before Tommy had a chance to respond, Jason asked, "Do you have clothes for the dance with you?"

"Ummm, no." Tommy rubbed the back of his neck. "To be honest, I was kinda expecting to be under house arrest."

Jason chuckled darkly. "If you hold sand too tightly in your hand, it will run through your fingers." He shook his head at Tommy's quizzical look. "Joni Mitchell? No matter. You have jeans, I assume? I'll take you shopping, and we'll get a couple of shirts. You're the same colouring as Kennedy, and she looks amazing in emerald green."

"You don't have to—" Tommy cut himself off at Jason's raised hand.

"I want to."

Chapter 2

♥

SATURDAY THE 8TH OF MARCH, 2003 - WESTMEATH, ONTARIO

Tommy expected to feel uncomfortable in his new dress shirt since all his formal clothes at home made him feel constricted. But the old ladies who ran Seams Likeable, where Jason had taken him to get fitted for his shirts, had dressed him in the softest, most comfortable clothes he had ever put on his body. They had made him try on a variety of colours, cooing over him until he almost begged Jason to get him out of there. In the end, he had left with three shirts; emerald green, turquoise, and a black with silver sparkles that you couldn't see unless you were looking out of the corner of your eye.

For the dance at The Hawaiian that night, he was wearing the green shirt with the collar open and the sleeves rolled up. Kennedy had informed him that he looked like he was going to church with them rolled down.

He fidgeted with the hem of the shirt, untucked as per Kennedy's suggestion as well, and glanced at himself in the mirrored wall by the coat check. The sight calmed him, slightly. The green made his hair look blonder and his eyes brighter, and rolling the sleeves made his forearms stand out in an attractive way.

"Hey, man. I wasn't expecting to see you here."

Tommy looked into Carter's grey eyes as he came up beside him, and his breath caught in his throat. Carter was dressed similarly in a dark red dress shirt, sleeves rolled up and collar open. Tommy tried to ignore the hammering of his heart and not to let his eyes linger on nicely muscled forearms. "Yeah, I didn't know this was happening until Jason told me on the way home."

"Well, you clean up nice," Carter said with a grin. "That's a great colour on you."

"Um, thanks. You look good too." Tommy flushed and hoped Carter couldn't see it in the dark.

Kennedy came up to them at that point. "Oh, good. I'm glad you're here, Carter. I don't think Tommy would have nearly as much fun with Jason and I as he would with you and friends your age." Turning to Tommy, she said, "If we leave, we'll be back. Please don't leave without us."

"Why would you need to leave?" Tommy asked.

Carter slung an arm over his shoulders. "Don't ask questions you don't want to know the answer to," he whispered, leaning in close to Tommy's ear and making the hair stand up on the back of his neck.

The scent of his shampoo and deodorant was incredibly distracting and Tommy found it hard to focus on the topic of conversation. "I don't— Oh!" Flustered, Tommy turned with Carter. Once they were far enough away from his sister, he whispered back, "Do they do that often?"

Carter looked amused. "Often enough that there's a running gag about it. If they *don't* leave, people ask them if everything's alright."

"They're so in love it's a little sickening to be in the same room with them." Tommy made a face.

"And you're living with them for a week!" Carter smirked. "You can visit anytime if you need a break."

"I'll probably wear out my welcome."

"Unlikely." Carter's eyes dipped down and back up again, and Tommy felt them like a brand. "Want to dance?"

"I... Uh..." Tommy's heart beat faster. "I don't think I'm into guys!" he blurted out and then wondered if he was lying.

Surprise flickered across Carter's face, followed by hurt. "It's a dance. You're supposed to dance. But if you're not comfortable yet, we can get some juice and sit at one of the tables."

"Right," Tommy mumbled, feeling very out of place suddenly. "Juice sounds good," he said, a little louder.

"Great." Carter led the way to the bar. "My favourite is guava. You?"

Tommy noticed that Carter left a little more space between them than he had earlier, and he was frustrated with himself for having caused the distance. "The fresh stuff? Jason brought some at Christmas, and I couldn't get enough of it."

"Yeah, that's it alright." Carter flagged down the bartender and ordered the drinks.

"I'll have to pay you back," Tommy said, flustered that he hadn't thought of money before this.

"All juice is on the house," Carter said. "Don't get yourself in a twist."

"Really?" Tommy breathed easy again. "Damn, I wish we had a place like this back home!"

"What's it like?" They got their glasses and Carter led them to a table off to one side. "In Parry Sound, I mean."

Tommy glanced at the dance floor and saw that it was full of people, all his age or a little older. Jason and Kennedy were dancing on the far side of the room, completely oblivious to everyone around them.

"You see the same faces in your class every year, and everyone remembers everything about you. Your teachers taught your siblings and expect you to be just like them." Tommy sighed. "In the summer, the town is inundated with tourists. That's when festivals and concerts happen. Lots of boating, especially sailing. But there's not much to do in winter except school. And it's not cool to like school," he added bitterly.

"Is being cool important?" Carter asked. "You're obviously smart, or else you wouldn't be here, going to one of the most exclusive tech camps in Canada."

Tommy opened and closed his mouth as he thought. If he'd

been asked that question the day before, the answer would have been easy. If you were cool, you got invited to the best parties, you weren't picked on, and there was this aura around the cool kids... One that he had wanted to be part of. But after only one day in Westmeath, he was already doubting himself.

He had been to a couple of those 'best parties,' and they usually just involved a lot of stinky beer and ridiculous games like spin the bottle or seven minutes in heaven. He'd only been chosen once for the latter, and it had been the longest, most awkward seven minutes of his life. "I thought it was, but now I'm not so sure," Tommy said slowly, and was rewarded by a grin from his tablemate that made his stomach swoop.

"Come on, I want to introduce you to some of my friends." Carter got to his feet and held out his hand. "But they're on the dance floor, so you'll have to dance with me to get to them, even though you're not into guys," he teased.

Tommy rolled his eyes, drained his glass, and put his hand in Carter's, ignoring the tingles that spread from the point of contact. "Lead the way."

On the way home that night, Tommy was full of things to say about Carter and his group of friends. "Leo and Steve have been his friends since forever, and he only met Elyse this semester in math class, but he says she's brilliant and it's no wonder Veronica picked her to sponsor as well. Carter's not sure how he ended up getting sponsored, because he says he feels like he's constantly struggling, but I think he's smart in different ways, and he'll probably shine under Veronica's guidance, not that I've met her, but if she's friends with you, then she has to be amazing."

"Sounds like you had a great time," Jason said, exchanging an amused glance with Kennedy that Tommy elected to ignore.

"I really enjoyed myself. This was ten times better than the boring parties back home. Why can't they have a place like this there?"

"Because there's nobody like Jason to run it," Kennedy said, smiling.

Tommy grimaced, but thought she made a good point. Doing something like this every single weeknight would seriously cut into any profits that the restaurant made, and offering free juice as well? It was obvious that Jason cared a great deal about the youth in the community if he was willing to take such a financial hit.

He frowned, thinking hard. He'd rather be like Jason any day of the week than the cool kids back home. But could he keep it up once he got back there? *Being a teenager is hard!*

MONDAY THE 10TH OF MARCH, 2003 - WESTMEATH, ONTARIO

Sunday had been a lazy day in the Johnson household.

Tommy had slept in so late that Jason and Kennedy had come back from the church they attended *and* had made pancakes before he'd stumbled out of his room, following the yummy scent of cooking into the kitchen.

After lunch, he had run errands with them, getting groceries and meeting the owners of the local shops, including Carter's dads at the bakery. He'd felt triply embarrassed over his comment about not liking guys the night before.

They had ended the day with dinner and games with Jason's sister Zoe, her wife Gabrielle, and their adorable daughter Brooke, who had somehow managed to spill water from her sippy cup on his shirt. He hadn't minded; he'd had too much fun laughing and hanging out with them. He had felt included and wanted, his opinions respected, *and* he hadn't felt like an extra wheel with no purpose.

Now, he was regaling Carter with descriptions of the previous evening as they walked, sending the other boy into peals of laughter over his imitation of Jason trying to act out *Chicken Little* in charades.

"How long did you make him keep trying?" Carter wheezed out, and then burst into laughter again when Tommy held up two fingers.

"I think he knew what I was doing after the first few failed guesses, but he played along because everyone was laughing so hard."

"You know," Carter said, wiping tears of laughter from the corners of his eyes, "Jason used to be so serious. I don't think Kennedy realizes what a difference she has made in him."

"He's still serious," Tommy protested.

Carter shook his head. "Not like before. He never smiled, never danced, never joked. He cared, more deeply than any of us realized, but he had difficulty showing it."

"Really?" Tommy was surprised. The Jason he knew was the opposite, especially when showing devotion to Kennedy. "He must have been really lonely."

"Yeah, he probably was." Carter's usual smile was gone, and he scuffed his feet on the snowy sidewalk.

"Hey, is this it?" Tommy asked, pointing at a high wall that surrounded the entire block up ahead.

"Looks like it."

Together, they walked up to the entrance where they were scanned, their picture taken for their passes, and signed in. They were led to a row of lockers where they left their winter gear. Finally, they were shown to a small lecture hall. A dozen or so other kids their age were sitting in seats and talking quietly in pairs.

"They probably know each other from other high schools in the city," Carter whispered to Tommy as they found seats together. They saved one for Elyse and kept an eye on the door for her as more students entered the room.

"How many high schools are in Westmeath?" Tommy asked.

"I'm not sure," Carter said thoughtfully. "Just over sixty or so, I would guess."

Tommy's jaw dropped. "I forget just how big Westmeath is compared to home sometimes."

"Why? How many are in Parry Sound?" Carter asked.

"Ummm... one," Tommy whispered. "Remember how I said

that you see the same faces in your class every year? I meant that literally."

"Wow." Carter was obviously trying not to stare. "I didn't realize you came from *that* small a town!"

"Yeah, yeah, I get it," Tommy said, rolling his eyes. "Small town hick kid in the big city—"

"I wouldn't think that about you," Carter hissed fiercely, leaning close. "It's just different from what I'm used to, that's all."

"Hey, you two. Is that seat for me?" Elyse interrupted their staring contest.

"Yes," Tommy said, settling back in his seat. "Us Oldtown kids should stick together."

"You're one of us now?" Elyse asked, raising an eyebrow.

"He's living there right now, his sister is marrying one of us... I'd say he is," Carter said defiantly.

"Hmm," Elyse said, glancing between them. She tossed her wavy brown hair over her shoulder. "We'll see."

Any further conversation was prevented by the arrival of two people on the stage. The audience quieted instantly.

"Good morning. My name is Quinn, and my pronouns are they/them. This is my colleague..."

Tommy was surprised to hear someone mentioning their pronouns; it was something he'd read about happening in Californian tech companies, but to hear it in Ontario was surprising. He found himself having a little more respect for the company.

"Tiffany. Pronouns she/her. We're your primary counsellors for the week."

"Essentially your tutors and lab leaders. You'll have teachers who are experts in the field, but your questions will be directed to us." Quinn flashed them a smile. Tommy liked their bright blue hair, shaved on one side and down to their jaw on the other.

"We'll also tell you any announcements each morning and give you special surprises!" Tiffany grinned at the murmur that greeted her statement. Her short brown curls shifted as she turned toward backstage and beckoned for someone to join them.

Out trotted what Tommy initially thought was a dog, but soon realized was a robot. The murmur grew louder, and some of the kids in the back stood up to get a better view.

Tiffany raised a hand for silence and got it immediately. "Meet LASS-C, Land Automated Scout and Supply Carrier."

Carter raised his hand. "Does that mean there are water and air robots as well?"

"Very good, Carter," Quinn replied with an impressed grin. "You'll probably get to see those in your tour this afternoon if your sponsor takes you to the robotics lab."

"LASS-C has a cutting-edge prototype smartphone for each of you." As Tiffany spoke, the robot descended the stairs at the side of the stage and started up the aisle, using its arm to reach into the basket on its back and hand each student a small package. "I must emphasize that these are loans *only*. You take it home with you each night, but we get it back on Friday at the end of camp."

"The phone is called the Able, because you are going to be *able* to do almost anything on it." Quinn paused for chuckles and then continued the spiel. "It has a touchscreen and a holographic keyboard, so you'll have no trouble taking notes during your classes. I suggest practising with it tonight." They winked and the students laughed. Tommy understood why; he couldn't wait to try it out either.

"Your sponsor will show you the Bug App this afternoon. If you find a bug, document it, and give us your suggested solution." Tiffany grinned. "The individual who records the most bugs and has the best solutions will win Door Tech's flagship phone: the DT 1701."

The students all applauded excitedly.

By this point, LASS-C had reached their row and handed each of them their new phones.

"Thank you," Tommy said politely to the camera at the front, where the face would be on a dog.

"It's a robot, dumbass," said a boy from behind him, kicking the back of his seat.

"You couldn't come up with a better insult than that?" Tommy asked, half turning around.

The boy sneered. "You don't have to be polite to it."

"Just because it's a robot doesn't mean we should forget our manners. Haven't you watched *Terminator* or *Star Trek*?" Carter snapped. "Thank you, LASS-C."

"Thank you," Elyse echoed, and glared at the boy.

After that, every student followed suit, to the bemusement of the counsellors.

"This is starting to *feel* like *Star Trek*," Tommy murmured to Carter, leaning close so the boy behind them wouldn't make fun of him again. "I wouldn't be surprised to walk outside and see that we've taken off into outer space."

"The robot, the touchscreen phone with a holo keyboard... Yeah, I'm picking up what you're putting down." Carter grinned.

Elyse leaned forward to join in their conversation. "I've never even *heard* of tech like this. Nokia has a smartphone, but not with a touchscreen. And RIM has developed something that can read an email and uses a special stylus, but a holographic keyboard? That's seriously sci-fi."

"Right? It's like they took people who wanted to make things happen, gave them a science background, and threw money at them," Carter said.

"That's almost precisely what we did, Mister Batudev," said a new voice from the aisle.

The three of them looked up at a well-dressed woman with perfectly coiffed red hair.

She smiled at them. "That makes two correct observations for you already, doesn't it? Not to mention starting a round of manners toward my LASS-C."

Carter raised his hand cautiously, and when she nodded at him, he said, "Tommy was the one who said 'thank you' first, Ms. Door."

"Integrity as well!" Ms. Door looked impressed. She shifted her glance to Tommy. "Ah, our out-of-towner." He nodded silently.

"And both of you were sponsored by Ms. Giles. That's... intriguing."

Then she turned to the boy behind Tommy.

"We don't stand for rude language at Door Tech. Watch your tongue, Mister Finch."

"Please put your hands together for Ellen Door!" said Quinn, up on stage. "The brilliant mind behind Door Technology and your host for this week!"

Ellen walked briskly down the aisle and climbed the stairs to meet the counsellors in the middle of the stage. The applause ceased the moment she regarded the audience. "Welcome to Door Technology. I started this camp a few years ago to give back to the city of Westmeath, and the sister city of Demers, Quebec, through its youth and to shape the minds of the future. If you do well this week, you will find many future opportunities opening for you, from summer camps to intern positions to scholarships, and potentially job offers after graduation."

Excited gasps met this statement and Ellen paused with a slight smile.

"We only take the best of the best. You were chosen, out of all the grade nine students in the city—and one beyond that—because your sponsor saw something inside you, something that made them think, 'This individual will excel with the influence of Door Technology.' And now, here you are! Thirty of the best young minds, all under one roof. I expect to see remarkable things from this group. I'm looking forward to it!"

There was another round of applause. Ellen bowed slightly and left the stage.

"Whew!" Carter said quietly into Tommy's ear. "That's not intimidating at all."

Tommy swallowed nervously. "I hope we're up for the challenge."

"Alright, let's start the icebreakers!" Tiffany exclaimed, clapping her hands together.

Quinn tossed an inflatable beach ball into the audience and a girl caught it. "As you may have noticed, *we* already know your names and faces, but you don't know each other. When you are holding the ball, please stand and state your name, school, and an interesting fact about yourself before passing the ball on to someone else."

The ball bounced around the room as the students introduced themselves. Tommy caught the ball early on. "Hello," he said, standing up awkwardly. "My name is Tommy and I go to Parry Sound High School. An interesting fact about me is that I'm learning guitar." He passed the ball on and sat, heart pounding.

"That wasn't so hard, was it?" Carter asked, leaning into his space.

Tommy shook his head with a shy smile.

Elyse was next in their group to catch the ball. "Hello, everyone. I'm Elyse, I attend Oldtown High, and I've been in gymnastics since I was three years old."

Eventually, there were only two students left, Carter and the boy behind Tommy.

"My name's Greg, and I go to Westmeath Prep. I've ranked first in my weight class provincially in boxing for the past three years." Greg smirked at Tommy and Carter as he sat down.

Carter stood up. "I'm Carter, Oldtown High. I've mastered four levels of belt in Kung Fu since September."

He was about to sit down when Greg scoffed from behind him. "What does that make you, a yellow belt?"

Carter stared at him impassively. "You obviously don't know the rankings, so why bother telling you?" He sat as the rest of the students *ooh*'d.

"Aren't you a black belt?" Tommy whispered.

"First degree," Carter whispered back.

"Is that more advanced than a black belt?"

"It usually takes a year of study to get the first Kata." Carter smirked proudly. "I had my exam last month."

"Damn," Tommy whispered, awed.

"How long have you been learning guitar?"

"Since last summer."

"Is it acoustic, electric, or bass? Do you sing while you play?" Carter asked eagerly.

"Acoustic, and yes," Tommy whispered back just before the counsellors started speaking again.

"It's time to get you out of your seats! Icebreaker bingo!" Quinn announced cheerfully. "Turn on your phones..." They walked the students through navigating to the app. "When you've found someone who has done the thing in your bingo sheet, get them to tap their phone against yours for verification. If there's a mistake, tap the undo button." Quinn grinned around at them. "Should be easy enough for geniuses like you."

Everyone laughed as they stood up and started to talk to one another.

"Have you ever smoked?" Tommy asked Carter, pulling up the first box in his bingo card.

Carter snorted. "As if! My dads would kill me. Ask me another."

"Have you made a loaf of bread from scratch?"

"Yup, that's definitely something I've done." Carter tapped his phone, and Tommy felt it vibrate as it accepted the phone's signature. "Okay, your turn. Have you ever been present at a birth not your own?"

Tommy chuckled. "Do animals count?"

"It doesn't specify species."

"Then yes, I guess I have." Tommy tapped his phone and they both turned to Elyse.

"No, I have not smoked, and I have the bread one too. Can you tap me, Carter?"

Tommy found himself enjoying the icebreaker. He and Carter stuck together as they met the other students, filling out the bingo sheet until, finally, one girl, who had introduced herself as Caitlin, called out bingo.

"What do you think they're going to have us do next?" Tommy wondered aloud when they got back to their seats.

Chapter 3

♥

MONDAY THE 10TH OF MARCH, 2003 -
WESTMEATH, ONTARIO

"We're going to split you up into your classes, so you can get to know your classmates better." Tiffany pulled out a tablet. "I'm going to list off the names that are to go with me. The rest of you are with Quinn."

Tommy held his breath, hoping their little group wouldn't be split. None of their names were called, but neither was Greg's.

"Alright, Team Q, follow me!" Quinn said, and the students filed out of the auditorium. Once they were all in the hallway, they said, "We're going to be in Gym A. Team T will be in Gym B. Once there, you'll be broken into smaller groups for an obstacle race. Whichever team completes the challenge first is the winner and will get some fancy Door Tech swag."

"A race?" Tommy asked the other two as they walked down the hallway. "I'm an okay runner, what about you?"

"I doubt it's just running," Carter said with a chuckle.

He was right. The gym had four stations set up with three sections each. The first section had a large circle with a bucket in the middle and a small pile of materials, the second section had a table with a wooden box, and the last section had two large barrels with narrow openings set about ten metres apart from each other.

"Hope you're good at lassoing there, Yee-haw," muttered Greg to Tommy.

"I'm sorry, are you talking to me?" Tommy asked, looking around.

Carter pulled Tommy and Elyse away from Greg before he could say anything further.

"I'm not from a ranch, I'm from a farm," Tommy told his friends indignantly.

"Let him dig his own holes," Carter whispered. "Don't give him the satisfaction of knowing he got to you."

"Alright, listen up, Team Q. 'Q' for Quinn, of course. I'm going to run through the rules with you, but first, your groups. Three groups of four and one group of three. Since one sponsor gave us three candidates this year, that'll be the team of three. Carter, Elyse, and Tommy, you're group one." Quinn gestured to the station on the right and continued listing off groups until all the stations were filled. "Each section contains tools that will help you in the next section. The end goal is to transfer twenty litres of water from the red barrel into the green one. Now, for section one, we want you to pretend the floor inside the circle is lava. We didn't have the budget to make it real."

Quinn paused for nervous laughter. "If the bucket or the contents touch the lava, I will reset it. Are there any questions?" When no one raised their hands, they pulled out their phone and tapped on it. "Ready? Get set, go!"

"Let's catalogue what we've got," Elyse said, moving to the pile of materials. "Some rope, a piece of wood, two bricks, and a pair of roller skates."

"That's a really odd set of materials," said Carter, puzzled. "Pass me the wood. Let's see if we can reach the bucket with that." Stretching forward, Carter was able to reach the bucket's handle. "I don't think I'd be able to lift it all the way to the edge of the circle."

Tommy was watching the group next to them, who were attempting that technique. The bucket was heavy enough that it fell off close to the centre. "You're right, one piece of wood isn't enough. But if we had two, I could go on the other side of the circle and support you."

"But we don't have two," Elyse pointed out.

"Not right now." Carter put his piece down and walked over to the group next to them, who were waiting for Quinn to reset their bucket. Tommy followed. "I propose an alliance."

Greg sneered at him. "We're not going to help you."

"But it would help you, too," Tommy tried to reason with him.

"Not a chance," Greg sneered. "Get lost."

"Come on, we'll try the next group," Carter said.

Group three was more than willing to ally themselves. They had tried to hit their bucket like a golf ball; Quinn was still collecting the pieces. Group three followed Carter and Tommy back to station one, bringing their wood piece with them.

"Let's give this a shot," Carter said. Tommy grabbed the other piece of wood and went to the other side of the circle. "Ready?" At the same time, they slid the wood into place and slowly lifted it.

"Move toward Elyse," Tommy said, gasping from the effort of holding up the pail.

Together, sidestepping like crabs, they walked to the side furthest from group two. Elyse grabbed hold of the pail and group three applauded them. Both boys surrendered their pieces of wood and wished them luck before turning to Elyse, who was heading toward the table in section two.

"There are a whole bunch of items in here," she said, dumping them out onto the table.

Tommy spread them out and picked up a folded piece of paper. On it was a series of numbers. "Anything else have numbers on it?" he asked. "This looks like part of a cypher."

"Not yet, but I've got pieces of a children's puzzle. Maybe if we put it together, it'll have a clue in the picture."

They started separating the contents into piles. The biggest pile contained screws, nuts, and bolts.

"This is starting to feel like we're missing something," said Carter.

Tommy frowned, nodding thoughtfully. "Hey, we haven't looked at the box yet. Maybe it has some clues."

Their box was locked with a standard combination lock.

"You know..." Carter said thoughtfully, watching groups two and four struggle to get at their bucket, "I have a theory."

"Lay it on us, because I can't make heads or tails out of what they want us to do," Tommy said, defeated. "At least you were able to put some of the puzzle together, but there are missing pieces." He glared at the chest. "They're probably in there."

"Tell us," Elyse urged Carter.

"At the beginning, Quinn said that the winning *team* would get a prize," Carter said slowly.

"Yeah, and?" Elyse said. "Spit it out!"

"Oh!" Tommy's eyes lit up, and he grabbed Carter's shoulders. "We're *team* Q! They split us into *groups* within the team! We all have to work together!"

"We're missing pieces because the other groups have them," Elyse said, getting excited. "That makes sense!"

"Okay, Tommy, you go tell group three. I'll talk to four, and Elyse, can you try to get through to two? Maybe try getting one of the ones who *isn't* Greg to agree. We need them if we're going to succeed."

Tommy shook off the tingles touching Carter had elicited and approached group three at their table. "Hey, ummm, can we talk for a minute?" He explained their theory, and they let him look at their table, which they had already split up into similar piles. Their box was locked with a set of differently shaped buttons. "Why don't you take your puzzle pieces over to table one. See if you can build onto the puzzle that Carter started. Did you get a piece of paper in yours?"

A girl, who he thought he remembered was named Caitlin, held out her hand, and Tommy saw their paper had letters of the alphabet, but all out of order. "We can't make heads or tails out of this."

"Hang on, I got a number code. They must be linked. Maybe one of the other groups has the cypher." Tommy jogged over and grabbed the paper from table one. He noticed that the puzzle was taking shape, and on the way back, he saw that his group members had convinced the other two groups to work together as well. "You have building supplies in yours, too," he said when he returned. "I feel like they're a red herring."

"I agree." The girl with the other paper said. "Maybe we should take a look at the other boxes, see what we're up against. My name's Caitlin."

"Nice to meet you, Caitlin. I'm Tommy. Good idea."

The group split up, and he joined the ones heading for group four, who had just dumped their bucket.

"Puzzle pieces are on table one," Tommy told them, and a boy grabbed them and headed off in that direction. "Hey, this box has a word lock!"

"What's on your paper?" Caitlin asked eagerly.

They unfolded it and found numbers, spaced out in various groupings.

"Ah ha!" exclaimed Tommy. "Alphanumeric cypher! Hey, Quinn," he said, raising his voice, "can we use our phones to make notes?"

At the counsellor's nod of approval, he, Caitlin, and a boy who introduced himself as Brandon put their heads together. On Caitlin's phone, they slowly typed out the phrase written in the cypher.

"I got a paper too," said a small voice, and they moved aside to make room for the group two member, who introduced herself as Dildeep. "Mine has math, but it's all written in letters."

"Oh, that's going to be fun," Tommy said with a grin that the other three echoed.

"Box three is open!" shouted a voice, and everyone cheered.

The cypher group finished writing the phrase and realized it was a riddle.

"Hey, is anyone good with riddles?" Tommy asked loudly to the rest of the gym.

Two people headed over to them, and Caitlin sent them the phrase by tapping her phone against theirs.

"Box two is open!"

"Okay, let's look at this math," Tommy said, rubbing his hands together.

There were three separate problems in varying levels of difficulty. Tommy chose to work on the first problem, Dildeep and Brandon the second, and Caitlin the third.

"Done," Tommy said after a few minutes. "It's a three. Probably the first digit in the combination lock at station one."

"Box four is open!"

"Done! The third digit is a nine." Caitlin looked proud of herself.

"Can you check my work?" Tommy asked. "Best to be sure about this. We're the last ones."

"Only if you check mine too."

They exchanged phones, and by the time they had corroborated each other's answers, Dildeep said, "Forty-five."

"Let's go!" Tommy said excitedly, leading them over to station one. Heart thumping loudly in what felt like his throat, he spun the dial carefully to each number and gave it a tug.

The lock opened.

"Box one is open!" the four chorused, grinning at each other.

Inside was a section of hose.

"Oh, good. That'll make things go much faster," said Carter over Tommy's shoulder, grabbing the hose and carrying it to station two where a bin too large to fit inside the barrel was waiting. At station three, another section of hose was draining water into another large bin.

Tommy glanced at the completed puzzle on table one and noticed the black light pen beside it. He clicked it on and shone it at the puzzle, showing a row of shapes. It must have been the order to press the buttons on the box at station three.

"Why can't we use the buckets from section one to scoop the water from the other two stations?" Tommy asked Elyse.

"They're all cracked. Greg already suggested it."

Tommy nodded slowly. "Too bad."

They watched as Carter organized people to hold the bin from station three off the floor, switching the hose to the narrow opening of the green barrel. When water poured in, everyone cheered.

After several more minutes of everyone helping to hold the bins, each green barrel had twenty litres of water, and Quinn was smiling.

"Great work, everyone! I am extremely impressed," Quinn said, nodding at them. "I'll have to compare times with Tiffany, but it wouldn't surprise me if you won by a landslide. Let's head back to the auditorium for debriefing before lunch."

"The three of us ate lunch with Veronica, and then she gave us a tour of the campus. In the robotics lab, they have robots that travel over land, water, and air. They're called Automated Bots, or ABs for short. It's like *Star Trek*, it's so futuristic! They've got drones and they let us race them! Carter won, but I was so close to beating him. And they've got laptops and tablets with touch-screens! And have you *seen* these phones? There's a holographic keyboard!"

Tommy knew his dinner was getting cold, but he was so excited about his day that he wanted to share it with the avidly listening audience of Kennedy and Jason. "And there's this printer, but it doesn't print words on paper, it prints in 3D, and with any material! Veronica said we could each make two things, if they were small. So..."

He dug into his pocket, pulling out the ring and sword pendant he had made, shy all of a sudden.

"I wanted to give you something as a thank you for, well, everything. This is Galadriel's ring." He handed Kennedy the pure white ring. "It's not a diamond, just some sort of polymer crystal. I don't remember the ring's name, but I'm sure you know it." The ring had an intricate flower pattern in silver metal wrapped over the white crystal.

"Nenya," Kennedy said with a smile, putting the ring on the middle finger of her right hand. "It's beautiful, Tommy. Thank you."

"Veronica told me that you're not as into Middle-earth as Kennedy, but that Everdome was more your style." Tommy smirked. "She said that she got the specs for Demetrius's sword from the video game, and not to tell anyone." He handed Jason the sword pendant. "I hope you like it."

Jason looked shocked. "This is incredible. The game isn't supposed to be out until this summer." He pulled out the chain around his neck, revealing a yellow stone, and undid the clasp, placing the sword on the chain next to the stone. "Thank you, Tommy." He tucked the chain back under his shirt.

"There's so much security. Carter and I noticed cameras in every hallway and room, and there are patrols, and why is there a ten-foot wall around the campus?" Tommy finally picked up his fork to dig into his dinner.

"There are many different tech companies in Westmeath, and they're all pretty paranoid when it comes to their research and development," Jason said thoughtfully. "I'm actually surprised that they let you take *that*," he indicated the smartphone on the table, "home with you. Be careful not to flash it around on the street."

"I'll be careful," Tommy said before humming around a bite of food, making Jason chuckle and smirk at Kennedy, who grinned at him. "We have to look for bugs, try to figure out ways that it doesn't work for us." Tommy got excited again, letting his fork fall from his hand onto the plate. "I already found one! While I was waiting for you to get home, I was texting with Carter in my room, and I moved from the table to the bed, and the keyboard started going all wonky! Instead of the hologram being a certain distance from the phone, it projects to be a certain distance from whatever the phone is on! I tested it on a variety of different surfaces after that; a mirror, carpet, a cookie sheet, as well as being half on different surfaces, like half on a desk and half over empty space. The keyboard really didn't like being over nothing. I feel like that's a pretty big flaw in the design."

"That's great!" Kennedy enthused. "I'm really impressed."

Tommy grinned and picked up his fork again. "Veronica also showed us her office. Did you know she keeps a robot head in her desk drawer?"

Jason started coughing, tears streaming from his eyes. He rubbed down his sternum a couple times, trying to draw in air. "A *what*?" he asked once he could breathe again.

"A robot head. She said we weren't allowed to tell anyone, but I don't think she meant you." Tommy took another bite. "Oh, I almost forgot the best part about lunch! The CEO, Ellen Door, came to talk to us! She said we should call her Ellen! She said that Carter and I showed strong leadership and creative problem-solving skills."

"Wow!" Jason's eyes widened. "Those are quite the compliments."

"Yeah, I guess they are," Tommy said shyly. He ducked his head, but then remembered something else. "She also said..." he paused, trying to remember Ellen's exact words. "'Ms. Giles, you've been holding out on us, to give us two strong individuals in one year.' And then Veronica said something about us not being in grade nine before this year, and that all three of her choices were the best of the best. And Ellen said Elyse would get her time to shine in the coming days." Tommy paused again. "I didn't like her condescending tone, but Carter said that she's probably really busy and the fact that she took the time to come see us was a pretty big deal."

"Elyse is Rachel's sister," Jason said to Kennedy. "She was so little when I used to babysit them. It's hard to believe that she's old enough to be in grade nine."

"I thought she looked familiar at the dance the other night!" Kennedy exclaimed.

"You saw her?" Tommy smirked. "I'm surprised. Every time I glanced over at you two, you were completely oblivious to your surroundings."

"Surely not *every* time!" Kennedy protested.

"No, that's true," Tommy said mischievously. "You weren't there at all one time when I looked up."

"Oh." Kennedy glanced up at Jason, who smirked at her. She blushed, smiling. "Well, I *did* look at who you were hanging out with, if only to be able to describe them to Mom when she called." She sighed. "I hate feeling like I'm hovering over you. I hope you're okay with it."

"Honestly, I forgot about Mom's check-ins." Tommy tilted his head questioningly. "Obviously, she's okay with how things have been going, because she hasn't come to collect me yet."

Jason chuckled. "She wasn't too thrilled that we took you to a dance, but Kennedy reminded her that you weren't grounded here. And Lilah knows Carter, so it could have been worse. Then last night..."

"Last night she seemed sad," Kennedy said thoughtfully. "I told her about how much fun you had at game night, and she seemed surprised by how much you participated. I think she misses you."

"Really? She has a funny way of showing it," Tommy said bitterly.

Kennedy shrugged. "Changing the subject, are you feeling pressure to perform to a higher standard now that you know that Ellen has her eye on you?"

Tommy wrinkled his nose. "Carter and I talked about that on the way home. We're going to try not to think about it and just do our best."

"I think that's a good thing to do." Jason nodded approvingly. "What's on the schedule for tomorrow?"

"Tomorrow we've got," Tommy unlocked his phone the way Veronica had shown them at lunch, using his fingerprint on the screen, and navigated to his schedule, "engineering in the morning and biology in the afternoon, with an hour after lunch to get help from Veronica."

"You're taking classes during your vacation?" Jason asked with a smirk.

"Yeah, sort of. But it's not like in school."

"Please, do go on." Jason leaned his chin on one palm.

"There will be actual real-world applications involved. It won't be busywork."

"You're telling me that high school is boring," Kennedy said.

"Well, yeah. It is."

"You know you're allowed to skip ahead. You just have to pass the testing," Kennedy pointed out. "My friend Basil, he's an engineer, did that with a couple of his math classes in the lower levels. It gave him the space in his schedule in grade thirteen for university-level math, although he could have taken spares."

"I didn't know you could do that," Tommy said, surprised. "But I'm not going to get grade thirteen. This is the last year of it."

"All the more reason to reach ahead." Kennedy shrugged. "Then you have enough room in grade twelve to take all the courses you want to take."

"Good point. What will I have to do?"

"You need letters from a couple teachers and your parents, but yeah, I think it should be something to consider for next year."

"Cool. Thanks, Kennedy." Tommy snapped his fingers. "Ah! Now I place the name! I know Basil's youngest sister, Faith. She's in my grade."

"Is that how you skipped ahead?" Jason asked her.

"No." Kennedy blushed, and Tommy smirked.

"What?" Jason looked confused.

"I skipped one year of kindergarten. I could read before I started, and I was pretending I couldn't because none of the other kids could." Kennedy traced a pattern in the wooden table. "Mom talked to my teacher and bumped me ahead. It wasn't a big deal."

"Our little genius," Tommy teased.

"Right, because that's so much more impressive than your accomplishments," Kennedy said with a roll of her eyes. "I was *four,* and I wanted to read to be able to keep up with my older siblings." She paused. "It's not like they had the time to read me stories," she finished softly.

"You taught yourself?" Jason asked. "That's quite the accomplishment."

"Is that why you never said no when I asked you to read to me?" Tommy had many fond memories of cuddling up with Kennedy while she read to him.

"Partially," Kennedy admitted. "I also loved being around you. You were so cute. What happened?" She reached out to ruffle his hair, and he ducked away, pretending to be annoyed.

Later that evening, after Tommy had finished his math homework for school, his stomach rumbled, and he decided to get himself a snack. With the door open and his head in the hall, he could hear Kennedy on the phone in the kitchen.

"Seriously, Mom, he's flourishing here. You should have heard him at dinner, he's so excited! Really! I think he's bored in school. He seems to be a more hands-on kind of learner, and Parry Sound didn't have the resources for things like robotics when I was there, not even a club, so maybe you can look into some long-distance learning? He's got quite the schedule for the week. Once he's tried a whole bunch of different things, he's bound to have a focus on one of them. You can ask him then. I'm so glad he's here."

There was silence for a minute, during which Tommy assumed their mother was speaking.

"I'm serious, Mom. He's not even here right now, he's doing homework in his room. It's been great to get to know the older, more mature Tommy. I'd keep him here for the rest of the semester if I could."

Tommy drew in a sharp breath and felt tears stinging his eyes. He hadn't realized how much he wanted that until he'd heard it said out loud.

"I think that's enough eavesdropping for one night, don't you?" a quiet voice whispered from behind him in the hallway.

A squeak escaped him, and Tommy turned, heart pounding, to face Jason.

"Heard enough?"

Tommy said, "It's nice to overhear compliments."

Jason nodded thoughtfully. "It's even nicer to hear them to your face. I'm guessing you were hungry?"

"Yeah," Tommy said sheepishly.

"Then let's go save your sister. I think your mom is about to start the wedding questions again." Jason smiled at him.

"That reminds me, I think Mom's been making changes behind your back."

"Oh, really?" Jason said and sighed. "Any idea who she's been in touch with?"

"I heard her mention roses, so probably the florist, and table-cloths, so the venue?"

"The restaurant isn't an issue," Jason said. "Nick told me about the call, and he knows not to change anything without one of us confirming it. But the flowers..." He sighed again. "Kennedy says she doesn't care about anything except that she ends up married to me, but there are some things that I don't think she'd be happy about if they got changed. The dress, for one, although we don't need to worry about that with Zhanna and Lydia."

"Weren't they the women at Seams Likeable?" Tommy asked.

"Yes, they own it. They're making all the dresses and suits."

"If all their clothes are like the ones you bought for me, I'm envious."

"They are very good at what they do," Jason said, nodding. "Now, the flowers. The only thing I remember Kennedy saying is that she wants peonies to be the focus. White peonies. If your mom is mentioning roses... I'll get Rachel to investigate and make sure the florist knows to check any changes with us." Jason pulled out his phone and tapped at it. "I don't want Kennedy to get angry at your mom—"

Kennedy's volume increased and they heard her say, "What's wrong with white and green for our wedding colours?"

"Make that angrier. Better go." Jason urged Tommy into the kitchen before finishing his text to Rachel.

"Hey, Sis, do you want a late-night snack?" Tommy asked, walking in.

Kennedy held up a finger. "Tommy's here, Mom, and wants food. Don't you dare try to make changes to our colour scheme and leave the band alone! They know what songs we want played, and they're going to do a fantastic job. Goodnight!"

There was a pause as their mom said goodnight.

"I love you too, Mom." Kennedy hung up. "Can I throw my phone? I want to throw my phone."

"No, but you can go downstairs and punch the bag for a while," Jason said, walking into the kitchen.

"She just told me that the restaurant isn't agreeing to change the tablecloths to blue and pink! Why would we want them blue and pink?" Kennedy seethed for a minute. "And she wants the phone number for the band so she can *suggest songs*! I just...! What? No!"

She turned to Tommy, eyes pleading. "Am I turning into a bridezilla? Is that what's happening here? You'd tell me honestly, right?"

"Take a deep breath," Tommy advised. "You're not. Mom's trying to undermine all the work you've already done. It's no wonder you're stressing out."

"Here's what we're going to do." Jason wrapped her up in his arms and rocked her gently. "We're going to call everyone we've already booked and make sure they know that no changes are to be made without approval by us. Any future bookings will be told the same thing. Then your mother can call them all she wants, and we don't have to worry, alright?"

Kennedy nodded and relaxed in his hold. "Yeah, that's great. Thanks." She tilted her head up for a kiss. "Tell me again why we can't elope?"

"Because we want a big party."

"We can just... sneak away and get married now and then pretend to get married in June," Kennedy suggested.

Jason laughed. "What's the point of doing that? What would be different from how we're living right now?"

"Yeah, you're right." Kennedy sighed. "Mom would still try to micromanage everything."

"We'll just beat her at her own game." Jason pressed their foreheads together.

Tommy pretended not to watch them but seeing them together like this made something warm and fuzzy well up inside of him.

"What do you want to eat, Tommy?" Kennedy asked, pulling away after a moment. "Pancakes are our usual go-to for late night snacks."

"Pancakes sound great."

Chapter 4

♥

WEDNESDAY THE 12TH OF MARCH, 2003 -
WESTMEATH, ONTARIO

"What did you think of the electronics class this afternoon?"
Carter asked Tommy on the way home.

"You know, my science class is doing an electronics unit right now, and I did the homework the day I got here. I expected this class to be repetitive or boring." Tommy shook his head. "It was anything but! Why can't learning always be this way? Figuring out how to power a boat, learning how to run wires through a robot... This camp is amazing, and I'm going to have a lot of trouble settling back into regular school." He pulled his navy Door Tech Camp tuque further down over his ears and dug the matching mittens out of his pockets. "There's quite the wind tunnel with all these large buildings, isn't there?"

Carter copied him with his own matching tuque and mittens. "We can take the back roads to get to my place. It's a little longer, but fewer high-rises."

"Nah, this is fine," Tommy said, tucking his red nose into his scarf. "The wind will calm down once we reach Oldtown. Back home, the wind off the water rarely dies down."

"I looked up the geography of Parry Sound. There's an awful lot of lakes in the area. Do you get flooded often?"

"As much as any other region near water. Our farm is built higher up than the water table, so it doesn't really affect us personally. We've helped others out in the past. What about Westmeath? It's surrounded by the river. Do you get flooding?"

"Some areas do, mostly in the northwest, but the houses there were built with that in mind, so they don't have basements, or they have extra sump pumps. My dads took me to see a house there that was for sale last year, not because they wanted to buy it, but because they wanted me to see the architecture." Carter chuckled. "It sounds kinda funny when I say it out loud."

"No, it's cool that you understand how your city works, so you know how to fix it if you need to." Tommy smiled at him, forgetting his face was covered by his scarf. "Kinda like our smartphones. We're understanding how they work, and that's giving us insight on how to fix the bugs. The coding class this morning gave me an idea for a fix on a bug I found last night."

"We should test out the video functionality when we get to my place," Carter said.

"Sure. What do you want to film?" Tommy chuckled. "Bread rising in the bakery?"

"Actually, that's not a bad idea. See how well the fast replay works." Carter grinned. "Not today, though. I want to see the slow-motion replay. Let's film me throwing knives!"

"This I can't wait to see."

It didn't take them much longer to get to Oven Baked, and they clattered up the stairs to fetch Carter's knives.

"Did you want to try throwing them?" Carter asked.

"Uh, no thank you. I think one Fairfield throwing sharp objects is enough," Tommy said. "I'll stick with being your videographer."

"As long as you're sure."

They headed out into the backyard where Carter's target was set up, and he placed the knife case on the bench to one side. "My dads gave me these for Christmas. They're custom made," he said proudly as he opened the case.

They were well taken care of, the matte finish shining dully in the late afternoon sunlight. Tommy thought they looked elegant and deadly and told Carter so.

Carter laughed. "Well, they *are* knives! Why don't you stand here..." He shifted Tommy to the side, as far as the small yard would let him go. "You should be able to get the target and me in the shot at once."

Heads together, they checked the screen as Tommy pretended to take a video. It took all his energy to keep the phone from shaking; Carter's proximity was making his stomach do flips.

Satisfied, Carter took his place and picked up all five knives. "Keep it going until I'm done, 'kay?"

"Okay." Tommy pressed record. "Go."

Carter focussed on the target and sent the knives, one after the other, directly into the centre. He smiled. "You can stop." He headed over to where Tommy was standing, jaw dropped.

"How does it look?" Carter asked, nodding at the screen.

As if in a trance, Tommy pressed the replay and slow-motion buttons. Together, they watched the video. When it was done, Tommy, a little dazed, said, "That was super hot."

Carter glanced at him, surprise written on his face. "I'm sorry?"

Tommy blinked and then slowly started to flush. "Did I say that out loud?" he whispered, embarrassed.

"Did you want to?" Carter kept his voice quiet.

"I... I don't know." Tommy could feel his heart rate picking up, his throat tightening with anxiety. "I think I should go home. I... I'm sorry." He swallowed hard, trying to fight against his urge to run. "Let me get you the video." He held up his phone, ready to tap it against Carter's.

Carter dug his phone out of his pocket and held them together. "Text me tonight?" he asked, face blank.

Tommy wished the video transfer would hurry up so he could get away from the awkward situation. "Course. I just... I need to..."

He took a deep breath, surprised at how shaky it sounded.

"If you decide that you wanted me to hear it, I liked hearing it from you," Carter said shyly, gaze fixed on the progress bar.

Their phones beeped that the transfer was complete. Tommy gave his friend a wobbly smile, turned, and jogged away.

A block later, he slowed to a walk. He couldn't run any longer with his heart racing so fast. He didn't want to think about it, but he owed Carter an explanation. The whole way home, he tried to figure out what was going on in his head… and his heart.

I feel like such a cliché! he thought. *Every teen romcom wrapped up in one!*

When the little bungalow came into view, he suddenly realized that he thought of it as home. But he didn't want to go in just yet. Instead, Tommy pulled out his phone and queued up the video again, watching it at regular speed. The lethal grace of the boy on the screen made him feel like he'd just run a marathon.

I'm not ready for this! he wailed internally.

Stuffing his phone back in his pocket, he paced the length of the property a couple times until movement from the porch next door caught his attention.

Gabrielle, with Brooke dressed like the Michelin Man in her arms, was leaving their house. "Hi, Tommy. Is everything okay?" Gabrielle put Brooke down in the front yard and the toddler threw herself into a snowbank, shrieking with laughter. "Is your fingerprint not working? You know you're welcome at our house."

"No, I… I wanted the fresh air." Tommy stumbled over his words, his thoughts a tangled mess. "I needed to clear my head."

Gabrielle hummed thoughtfully and joined him on the sidewalk. She pulled a hat out of her pocket, covering her short light brown hair and unusually pointed ears with it. "Is camp going as well as you hoped?"

"I'm loving camp. It's so much fun!" Tommy could be sure of that.

"Ah, then it's affairs of the heart," Gabrielle said with a smile. "What seems to be the trouble? Worried about what will happen after you go home?"

Tommy's breathing picked up again. "I *wasn't*," he said, pressing his knuckles to his sternum.

"Would a hug help?" Gabrielle looked concerned.

"No, I'm okay." Tommy stared at Gabrielle's feet. "Can I ask you a question?"

"Of course."

"How did you know you wanted to date Zoe?"

Gabrielle chuckled lightly. "At first, we were friends. A boy was bullying me, and she... took him to task. After that, she took my hand, and told me that she would stand by me forever."

Tommy looked up to see she was smiling.

"We were twelve years old. Then, in grade nine, I asked her to be my girlfriend. We got married the summer after grade thirteen."

"But how did you know whether you were feeling friend-feelings or romantic-feelings?" Tommy asked anxiously.

Gabrielle laughed and put a hand on his shoulder. "I'm going to ask you some questions. You don't have to answer out loud, but I think they might help clear things up for you."

Tommy nodded.

"Close your eyes. I want you to picture a friend from home. Got them? Okay, now imagine holding their hand, gazing into their eyes, leaning in for a kiss."

Tommy wrinkled his nose, remembering the time Cindy Lou had chosen him for seven minutes in heaven. The stuffy closet full of fall coats in her parent's basement, him trying not to trip on rain boots, her grasping fingers on his arms, and the demanding pressure of her lips against his. The memory of her slimy tongue slipping into his mouth made him shudder, and Gabrielle chuckled.

"Now picture this friend you're unsure about. How do you feel when you imagine holding their hand? Gaze into their eyes. How do you feel about leaning in for a kiss?"

Tommy felt his cheeks flush with colour as he imagined getting closer with Carter. Imagining kissing him sent pleasant shivers up and down his spine. He opened his eyes with a gasp.

Gabrielle smiled gently. "Did that help?"

"What do I do?" Tommy asked frantically.

"*That* is up to you. Do you think this person would be open to a relationship with you? What do you have to lose if they aren't interested?" Gabrielle gestured to Brooke, who was throwing clouds of snow over her head and giggling when the tiny crystals landed on her face. She had white eyelashes, and her cheeks were red from the wet cold. "But if they are, you're opening yourself up to something magical."

"I... Okay." Tommy took off his hat and ran his fingers through his hair. "Okay. Thank you, Gabrielle." He turned to go into the house.

"Whatever you decide, I hope it goes well," Gabrielle said softly.

"Me too."

He half ran to the door, unlocking it and disarming the alarm with barely a thought. He closed the door against the cold March wind and checked the clock. Kennedy wouldn't be home for a while. He stripped out of his winter gear, hung everything in the closet, and then paced back and forth.

I like him. I really like him. It sounded strange, even in his head. He thought about his family, and how they might react. Kennedy wouldn't be upset that he liked her friend, would she? *And Carter...* Just thinking his name made him want to melt into a puddle. He swallowed hard.

I like him. I really like him, he repeated to himself. *Holy crap, I didn't know I could like someone this much!*

Tommy sat on the couch, elbows on his knees, and pressed his hands over his eyes until he saw sparkles behind his eyelids.

"I need paper." He shot to his feet and ran to his room, determined to get his feelings down in print. "Maybe this will help me organize my thoughts."

Half an hour later, he heard Kennedy call out a greeting to Gabrielle, and he groaned. Tommy looked at the song he'd managed to write, the page half-scribbled out, and felt a bit better. He watched from his window as Kennedy hugged Gabrielle and tossed a handful of sparkling snow over Brooke. Gabrielle said something, and Kennedy looked back at the house. She gave Gabrielle another hug and hurried up the walk.

"Tommy?" Kennedy called the instant she was through the door, shedding her hat and coat and kicking off her boots.

"Did she say anything?" he gasped, running into the front hall and skidding on the floor in his socks.

"Just that you were home. It's early. I thought you were going to hang out with Carter after camp today?" Kennedy took his face in her hands, and he was startled to realize they were almost the same height. "What happened? What's wrong?"

Tears prickled his eyes at her concern, and he felt his lower lip wobble. He buried his face in her shoulder and felt her arms wrap around him in a warm embrace. "Dee, I..."

When he'd been first learning to talk, Kennedy's name had been too hard for him to say, and she had been dubbed 'Dee' by the toddler. She'd loved it, so he still used it occasionally, mostly when one or the other was feeling particularly sappy.

His voice broke. "I really like Carter. *More* than like. I want to be with him all the time."

Kennedy held him tighter and swayed him back and forth. "That's wonderful! Why are you crying?" She walked him over to the couch and sat down, pulling him against her shoulder. "What can I do?"

Tommy wiped his eyes and sniffled. "That's the first time I've said it out loud."

"Why were you so worried to tell me?" Kennedy put a hand to her heart. "Am I that horrible a person?"

"He's one of your closest friends. I didn't want to harm your relationship." Tommy squinted at her suspiciously. "It feels like you already knew."

"Tommy, I love you, but you are a bit oblivious," Kennedy said with a chuckle. "It's not your fault. You were just too close to the situation."

Something in his expression must have made her pause because she ran her fingers through his bangs, pushing them off his forehead. "Think about it this way." She cleared her throat and tossed her hair back. "When I look at Jason across the table, what do you see?"

"That you want to be closer to him," Tommy said with a smirk.

"Exactly." Kennedy booped his nose with her finger and he wrinkled it. "Now, what do you think I see when you're looking at Carter?"

Tommy flushed. "I don't know."

"Longing, mostly. A bit of lust." Kennedy grinned.

"I didn't realize I was so obvious," Tommy said sheepishly.

"It's okay. I don't blame you." She laughed and then sobered. "Now tell me. Why aren't you at Carter's?"

Tommy squirmed at the knowing look in her eye. He avoided her gaze. "I panicked. I've never had a crush on someone before," he whispered. He told her the whole story.

"You came back here to figure out... what?" Kennedy asked. "What you want?"

"Well, first I needed to figure out that I actually liked him like that," Tommy said, half smiling.

Kennedy laughed. "And now that you've figured it out, what's next?"

Tommy cleared his throat. "Ummm. Can I ask Carter over? Now? We need to talk."

Glancing at the clock on the mantel, Kennedy nodded. "Invite him for dinner. But no sleeping over tonight; you've got camp in the morning and need to be rested."

"Sleepovers are an option?" Tommy asked, surprised, and blushed.

"Tommy." Kennedy patted his cheek. "We trust you to ask for consent and be safe. Once you talk to Carter, keep the communication going, and we can talk about a sleepover after camp is over."

"Wow. I'm not sure I'm ready for, you know, *sex*. Let me get a boyfriend first? Hang on, I'm going to text Carter."

"Sleepovers don't have to mean sex. I'm going to start dinner." Kennedy got to her feet. "Spaghetti okay?"

"Yes, please."

Tommy was still reeling from Kennedy's most recent revelation as he pulled out his phone and opened the texting app. Clicking on Carter's name, he took a moment to compose himself and figure out what he wanted to write.

Finally, he texted, "I didn't mean to say it out loud, but I'm glad I did. Can you come over and stay for dinner? I would like to say some more things out loud, intentionally this time."

Tommy hit send and waited for the panic to set in. It didn't. Less than two minutes later, he received a *ping* of notification.

Carter's reply was short; "omw."

Beaming, Tommy headed into the kitchen and wrapped his arms around his sister from behind. "He's on his way."

"You sound a lot calmer," Kennedy remarked happily. "Feel steady enough to help me cut veggies?"

Tommy held out a hand for the knife. "I have a plan. I wrote him a song that I'll sing, and then I'll tell him I like him as more than a friend."

"Solid plan. Definitely swoon-worthy."

"Don't joke."

"I'm not! Jason sang to me on our first date. Swept me off my feet."

"What song was it?" Tommy asked, curious.

"'I Want You' by Savage Garden," Kennedy replied, smiling dreamily. "He knew all the words to the verse and even sang them at tempo! Pro tip, singing quietly into your partner's ear while dancing close is super hot."

"I'll keep that in mind," Tommy said dryly.

The front door opened, and Jason walked into the house. "Honey, I'm home!"

"Are you going to tell Jason?" Kennedy asked quietly. "We had already guessed that you might like Carter, so it's not going to be a huge surprise to him."

Tommy put the knife down next to the chopped green peppers, heart leaping with nerves. "Yeah, it'll be good practise."

He washed his hands as Kennedy left the kitchen to greet Jason. He gave them a moment, but not long enough. When he entered the hallway, they were still kissing, Kennedy's dirty hands held up above her head by Jason's larger ones as he pressed her against the wall. Face flushed, Tommy coughed and tried to avert his eyes from the enthusiastic display.

"Sorry, didn't realize you were home," Jason rasped, pulling away from Kennedy with what looked like great reluctance.

Tommy felt shivers go up and down his spine at his tone. "It's okay. Sorry for messing up your plans."

"Why *are* you home? Is everything okay with Carter?" Jason put a hand on Tommy's shoulder, the heavy weight comforting.

"He's coming over now, actually." Tommy took a deep breath and met Jason's hazel eyes. "I'm going to ask him to be my boyfriend."

A grin immediately appeared on Jason's face. "Yeah? You think he'll say yes?"

"I really hope so," Tommy said nervously.

"Good for you." Jason squeezed his shoulder. "You've discovered another piece of yourself. Thank you for trusting us."

The doorbell rang, cutting off any reply, not that Tommy could think of anything to say. Jason stepped out of his way, and he moved as if in a daze toward the door, opening it to Carter's smiling face. "Come on in." Tommy hung his friend's coat and waited impatiently while he unlaced his boots. "Let's go to my room."

Tommy noticed that Jason was now in the kitchen helping Kennedy make the sauce for dinner. He towed Carter into the hallway that led to the bedrooms.

Once inside, he sat Carter in the desk chair and paced in front of him. "Okay. I'm not great with words in person. I'll probably mix things up and screw up and, actually, I've kinda already done that. You've been... *so* patient with me, and I really don't deserve it, but I appreciate it—" Tommy cut himself off. "Sorry, I kinda go on when I'm nervous. Let me..."

He held out his hands, indicating that Carter should sit tight, and grabbed his guitar case, placing it carefully on the end of the bed and opening it. He picked up the paper on the desk and winced at the scribbles.

"I wrote this when I got home, and it's a bit of a mess, but I think it'll help me say what I'm trying to say."

Tommy sat on the bed, one leg bent in front of him and one hanging off the edge. He pulled the guitar out of its case. He strummed over the strings, tuned one slightly, and shifted the paper in front of him on the bed.

"I didn't get a chance to write music to go with this, so it's going to be very rough." Tommy put a capo on the third fret and played a couple chords, trying to decide which ones he liked best. "Okay."

Tommy glanced up at Carter's rapt expression and took courage.

Tommy kept his eyes glued to the paper throughout the first verse.

> *When I first saw you, I was looking through a window,*
> *Didn't get why I felt the way I did, I didn't know,*
> *Then when you touched my hand,*
> *I needed to understand...*

He felt his cheeks redden as he sang the chorus.

> *Ooh, I wanna get to know you,*
> *And, ooh, I maybe want to kiss you,*
> *I want to hold your hand,*
> *As beside you I stand,*
> *Ooh, you know, I think I might be—*
>
> *Today I saw you moving with such lethal grace,*
> *Carved open my chest just to watch my heart race,*

It's like I was hit by a meteor,
I think I'm ready to open the door...

Ooh, I wanna get to know you,
And, ooh, I maybe want to kiss you,
I want to hold your hand,
As beside you I stand,
Ooh, you know, I think I might be—

He looked up and locked eyes with Carter, whose mouth hung open. Tommy forged onward to the bridge.

I can almost see the lightbulb when you're learning,
You're so bright it's almost like you're glowing,
I can't look away...

Ooh, I wanna get to know you,
And, ooh, I maybe want to kiss you,
I want to hold your hand,
As beside you I stand,
Ooh, you know, I am—

Tommy swallowed hard, took his fingers from the strings, and laid the guitar flat across his lap.

"I lied to you at the dance on Saturday. I'm sorry. I was feeling... I panicked," Tommy whispered to the guitar, fiddling with the capo once he removed it. He looked up at the boy sitting in the chair.

"Carter, I *do* like guys. And I..." He took a deep breath. "I'd really like you to be my boyfriend."

"I'd like that a lot, too," Carter said, beaming at him. "I have a couple questions."

"Yeah?" Tommy mentally told his heart to calm down.

"You wrote that? Today?"

"Yeah, I did." Tommy blushed and ran a hand through his hair. "It's not perfect. The first verse is a bit rough, and the rhyming could use some work..."

"It was amazing! Don't change a word of it!" Carter's grin morphed into a smirk. "Was I, like, your sexual awakening?"

Tommy laughed and put his guitar back in its case. "If a sexual awakening is my heart doing a samba when watching you throw knives, then yeah, you are. Seeing you made me finally figure out why kissing Cindy Lou felt like a chore and why I was envious of my sister. I've never felt like this about anyone before."

Carter stuck out his tongue but laughed. "Yeah, Jason's hard to compete with."

"No, that's not it." Tommy shook his head and shifted closer on the bed to the chair. "I'm a little bit in awe of him, and yeah, he's hot, but you..."

Tommy flushed but reached out and took Carter's light bronze hand in his, noting the olive undertones against his pink ones, fingers brushing over callouses until he laced them together. "I see your face and my heart races. I touch your hand and my nerves are singing. I talk to you and my day is brighter. You're not competing, because you're in a whole other category."

"Damn, I thought you said you weren't great with words!" Carter said with a grin. "First you write me a song, we become boyfriends, and then you compliment me until I can barely think. Where's the catch?"

"There's a couple of pretty big ones, actually," Tommy said sadly. "Like the fact that I'm leaving on Sunday."

Carter wrinkled his nose. "Yeah, that really bites. What's the other one?"

Tommy worried at his lip. "I'm not ready to tell my parents that I'm dating. It's not about being cool... I just... My mom and I don't have the best relationship. I don't know what'll set her off, and I definitely don't want her nagging me about you. When Mom picks me up, you'd have to be my friend Carter. I can't... I don't want her to know yet, but I don't want to hurt you either."

Tommy searched Carter's face for understanding and found it.

"Hey, it's okay. I get where you're coming from. We'll lay some ground rules after dinner, alright? Do Kennedy and Jason know? Can we tell them?" Carter asked anxiously.

"They know." Tommy grinned. "They're incredible."

"They really are."

"Even if I have to walk in on them making out in the hallway."

"They are unfairly hot together."

"That's my sister. I don't think that about her!" Tommy slapped Carter's arm lightly. "Wait, you think that about her?"

"I'm bisexual. I think everyone's hot." Carter smirked.

"But I'm the hottest?"

"So hot I'm worried I'll burn my fingers if I hold your hand too long."

Tommy smiled and ducked his head shyly.

"But it's so worth it," Carter whispered, leaning in close to Tommy's ear and making him shiver. "Shall we?"

"Yes."

"Can I hold your hand?" Carter asked, not letting go as he stood.

"I'll learn how to eat and write left-handed if it means that you don't have to let go," Tommy said gallantly.

"Awesome," Carter replied, leading him to the door. "What about the dance on Friday? Are you going?"

"I haven't asked to go, but I'm pretty confident that they'll say yes. They probably want the house to themselves after a week of me being underfoot. We can definitely hold hands there."

They turned the corner from hallway to kitchen and found Kennedy straddling Jason on a kitchen chair, his hands on her ass while they made out.

"See?" Tommy said to Carter, making Kennedy jump. "Did you not hear the floor creak?"

"I did," Jason said with a wicked grin. "But it's my house. And if we left the room, the sauce could burn."

"Speaking of," Kennedy said, getting up and going over to the stove to stir. "We should put the pasta on."

"Yeah, alright." Jason got to his feet to help her. He nodded at their linked hands. "I'm glad."

Tommy grinned and squeezed Carter's fingers.

"So, Tommy," Kennedy said, and he braced himself. "You sing and play beautifully. Would you be willing to play some more another time?"

Letting out a breath he didn't realize he was holding, Tommy said, "Yeah, I'd love that. I heard you singing on Saturday. Your voice is pretty great too. I can play songs that you can join in on."

"Great idea!"

Chapter 5

♥

"I am so proud of you for winning the phone!" Tommy said to Carter, swinging their linked hands together as they headed for their lockers at the end of their last day of camp. "You totally deserve it."

"There were a couple really close contenders, you included," Carter protested. "I wish they'd given out more than one."

"But then it wouldn't be special." Tommy grinned at his boyfriend. "Besides, I'm not jealous. I got awards for best student overall *and* leadership. I think my parents will be over the moon."

"My boyfriend, the genius," Carter said, bringing their joined hands to his lips and pressing a light kiss to one of Tommy's knuckles.

"*My* boyfriend, the out-of-the-box thinker with innovative solutions," Tommy replied with a smile, heart fluttering at Carter's casual display of affection.

They opened their lockers, pulling out their winter gear.

Tommy patted his pocket reflexively, chuckled at himself, and said, "It feels weird not having a cell phone again. I really got used to having it this week."

"I—"

"Hey, Yee-haw," Greg interrupted Carter. He leaned against his own locker a few doors away from Tommy's. At his back were a couple of his friends. "It's a good thing there wasn't homework, eh, or else it would have interfered with you going at it all the time."

Tommy was confused. "Going at it... Like walking home?"

Carter chuckled and leaned in, draping himself over Tommy's back. "He means sex," he whispered in his ear.

"Oh!" Tommy widened his eyes dramatically. "Why do you care? So that you can visualize your fantasies properly?"

Carter collapsed in laughter, clinging to Tommy's shoulders.

Greg snarled and slammed open his locker, the door banging off the one next to it. "You're going to pay for that, Yee-haw."

"In your dreams," Tommy said dismissively, turning his back on the bully.

Greg pulled on a purple leather coat and Carter inhaled sharply. "He's one of *them*. They recruit teens now, like some sort of fifties greasers? That's messed up," he whispered to Tommy.

"One of who?" Tommy asked, yanking on his coat.

"Blue Bloods. They're a gang that was trying to take Oldtown. Judy's not going to be impressed."

They stayed to say goodbye to and compliment the other students as they arrived at their lockers, and the next time they looked for Greg and his friends, they were gone.

"See you at the dance tonight, Elyse?" Carter asked. "Or will your parents want to celebrate your physics award?"

Elyse grinned. "They can celebrate my achievements tomorrow. I'm coming to that dance. We only get to see Tommy for a couple more days. I'm really going to miss you," she said, giving Tommy a hug.

He squeezed her back awkwardly. "I'm going to miss being here a lot, but I've got your email for MSN, and I'll be back for the wedding in June, as well as a whole week before it."

"Your parents are letting you take a week off from school right before exams?" Elyse asked, surprised.

"Yeah, but I'm going to have to keep up with the work. It's not a *complete* vacation."

"You'll stay out of trouble so they don't change their minds, right?"

"Who, me?" Tommy grinned innocently. "I'm an angel!"

"Mmhmm." Elyse raised one eyebrow skeptically. "I seem to recall it was *your* idea for the prank we pulled this morning."

"Well, I will be," Tommy amended. "When I go home, I'm not going to hang out with those losers I thought were my friends anymore. And Jason suggested I join a couple clubs if they're still accepting members. That should keep me busy and distracted from missing you, my real friends."

"Aww!" Elyse hugged him again.

"Come on, we've got to get home," Carter said. "I want to shower before the dance."

"Yeah, good call," Tommy agreed. "See you!"

There was a chorus of goodbyes as they left, and they linked fingers until they reached the gate to the outside world.

Tommy returned his pass first, signing out for the last time, and then waited for Carter on the sidewalk, pulling on his mitts.

"Not so tough without your big-shot boyfriend, are you?" snarled a voice behind him.

Tommy was pushed, stumbling, into an alley beside the campus and thrown back against the stone wall.

"So courageous of you, attacking someone while their back is turned," Tommy spat at Greg. He looked beyond him at the lackeys. "You must be so proud of your leader."

They shifted awkwardly but didn't leave.

"You wanted to get me alone so you could, what? Beat me up?" Tommy tilted his chin up and looked Greg in the eye, unafraid. "Am I *that* intimidating to you?"

Greg roared and pulled his fist back. Tommy ducked at the last second, and Greg howled as his fist crunched into stone.

"You should probably get that looked at," Tommy said, squeezing past the whimpering bully. "Excuse me," he said politely to the lackeys, and they stepped aside so he could walk back out onto the sidewalk.

"There you are!" Carter ran up to him, obviously relieved. He paused as he caught sight of the purple jackets in the alley. "They give you any trouble?" he asked, concerned.

"Nah." Tommy turned his back on the gang members and started walking home. "Greg had a brief conversation with the wall, and then I left."

Carter whistled and grinned. "That is so hot."

"Says the black belt who would have mopped the floor with him," Tommy scoffed. "All I did was duck."

Carter shook his head. "And that's exactly what you should have done. I would have done the same. Least amount of effort for maximum return. I wouldn't beat him up, just hurt him enough to get away." He grinned. "Change of subject; I'm looking forward to sleeping over tonight after the dance." Carter bumped his hip into Tommy's. "Get our cuddle on, maybe share our first kiss?"

Tommy blushed, shyly glancing at Carter. "I used to think I wasn't all that into kissing."

Carter snorted. "Used to, as in up until a couple days ago?"

"Yeah," Tommy said sheepishly. "Let's just say that seven minutes in heaven isn't the way *I'd* describe it."

They managed to take a few steps before they broke, laughing so hard they had to stop walking.

"Well," gasped Carter, clutching at his stomach and trying to catch his breath. "I think you'll find that kissing *me* will be a very different experience."

"That sure of yourself, are you?" Tommy asked, smiling shyly.

"Even though I've never kissed anyone before, I've been imagining a kiss with you for almost a week," Carter admitted.

Tommy swallowed hard. "Jeepers, that's not intimidating at all."

"I think Kennedy's starting to rub off on you. I've never heard anyone else say 'jeepers' before," Carter said with a chuckle.

"Don't distract me. Almost a week?"

Carter grinned. "I thought we already had this conversation. You're hot. I'm glad that you think I am, too."

They walked in shy silence for a little while.

"What did you think of our classes this week? I, for one, am going to be so bored when I get back to school." Tommy groaned dramatically. "As if I wasn't already."

"The classes were advanced, but the way they taught them made it feel so easy, and the lab work we did really helped stick the concepts in my brain." Carter pouted a bit. "I'm going to miss that."

"At least you know how you study now. Exams are going to be a breeze once you set up your study notes," Tommy pointed out.

"I wish we could study together." Carter pouted even more. "It's not fair that you live so far away."

"We can quiz each other over MSN. I'm in science and math this term, same as you. The curricula can't be that different."

"It wouldn't be the same, but I'll take what I can get." They had reached Carter's home, and they made the detour to get his overnight bag and promise his dads that he wouldn't miss his Kung Fu lesson the next morning.

"Don't worry, Jason's in my class. He'd never let me miss it, even if I wanted to." Carter hugged each of his dads. "I promise I won't stay too late at the dance or be up too long talking."

They walked the few blocks to the Johnson home and met up with Kennedy getting off her bus.

"Wave at my co-workers, Tommy. They've been hearing about you all week and will be happy they caught a glimpse of you," Kennedy said.

Tommy dutifully waved, and they all walked home together. It was strange to wave at tinted windows; he couldn't even see a silhouette.

Later that night, after the dance, and after brushing their teeth side by side over the sink, Tommy and Carter stood awkwardly in front of each other in the bedroom.

"I... We don't have to kiss if you're not ready," Carter said, running a hand through his hair and messing up his curls. "I still want to, but I don't want to pressure you into anything you don't feel comfortable with."

Tommy laced his fingers through Carter's and shuffled closer. He gazed into grey eyes and leaned until their foreheads pressed together. "I want to," he breathed. He shifted to touch their noses and exhaled shakily. "I *really* want to."

Breath mingled as they hesitated. Tommy's eyes drifted closed, and he focussed on other sensations; the soft skin against his nose, Carter's scent surrounding him, hot breath, spicy with mint toothpaste, against his lips, his heart thundering in his ears... A slight shift of Carter's head and soft lips brushed against his own.

Oh, he thought as he lightly pressed back, dizzy with sensation, this *is what it's supposed to feel like.*

They both gasped, pulling back a short distance.

"Okay?" Carter said, breathing hard.

Tommy laughed happily and hugged his boyfriend close, burying his face in the collar of the purple dress shirt Carter had worn to the dance. "So much more than just *okay*!" he said. "Can we do that again? Did you like it?"

"I can barely catch my breath, and I feel like I could fly!" Carter said, grinning. "Yeah, let's try again."

More confident now, Tommy cradled Carter's face in his hands and brought their lips together.

It's hard to kiss while smiling, Tommy thought after a moment. *Good to know.*

They giggled at each other when they pulled away.

"Maybe we should get in our pyjamas," Carter said, tugging on the shirt tails of Tommy's sparkly black button-down. "I do have a pretty early morning tomorrow."

"Yeah, good idea," Tommy said. "Ummm, I usually sleep in just my boxers, but I was thinking of wearing a shirt, too?"

Carter bit his lip. "Yeah, me too. I... I'm not sure I'm ready for so much skin-to-skin contact."

Tommy blew out a breath of relief. "Glad we're on the same page."

"I'll just..." Carter picked up his shirt and indicated the door.

"No, we'll just turn away while we change. Then there's no awkward 'is he done' moment," Tommy said.

They got into their pyjamas quickly, turned off the light, and climbed into bed, lying facing each other in the semi-darkness.

"Good night," Tommy said softly.

"Good night," Carter replied. He put his hand in the space between them, and Tommy covered it with his own. Carter wiggled his feet closer, touching Tommy's ankles with his cold toes. "Sorry," he whispered in response to Tommy's squeak. "They'll warm up quickly."

"Cold feet? Really?" Tommy teased.

"Not about us," Carter said fiercely. He pushed himself up on his hands, shifting to loom over Tommy's upper body, who rolled onto his back. He took in a shaky breath. "Why does it feel more intimate now that we're lying down?"

"Gravity?" Tommy suggested, relieved that Carter had kept their hips apart. He wasn't ready for *that* much intimacy. "Pressure?"

"Maybe."

"Are you going to kiss me?" Tommy quirked a half-smile. "Or is this too much?"

Carter lowered himself to one elbow, bringing their faces close together.

"You are so hot," breathed Tommy, tilting his chin up.

"Mmmm, I think we already decided that I'm the one who has the *cold* feet," Carter said with a smirk, brushing their noses together.

"Carter," moaned Tommy, startling them both. He swallowed hard and asked, "Please, kiss me?"

"Yeah," gasped Carter. His first attempt landed on the corner of Tommy's lips, but Tommy turned his head to meet him.

They settled into a rhythm quickly, a gentle press and pull back that made Tommy dizzy and grateful he was lying down. He realized his hands were motionless beside his body like dead fish, and moved them onto Carter's back, feeling the strength in his muscles as he supported himself. He fisted one hand in the material of Carter's shirt, the other climbing higher and curling over his shoulder.

"Tommy," breathed Carter, settling more firmly on top of him, chest to chest.

Nerves firing, Tommy opened his mouth and traced Carter's bottom lip with his tongue.

Carter pulled back, panting, pupils blown wide.

"Sorry," Tommy said, apologetic. "Too much?"

"No." Carter pressed their lips together again, and then opened his mouth.

Tommy chased the flavour of toothpaste and Carter into his mouth and groaned.

"Oh," Carter gasped and rolled away, breathing hard.

"Sorry," panted Tommy, staring up at the dark ceiling. "I wasn't... I didn't..."

"Don't apologize. That was amazing." Carter grasped Tommy's hand and squeezed his fingers tightly. "I had no idea kissing would be like that."

"Me neither." Tommy scrubbed his free hand over his face. "Think you can sleep now?"

Carter chuckled. "Give me a minute or two."

"Yeah, I hear that."

SUNDAY THE 16TH OF MARCH, 2003 - WESTMEATH, ONTARIO

The sunlight streaming through the window woke Tommy, and he groaned, annoyed with himself for having forgotten to close the curtains the night before. He rolled over, ready to bury his face into the pillow and hit another warm body. "Oh oops, sorry!"

Carter lifted his head, eyes bleary with sleep. "Forget I was here?" he rasped, voice hoarse with disuse.

"I'm not exactly used to sleeping with someone else," Tommy said sheepishly. "It's only been two nights."

"Time?" Carter asked, covering a yawn with a hand.

Tommy rolled in the other direction and picked up his watch. "Seven."

"You're not leaving until after lunch, right? Wanna cuddle?" Eyes mostly closed, Carter held his arms open.

Tommy could hear noises from the kitchen and smelled bacon cooking. His stomach rumbled, but the appeal of snuggling up with Carter was overwhelming. "Yeah." He shifted closer, pressing his forehead to Carter's sternum and wrapping his arm around the other boy's waist.

"Delaying food for me?" Carter murmured, nuzzling into the top of Tommy's head. "I heard that thunder. I must be something special."

Tommy flushed. "You are," he whispered back, clutching the back of Carter's shirt in his hands. "You are to me."

A little while later, a knocking on the door startled them awake. "If you want breakfast, boys, it's time to wake up," Jason's voice called through the door. "Can you hear me?"

"Yeah, we hear you. We're up," Carter croaked.

"I didn't mean to fall asleep again," Tommy said, his body protesting as he rolled out of bed. "It was nice to sleep wrapped up in you."

"It was, wasn't it?" Carter said with a grin. He grabbed his clothes from his bag and headed for the door. "I'm going to wash up."

Tommy pulled pyjama pants over his boxers and followed his nose into the empty kitchen. He grabbed a clean plate from the table and served himself from the plates keeping warm in the oven. He could hear grunts and sounds of skin slapping skin coming from the basement. He wrinkled his nose. Coming from any other couple, those noises would mean something entirely different.

Right now, though, they meant that Jason and Kennedy were practising some of the moves they'd been working on in class the day before, and, given the absence of his mother on the main floor, they were showing her. The sound of applause met his ears, confirming his guess.

Carter entered the kitchen and Tommy waved him over. "Good morning kiss before Mom comes up," he whispered.

Leaning over him, Carter pressed a chaste kiss to his lips as he grabbed his plate. He was filling it when all three adults entered the room.

"Hello, boys," Kennedy said, giving Tommy a kiss on his head and hugging Carter when he stood up from the stove.

He pushed her away with a grin.

"I hope you didn't stay up too late talking last night."

"Late enough," Carter said with an exaggerated yawn. "He just wouldn't shut up."

"Uh, no, I seem to recall that you were an equal participant in the 'just one more thing' and 'oh wait, we haven't talked about this.'" Tommy pouted. "We *were* asleep by midnight."

"Not bad. Could have been worse," Jason said, interrupting the frown Tommy saw on his mother's face. "One time I stayed up until four in the morning talking with my best friend. And that had been a school night!"

"Speaking of Veronica, she's coming over, and she'd like to say goodbye to you, Tommy. Were you planning to have a shower before packing?" Kennedy asked. "We don't want her coming while you're busy."

"I can take a break from packing. My shower shouldn't take more than ten minutes. I plan to hop in right after I finish eating." Tommy stuffed a bite of bacon in his mouth. "Thanks for keeping it warm for us."

"I'll let her know." Kennedy typed away on her phone.

Tommy's shower didn't take long, and he was even able to pack most of his dirty clothes in his suitcase before he heard the doorbell ring.

He skidded in the hallway, his socks slippery as he turned the corner too quickly, running past the others to the door. Veronica didn't look much different in her everyday clothes compared to her work ones, still the same pale, petite brunette. The only difference was the punk skater dress instead of a business skirt suit. She was carrying a large paper bag that instantly piqued Tommy's interest.

"Thank you so much for sponsoring me, Veronica. I really appreciate it."

Veronica laughed. "You said that on Friday at lunch, and again after the award show that afternoon. I couldn't be prouder of all three of you. You really covered yourselves in glory."

Out of the corner of his eye, Tommy noticed his mother puffing up with pride.

"And, to make it easier for you to keep in touch and keep up with schoolwork, Jason, Kennedy, and I decided to give you an early birthday present."

Tommy's jaw dropped. "But my birthday isn't until May!"

"Yeah, but we won't be able to come down to celebrate it with you properly, and we won't see you until the wedding, so..." Jason trailed off.

Veronica handed him the bag, and Tommy peeked inside. "No way."

"Yes way. I built it myself." Veronica looked proud. "It was Kennedy's idea, once she saw how well you were doing at camp. It's got all the latest specs, minus a touchscreen, sorry, I couldn't get my hands on one, and it'll do pretty much whatever you want it to. If it doesn't, you've got my email."

"What is it?" Carter asked, peeking around him into the bag.

"It's a laptop," Tommy breathed, pulling it out. It was sleek, black, and much lighter than he thought it would be. He moved into the living room and sat down, opening it up. He placed his fingers over the keyboard as if to type and pressed a few keys, liking the way they responded to his touch.

"There's a camera here," Veronica said, having followed him into the room, and pointed it out. "You can do video chats with anyone else with the same program."

"Who else has the program?" Tommy asked.

Kennedy and Jason raised their hands, as did Veronica. She nudged Carter, who looked surprised. "I have it too?" he asked.

"Wasn't it your birthday last week?" Jason asked, amused. "We didn't get you anything then, but Veronica's almost finished building yours."

"I had to wait for a duplicate part," Veronica said, wrinkling her nose. "Sorry I couldn't give it to you today. You'll have it by the end of the week."

"Thank you," Carter said to her. "Thank you," he repeated, looking from Kennedy to Jason. "I wasn't expecting... anything, really."

"You're practically family," Jason said. "And I know Tommy will want to keep in touch with the friends he's made here. This makes it easier for him."

"Thank you, all of you." Tommy could feel tears pricking at his eyes and blinked furiously. "This is amazing. I..." He choked up.

Putting his new laptop aside, he got up and hugged Kennedy. Jason and Veronica joined in, squishing him. "I couldn't have asked for a better family."

"Awww, love you, too, Tommy." Kennedy kissed his cheek.

"Alright, now that presents, hugs, and goodbyes have been delivered, I have other errands to run. See you online, Tommy. Keep up the good work!" Veronica slipped back into her boots and left with a wave.

"Why don't you two finish packing and we'll get lunch ready?" Kennedy suggested to the two boys. "I don't want you driving in the dark on those roads."

Tommy sighed but agreed. Night driving in the country wasn't much fun. He scooped up his precious new laptop and followed

Carter into the bedroom for the last time. "I'm almost done. Just have my school stuff to put in my backpack."

"Great, that gives us plenty of time to say our goodbyes," Carter said.

Tommy carefully put the laptop in his suitcase, protected from banging around by his clothing. While Carter zipped it up, Tommy hurriedly packed his backpack with his binders, textbooks, and sheet music.

"I think that's everything," he said, looking around at the small room that had become home. "I'm really going to miss this place."

Carter looked sad. "I'm going to miss you."

"I'll be a phone call away," Tommy said. "Or email. Or MSN." He tapped his suitcase. "Soon to be video call, too. And now I'll have the privacy of my room."

He pulled Carter into a tight hug. "But I won't have anyone who can hug me like you."

"Or kiss me like you," whispered Carter, joining their mouths.

They said nothing for a long time. A knock on the door startled them into breaking apart.

"Lunch is ready. Everyone's in the kitchen," Kennedy's voice came through the door.

The boys took a moment to breathe, foreheads pressed together as they gazed deep into each other's eyes.

Reluctantly, Tommy pulled away to pick up his backpack and guitar. He opened the door while Carter grabbed his own bag and Tommy's suitcase.

Kennedy was still standing outside the door. "Good thing I waited," she whispered with a grin. "If you want to keep Mom in the dark, be more subtle. Go to the bathroom, splash water on your faces, and fix your hair." Louder, she said, "Wash your hands before lunch, please."

She winked at their flushed faces and headed to the kitchen.

Lunch was boisterous, at least on the part of the adults. The boys ate quietly.

"Tommy, dear, I'm glad you enjoyed your time here. I'm really impressed with everything you accomplished," Tommy's mom said. "I hope you can keep that focus when we get back home."

Tommy rolled his eyes. "I'll try, Mom."

His mom sighed. "I feel like you're already crawling back inside your shell to hide. Where's the happy boy I heard so much about over the phone?"

"He's staying here in Westmeath," Tommy murmured.

"What was that?"

"I think he's sad to be leaving his friends. They developed a strong bond this week," Jason said, giving Kennedy a concerned look that Tommy caught.

He didn't want them worrying about him, not after all they'd done for him already. He plastered on a smile that felt fake. "I'm going to try to join a couple clubs at school tomorrow, see if that can keep me busy. And I'm not going to hang around with Cindy Lou and the others. Now that I know what real friends are like," he flashed Carter a smile, "I don't want to deal with them anymore."

"Hallelujah!" his mother cried, flinging her hands in the air. "If nothing else, that was worth this trip."

After lunch, more hugs were given, and Jason brought their things to the car.

"Time to go, Tommy."

"Just a sec, Mom." Tommy hugged Kennedy one last time. "Thanks for being there for me, Dee," he whispered. "You really had my back. You and Jason, both. Thank you."

"I love you," Kennedy replied simply, holding him close. "You're welcome anytime."

Tommy pulled away from his sister and launched himself at Carter, squeezing him tightly. "Don't forget me," he whispered into his neck.

"Never," Carter whispered back.

A lump in his throat, Tommy stepped back. "I'll call when we get in."

"You'd better," Kennedy said.

Carter nodded, looking miserable.

They got in the car and his mother pulled out onto the road. She let him sit in silence until they had exited the city limits, condos and technology centres barely visible in the distance behind them. "I'm glad you had a good time," she said softly.

"I didn't." Tommy blinked back tears. "I had the best time of my life."

Interlude - Appearances

**SUNDAY THE 16TH OF MARCH, 2003 -
WESTMEATH, ONTARIO**

Carter watched from the front window as the car carrying his boyfriend backed out of the snowy driveway. His throat felt tight with tears, and he swallowed hard, trying to get rid of the discomfort.

"—Food, cuddles, or sparring?" Kennedy asked from beside him.

"Sorry, what?" Carter turned away from the window. The car was out of sight now.

"What would help distract you and make you feel better? Food, cuddles, or sparring?" She rubbed a hand over his shoulder and down his arm, lacing their fingers together. "All three of them help me."

Carter stared at their interwoven fingers, hers so delicate between his, a marked difference from Tommy's that made him miss him even more. He took a deep breath. "Can we bake some bread?"

"Ooooh, I love that idea!" She tugged him toward the kitchen.

Jason joined them, and Carter taught them how to knead bread to make it fluffy. While their loaves were baking, they sat around the kitchen table.

"It's been a while since we arm wrestled," Jason said with a smirk. "Do you still remember how?"

Carter chuckled. "Actually, I arm wrestled with a dude at camp on Thursday." He rolled his eyes. "I was worried I'd break his arm. Made me nostalgic for wrestling you. I have to actually *try* to win against you."

Jason held out his hand. "Bring it, kid."

Carter grinned and slipped his hand into Jason's larger one, the memory of Thursday surfacing as he tensed his arm muscles.

Carter, Tommy, and Elyse made their way into their afternoon class on Thursday after their sponsor session. They were planning a prank for the next morning in their biotech lesson, and Veronica had added the finishing touch. Carter swung Tommy's hand between them with a grin, excited to put their plan into motion.

They found their seats and set up their phones to take notes, before Carter tuned into the conversations around him.

"There's no way robots will take over for real people in the boxing ring," Greg was saying behind him. "They're all programming and no grit. I could easily take one on and beat it."

Carter scoffed.

"What, you don't think I could, Yellow Belt?" Greg sneered.

"No, I don't," Carter said dismissively. "I'm not sure *I* could."

"You say that like you think you're stronger than me!" Greg marched around his lab bench, pushing Tommy out of the way to loom over Carter.

"It's not necessarily a matter of who's stronger," Carter pointed out. "Kung Fu and karate allow for a wide variety of moves, whereas boxing is inflexible. It doesn't really matter though. Robots won't be used for performance entertainment for a long time yet." He glanced at Tommy, who was rubbing his ribs. "Apologize to my boyfriend for hurting him."

"Nah," Greg snarled. "He shouldn't even be here. This camp's for Westmeath students."

Carter felt cold anger burn in him. "You're jealous that he's smarter than you, just like you're insecure because I'm stronger than you."

"Prove it." Greg got in his face. "Arm wrestle. Now."

"If you wanted to hold my hand, you should have asked before I got a boyfriend," Carter said flippantly, winking at Tommy as he rolled up his right sleeve.

"Left hand," was all Greg growled as he stalked back around the bench.

"Carter, he's left-handed," Tommy whispered.

"Yeah, and?" Carter busied himself with his other sleeve.

"You're not!"

"You think he's going to win, don't you?" Carter smirked at his boyfriend.

Tommy gestured at Greg's massive frame and then at Carter, who was thin and gangly.

"Ouch. You should know that appearances can be deceiving by now." Carter held out his left hand. "Kiss for luck?"

Tommy kissed the back of Carter's hand lightly, sending tingles up and down his spine. "Good luck," Tommy whispered, green eyes shining.

"Don't worry. I don't need it." Carter scooted his stool closer to the lab bench behind him and held up his left arm, right hand holding his elbow steady. "Whenever you're ready," he said loudly to Greg, who was posturing to his friends.

"Ready to lose?" Greg snarled at him. He slid his hand into Carter's, but instead of gripping for an arm wrestle, he pushed down hard, trying to get a rise out of him. When he met nothing but a strong grip, he settled into the traditional position. "First one to touch their knuckles to the bench is the winner."

"I know how it works," Carter chuckled. He tensed his arm muscles, prepared for Greg to cheat the start, especially after the show of force.

Elyse counted from three, and just as Carter had expected, Greg started straining to move his arm early, not that anyone watching would have been able to tell. Carter's rock giant heritage meant he was stronger than an average human and although Greg was strong, holding him still was nothing compared to arm wrestling with Jason.

Carter looked up at Greg's reddening face and smirked. "It's like you're not even trying, big shot." He glanced at Tommy's awed expression and felt his heart beat faster. *I want to impress him so much it's kinda scary,* he thought.

"The teacher's here!" exclaimed a student.

"Ah. I guess I should end this then," said Carter and carefully pressed down until he felt his knuckles brush against the black top. If he was being honest with himself, the hardest part of arm wrestling was not hurting the other person; yet another reason he preferred Jason as his opponent.

"What are you on?" Greg hissed, eyes wide with a combination of fear and respect.

Carter looked down. "I'm on my stool." He shook out his hand, tactfully not mentioning the sweat, and turned around to face the teacher. He left his sleeves rolled up.

Tommy's fingers grazed one forearm, making the hair stand on end. "That was incredibly hot," he whispered. "Sorry I doubted you."

"No offense taken." Carter grinned. "You're not the first person to make that mistake, and unlikely to be the last."

That was all the conversation that they had time for, as the teacher began talking. Carter caught a couple shy glances throughout the lesson from his boyfriend that made him want to jump up and run around the room from happiness.

After the lesson, when they were about to start the lab, Tommy caught Carter's hand and gave his fingers a squeeze as he was about to reach for a beaker.

Carter smiled and squeezed back, trying not to listen to the countdown in his head that told him Tommy only had three more days in Westmeath before he returned home.

Make the most of the time you do have. It'll work out. It has to.

Carter was snapped out of his memories by Jason pushing his arm over and brushing the back of his hand against the tabletop.

"You were distracted," Jason said with a frown. "Focus. Again."

Carter shook his arm out and prepared himself. "Okay. I'm ready."

Chapter 6

♥

Digging his mittened hands into his pockets, Tommy glanced down the street for what felt like the tenth time in the last minute.

Still no sign of the yellow bus.

The music on his iPod changed, switching from "Clocks" by Coldplay to "Survivor" by Destiny's Child, and he started dancing along with it, swinging his hips.

He knew he wasn't that great a dancer, but he enjoyed the memory of his boyfriend's body brushing against his own while they danced together on the last Friday of March Break. He flattened the snow at the foot of his family farm's long driveway as he danced his way across it.

He was in the middle of trying to do the moonwalk when a loud honk startled him, and he whipped around.

The bus had arrived.

Cheeks flushed with more than cold, Tommy boarded the bus and nodded to the driver. He spotted Faith halfway down the aisle and made a beeline for her.

"Mind if I sit with you?" he asked breathlessly, slipping one earbud out.

"Sure," Faith replied, flipping her long dark hair over her shoulder and nodding at the empty place beside her.

"Thanks." He swung his backpack off his shoulder and sagged into the seat. "How was your break?"

"It was alright. My older brother took me sledding. Not to be rude, but why are you sitting with me?"

Tommy winced and dug his iPod out of his pocket, turning it off. "Your name came up over the break, and I thought it might be nice if I talked to you more than once a week. It's a nice way to start fresh."

"You were talking about me?" Faith's brown eyes widened, and she blushed slightly.

"Not like that!" Tommy was quick to reassure her. "Sorry, I don't want you to get the wrong impression. Kennedy mentioned that Basil had done accelerated learning for math, and I remembered that you were his sister."

"Ah." Faith frowned. "I thought Basil said Kennedy was in Westmeath now?"

"She is. I stayed with her and her fiancé over the break."

Faith's eyebrows rose. "How was that?"

"Absolutely fantastic!" Tommy beamed at her.

"Yeah?" Faith smiled back at him. "You like him, then?"

"Jason is one hundred percent perfect for Kennedy. They're so in love," Tommy said.

"Basil saw them when they were here over Thanksgiving." Faith smirked. "He said they were all over each other."

"Oh, yeah, that hasn't changed," Tommy said with a chuckle. "I kept walking in on them all over the house."

"Oh, ew." Faith screwed up her face. "I would *not* want to walk in on my sibling doing the nasty!"

Tommy winced. "Not what I meant. They kept that stuff behind closed doors. No, just making out."

Faith laughed. "I suppose that's a *little* better. What did you do while you were there? Did you shadow them at their jobs? Did they take you to museums?"

"Ah, no." Tommy flushed. "I was at a science camp."

"Were you really?" Faith looked surprised. "I didn't know you were into that type of thing. You should join our STEM club!"

"There's a STEM club at school?" Tommy asked excitedly. He

knew that STEM stood for science, technology, engineering, and mathematics. "Yes, I want in! When do you meet?"

"Lunch period every day of the week. We do different things each day. It's totally fine to miss days. It's super informal. The older students help the rest of us out with writing reports and stuff if we need it."

"That's perfect!" Tommy exclaimed. "I didn't join any clubs earlier in the year, and I've been regretting that. I had no idea that we had a STEM club, though. I was going to see if Yearbook or something had any openings, but this is so much better."

Faith wrinkled her nose. "You sure it isn't going to be a problem with your... friends?"

Tommy shook his head. "My friends are back in Westmeath. Any people I used to hang out with here are not worth considering."

"Are you serious?" Faith's jaw dropped. "They won't take that lightly."

"Yeah, I'm not looking forward to that conversation," Tommy said, glancing toward the back of the bus out of the corner of his eye. He could see two of his ex-friends, Hunter and Louise-Ann, sitting beside each other. They were talking quietly with their heads together and kept glancing up in his direction. "I'll think of something that'll keep them off my back."

"Better think fast," Faith advised.

Tommy could see the school in the distance. He gulped. "Yeah."

The bus pulled up in front of the school and the kids filed out. Tommy waited for Faith, and they headed for the main doors together.

"I'm guessing the club meets in the science lab?" Tommy asked.

"You got it." Faith waved at a dark-haired girl walking up the sidewalk. "I usually grab my lunch from my locker after science and then head back there."

"We're allowed to eat in the lab?"

Tommy was surprised. The science teacher was particularly strict about food in class.

"Only at the table at the back, not at the lab benches." Faith shuddered. "Who knows what poisons are on those things. I'll see you in class. I want to catch up with Paisley."

"Yeah, see you," Tommy replied absentmindedly. He had caught sight of his ex-friends huddled together; Peter and Cindy Lou, having arrived on foot, had met up with the two that rode the bus in from the outskirts of the town like he did. "Don't believe anything you might hear about me."

Faith laughed. "Don't worry, I won't."

Tommy managed a small smile and returned to his path into the school.

He didn't quite manage to make it through the doors.

"How was your break, Thomas?"

Tommy groaned inwardly but turned to face Cindy Lou. Her cronies were behind her.

"It was pretty great, actually," he said, plastering on a fake smile. "How was yours?"

"*I* was grounded." Cindy Lou examined her nails. "*Someone* called my parents and told them I was skipping school." She turned her gaze on Tommy. "The same thing happened to Hunter, Peter, and Lou-Ann. Sounds like *you're* the snitch, since you weren't grounded."

"Yeah, no, my parents were called by the school at the end of February. I was most definitely grounded. But I went to Westmeath for a science camp that I'd been signed up for, and it turned out to be pretty awesome."

Tommy hoped that they'd consider him to be too nerdy to hang out with. He also briefly wondered why Louise-Ann had shortened her name before deciding he didn't care.

"A science camp?" Lou-Ann asked, wrinkling her nose. "Why would you—"

Cindy Lou held up a hand, and Lou-Ann stopped speaking. "You went to Westmeath for an entire week and didn't tell us?" She held out a hand imperiously. "What did you bring me?"

Tommy stared at the girl incredulously. *How did I ever think she was cool?* he thought. "Nothing," he said at last. "I was there for camp, not a shopping spree."

Cindy Lou laughed, a forced ripple that made his teeth ache from clenching so hard. "You're funny. So, when you skipped out on your 'camp,' where did you go? What did you do?"

"I didn't skip. I wanted to be there. I had a lot of fun." Tommy spoke slowly, hoping his words would get through to them. "I learned a lot of really cool things and made some great friends."

"Friends!" Cindy Lou practically shrieked. "*We* are your *friends*! Those big-city kids have already forgotten about you."

"Is that why you didn't sit with us on the bus?" Hunter chimed in, scowling. "Think you're better than us now that you've lived in a big city for a week?"

Tommy wanted to roll his eyes but knew that would only make things worse. "I don't think I'm better than you," he said, trying to sound sincere. "I came to the realization that I'm not cool enough to be in your group. I like math and science and would rather learn about engines than go to parties. I'm a lost cause, and I thought it would be better for you if I just stayed away. Don't want my nerdiness rubbing off on you."

Lou-Ann looked confused, and Tommy almost laughed at her.

Cindy Lou narrowed her eyes at him. "*You* don't get to decide if you're a lost cause. *I* do."

"But if I don't enjoy social activities, how will you manage to save me?" Tommy pointed out.

"Just because you don't enjoy them doesn't mean you won't come," Cindy Lou declared triumphantly. "I'm having an *intimate* party this Saturday. Some seniors will be there, too, and they promised they'd bring some of the good stuff."

Tommy scrunched up his nose. "Yeah, I'm going to have to pass on that. I have plans."

"What could *possibly* be better than a party?" Peter asked, eyebrows rising.

"Pretty much anything else," Tommy said carelessly. "Like I said, that's *really* not my scene. I'm going to be hanging out at home with a friend online, probably talking about our weeks and doing homework."

"Wow. You went to Westmeath and got boring," Lou-Ann said, her eyes wide. "I didn't think that was possible."

Cindy Lou still looked suspicious. "You're hiding something, Thomas. Nobody's *that* boring. Nobody turns down *my* party invitations."

"I am, and I just did."

The warning bell rang, and Tommy opened the door to the school.

"I don't want to be late on the first day back after break."

None of the others moved to enter the building, so Tommy shrugged and let the door close behind him.

"Yes!" he muttered under his breath, resisting the urge to do a happy dance while they could still see him.

"Hey, you two," Tommy greeted the smiling faces of his sister and her fiancé in the video call program on his computer. "Miss me?"

"More than I thought I would," Kennedy replied.

"Hey!" Tommy pouted.

Jason chuckled. "It's a compliment. She cried this morning when she remembered you weren't coming to breakfast."

Tommy's heart melted. "Really?" he asked softly. "Aww, Dee!"

Kennedy waved him off. "I'll get used to not having you here. Just give me some time."

"What she's saying is that you fit in really well here," Jason said. "And we're looking forward to having you again."

"I can't wait," Tommy said eagerly. "It's weird being back here. I feel like I changed so much in a week."

"How did your first day back go?" Jason asked.

Tommy saw Kennedy nudge Jason's ribs with her elbow and chuckled. "It went well. I joined a club that meets every day at lunch, and it's full of super awesome people, including Faith."

"Ooooh!" Kennedy squeaked. "Basil's little sister? What club?"

"STEM." Tommy smiled proudly. "The teacher supervisor gave us a past math contest to work through together today, and I was able to contribute to every single question. I was the only student younger than a senior to do that."

"Go you!" Kennedy's pride in him was practically visible through the screen.

"Did you run into any trouble?" Jason was fishing, and Tommy knew it.

"No trouble at all." Tommy paused and then laughed. "Thanks to your advice."

He grinned as Jason relaxed.

"Implying I'm not cool enough for them was definitely the way to go. They're very confused, but I don't think they're angry that I'm not hanging out with them." He left out Cindy Lou's suspicions. They weren't important.

Kennedy chuckled. "They *would* be confused! Turning down the 'cool' kids is highly unusual."

"Yeah, well, an 'intimate party' with seniors who are bringing 'the good stuff' really doesn't sound all that appealing to me," Tommy said, using air quotes.

Jason made a face. "That sounds like a recipe for trouble."

"Speaking of trouble, do you think Mom called their parents to tell them they were skipping?" Tommy asked.

Kennedy smirked. "Maybe. It sounds like something she might do. Why don't you ask her?"

"I wonder why the school didn't call them, too," Tommy said thoughtfully.

"Who knows." Jason shrugged.

MSN Messenger popped open in a new window.

"Carter's online. I'll talk to you later!" Tommy said, his mouse hovering over the 'end call' button.

"Oh, I see how it is," Kennedy teased.

"Like you wouldn't do the same thing if it was Jason waiting to talk to you," Tommy retorted.

"True. Love you!" Kennedy blew a kiss at the screen, and Tommy pretended to catch it, putting it against his cheek.

"Love you too, Sis. Bye."

SATURDAY THE 22ND OF MARCH, 2003 - PARRY SOUND, ONTARIO

"Only eleven weeks left," Tommy said with a sigh, gazing adoringly at his boyfriend's face.

"It sounds like your week wasn't so terrible." Carter's voice was slightly distorted as it came through the video call program. He had just received his laptop with the program that morning, as a belated birthday gift from Jason and Kennedy.

"Well, no, it wasn't so bad," Tommy conceded. "I'm really enjoying the STEM club. The teacher supervisor is talking about entering a STEM competition in early May in Toronto."

A brilliant idea practically smacked Tommy across the face. "You're in STEM club, too! You should suggest they go!"

Carter's jaw dropped. "That is genius! I'll make an MSN group chat with Elyse."

CarterIsARockStar started a group chat with ElyseBeautyA-NDBrains and MyNameIsNotTommy. "Hey! T was telling me about a STEM competition in Toronto. Have you heard of it?"

ElyseBeautyANDBrains responded almost right away. "Yeah, Ms. Rubens told us yesterday that we're entering. Why weren't you there?"

CarterIsARockStar replied, "There was a meeting for the play at lunch. I'm helping with the sets and doing fight choreo, remember?"

MyNameIsNotTommy added, "You're entering too? This is great!"

ElyseBeautyANDBrains typed quickly, "Ms. Rubens said that only 3 students from senior and 3 from junior are allowed to go. There's going to be a mini test in 2 weeks to decide the competitors."

Carter blew out a sharp breath. "Only three per level?" he said aloud to Tommy. "Besides Elyse and I, there are four other ninth graders *and* eight tenth graders in the club competing for the junior spots!"

"And who got selected for Door Tech, the most exclusive tech camp in Canada?" Tommy reminded him. "You're better than you think you are."

"I didn't win any of the subject awards," Carter protested.

"No, but you won the phone." Tommy looked earnestly into his boyfriend's eyes. "I know you freeze up with tests. You're just going to have to study your cute little butt off."

Carter blushed slightly. "You think my butt is cute?"

Tommy grinned. "*That's* what you got from my pep talk?" He noticed that the group chat was flashing. "Oops. We've left Elyse hanging."

"How many juniors are in your club, T?" ElyseBeautyAND-Brains asked. Then, "Hello?" Then, "You're chatting on that video program, aren't you?"

MyNameIsNotTommy replied quickly, "Sorry, giving C a pep talk. He thinks he's not good enough to get picked for the team to go to Toronto."

There was barely a second before ElyseBeautyANDBrains responded. "That's bullshit!" Her next reply took a little longer. "I'm not going to say that it'll be a breeze. I'll have to study hard to get in, too, but we can do it! We'll set up a study group, the 3 of us, and work hard."

Tommy looked at the program showing him his boyfriend's face. Carter seemed a little happier at that thought.

MyNameIsNotTommy said, "Are you sure you're comfortable studying with someone from a different team? What if I tell all your secrets to my teammates?"

Carter chuckled aloud, and ElyseBeautyANDBrains sent a series of laugh-react emoticons before adding, "Then we'd tell all your secrets to our team."

"Fair enough," MyNameIsNotTommy replied, grinning as he typed. "I'm one of 3 grade 9s and 2 grade 10s competing for the

3 spots. My friend Faith and her friend Paisley are the other 2 grade 9s. I don't know the others very well."

"Are you worried?" CarterIsARockStar asked.

"A bit. They're all smart. But if I study with you 2, I have a pretty good chance," MyNameIsNotTommy said.

"We should see if Veronica is willing to help us out," suggested CarterIsARockStar. "If I had to guess, she probably did these when she was in high school."

ElyseBeautyANDBrains said, "That's a great idea! We should write an email to her right now!"

Together they crafted their plea for help and sent it off to Veronica.

ElyseBeautyANDBrains sent, "And now we wait. I'm going to do some homework and let you 2 have your virtual date. Ping me when you get a response."

CarterIsARockStar replied, "Will do," and the group chat went silent.

"Do you think we're at a disadvantage because we're not in grade ten?" Carter asked Tommy quietly.

"Nah," Tommy said with a shrug. "We did more advanced stuff at Door Tech. And we'll all be studying the new stuff for this test."

Carter nodded thoughtfully. "That's a good point."

Tommy dragged his science textbook out of his backpack and put it on the table in front of his laptop. "Is it wrong that I feel guilty that I didn't think to form a study group with Faith and Paisley? Or should we suggest that they join our group?"

Carter chuckled. "You're too nice for your own good. You're trying to beat them to get into the competition. Hopefully, your friend will get in too, and then you can invite her to study with us. Until then, let's keep this group as the three of us."

"You think?" Tommy bit his lip. "It feels so... selfish?"

"Why don't you ask Kennedy for her advice? Or Jason? I'm a little too close to the situation," Carter suggested. "Do you think

Elyse and I should ask the other juniors at our school to study with us?"

"I feel like a hypocrite for saying no," Tommy replied. "I think it's mostly because I really want the two of you to be the winners."

"Why is it any different for you?" Carter asked. "I want *you* to be one of the winners at *your* school."

"Me too. But doesn't it feel a little like cheating to win?" Tommy asked.

"It's using the resources you have access to, in my opinion," Carter argued. "None of us are cheating! We're studying a little more intensely."

Tommy inclined his head in agreement. "Okay. I'm with you there."

"Besides, isn't Faith's brother an engineer? He's probably going to be helping her study," Carter pointed out. "You're not the only one with connections."

Laughing, Tommy had to concede. "Alright. Now, let's hope Veronica agrees to tutor us."

He glanced at his email inbox.

"She responded already!"

Opening it, he scanned her short reply quickly.

"She says of course, and she's making up a schedule for us right away! She wants to know if Elyse can go to your place after dinner tonight for a brief meeting through the video call program."

"Wow! That's awesome!" Carter said, typing in the group chat to notify Elyse. "I can't believe I'm looking forward to studying!"

Tommy chuckled. "It's going to be fun, studying in a group."

"Tommy, lunch is ready!" Tommy's mother's voice carried up the stairs.

"I'll talk to you after lunch, and we'll work on homework together?" Tommy suggested.

"For sure." Carter blew a kiss at the screen and Tommy caught it.

"You've been watching Kennedy and Jason again, haven't you?" Tommy teased.

Carter blushed. "It's hard not to. Especially when they're being lovey-dovey."

"I'll take your word for it."

Chapter 7

❤

"I'm going to get dizzy from refreshing my inbox over and over again," Tommy complained, blond hair in disarray. "I know Mister Travese said it would take a few hours to hear back about the tests, but it's been a few hours! Hasn't it?"

Carter grimaced in sympathy through the screen. "We finished writing ours at three-thirty. It's only five. I don't expect to hear from Ms. Rubens until nine at the earliest."

"Yeah, but she has to go over fourteen tests. Mine only has five!" Tommy ran his fingers through his hair again.

"Yeah, for our level. But what about the seniors?"

Tommy opened and closed his mouth. "Okay," he said sheepishly. "But still! They were Scantron tests! How long could it take to feed them into a computer to correct the little bubbles?"

"I'm going to guess a few hours," Carter teased.

Tommy rolled his eyes and refreshed his inbox again. Still no new emails.

"I can't believe I'm going to say this, but maybe we should both take a break from our laptops until just before bed," Carter suggested.

"Really?" Tommy asked, incredulous. "I thought we were going to hang out!"

"Yeah, but..." Carter sighed heavily, a brown curl flopping down over his forehead.

Tommy examined him. He looked stressed out, the lines at

the corners of his eyes and mouth tight from exhaustion. "But I'm not being a very good boyfriend right now, am I?" he whispered. "You're feeling just as anxious as I am. I'm sorry." Tommy wrapped his arms around himself. "I wish I could crawl through the screen and cuddle up with you."

Carter gave him a lopsided smile that made Tommy's heart skip a beat. "You're a great boyfriend. And cuddles sound amazing. Actually... maybe we should both go get toddler cuddles."

Tommy blinked. "You're really serious about leaving our laptops?"

"Yeah. I think it'll help lessen the stress. And I think Brooke and Arthur will be good distractions." Carter rested his chin on one hand. "As much as I love hanging out with you, I think we're stressing each other out right now."

"I... can't disagree." Tommy sighed. "I guess that's a good thing to keep in mind for the future. If both of us have a test on the same day, we shouldn't be around each other."

"So dramatic!" Carter laughed. "Who's taking drama this semester, me, or you? I don't usually get my test results by email. I think we'll be fine for a regular test!"

"I'm a musician," Tommy said, affecting a haughty expression. "Aren't we supposed to be all dramatic and stuff?"

Carter laughed harder, clutching his side. "Don't go emo on me now!" he gasped out, sending them both into peals of laughter.

"I do like Evanescence, though," Tommy said, catching his breath and setting them off again.

"Okay, so," Carter said, wiping tears from his eyes. "Toddler snuggles. Then we'll pop back on at ten tonight before bed. Sound good?"

"Sounds good." Tommy's mouse hovered over the end call button. "I... Bye."

"Bye," replied Carter, and Tommy ended the call.

He stared at his inbox, revealed by the video call program closing, and hit refresh again.

Still no new emails.

Tommy sighed and gave his desk chair a spin, his room passing in front of his eyes as a blur. Tommy slowed to a stop facing his bookcase. He pulled out the notebook he kept his song ideas in and flipped through them, reading lines here and there as they caught his attention. His gaze snagged on something Jason had said at Christmas that he'd thought was poetic and had written down. *I missed you the way shadow misses the light.*

"Huh," Tommy said thoughtfully. "If there's no light, then there's no shadow. It's like he was saying he doesn't exist without her."

Tommy thought about the week he had spent in Westmeath with the couple and what he'd learned about their relationship.

"Huh," he said again, grabbing a pencil and flipping to a blank sheet in his book. He jotted down a few lines, and then a few more. Halfway through a thought, the chorus popped into his head, and he wrote it along the edge of the paper before continuing.

After a few minutes, Tommy stared at the full sheet of paper. "That's not bad," he said, running a hand through his hair. He opened a new text document and transcribed the song, changing a few words here and there until he was happy with it.

After saving it, he composed an email to his music teacher, Mr. Gordon, explaining who the song was for, that he wanted constructive criticism, and attached it.

When he returned to the inbox, there was a new email... from Carter.

"Go play!" was all it said.

Tommy laughed and picked up his guitar. "He probably didn't mean it quite this literally, but Arthur loves it when I play for him, and I haven't been practising as much lately as I should have, thanks to cramming for the STEM test," he said to himself as he left his room.

Tommy found Arthur playing with his mother in the family room at the back of the house. "Hey, Sarah, want me to watch him for a bit? I thought I'd play him some songs." He lifted the guitar case.

"Oh, that would be so great!" Sarah pushed her brown hair off her forehead. "I desperately need a shower."

Tommy grinned. "Yeah, I can smell you from over here."

He liked his sister-in-law. She didn't treat him like a kid.

"Rude," Sarah said with a laugh, getting to her feet. "I just changed him, so he should be good for a half-hour at least, and if not, you know where his diapers are." She fled the room.

"Hey, kiddo," Tommy said to Arthur. "Want to sing some songs with me?"

"Kanks! Kanks!" Arthur said happily, clapping his hands and sitting cross-legged on the floor in the middle of the room.

"Okay, but first you need to tidy up a bit. There's nowhere for me to sit!" Tommy said, carefully leaning the guitar case against the wall. "I'll help. Can you collect all the books and bring them to their shelf?"

With Tommy guiding him, Arthur slowly put away all his toys. Once the room was clean, Arthur retook his place on the floor, and Tommy sat against the couch, his guitar case beside him.

"Now, do you remember what the number one rule in music is?" Tommy pulled his guitar out of its case and rested it on his right leg.

Arthur furrowed his brow in deep concentration. "Fun?" he said at last.

Tommy nodded solemnly. "Very good. And rule number two?" He picked at the top string, listening to make sure it was tuned.

Arthur rocked forward on his knees, one little hand outstretched for the guitar. He paused before sitting back down. "No touch."

"That's right. And if you're very good about following both rules, I'll let you strum a little bit at the end. How does that sound?"

Arthur clapped his hands and put them on his knees.

"Do you think one of your toys would like to listen to me play as well?" Tommy asked as he quickly tuned his guitar.

Arthur gasped excitedly. "Baby!" He got to his feet in the way that little kids so often did, putting his hands on the ground and popping his bum up in the air before getting up onto his feet. He ran over to his toy box and grabbed an old doll that had been passed down through the Fairfield children.

Tommy smiled, remembering that he had taken care of Baby when he'd been little, too, although his name for the doll had been 'Purple.'

Arthur carefully carried the doll back to his seat, smushed its head against the ground as he sat, and then gently placed it on his lap to face Tommy.

Stifling his giggles, Tommy focussed on his fingers, running through a scale, and then playing a couple chords. "What song should we start with? Star or Farm?"

"Tar!" Arthur exclaimed excitedly.

Tommy's fingers easily found the strings for his nephew's favourite song, "Twinkle, Twinkle, Little Star." He played through it once, finger picking the strings, and then with chords. Then he added the words, singing along with his music.

"Do you want to sing, too?" he asked his rapt audience.

"Ess!"

Tommy led Arthur in the tune, slowing the song down so that the little boy could keep up with the words. "That was so much fun!" he said at the end, beaming at his nephew. "Would you like me to play another song for you?"

"Am!"

"'Old MacDonald Had a Farm,' it is!" Tommy said enthusiastically, even though inwardly he groaned. The song had a way of getting stuck in his head all night. In order to challenge himself, he added extra finger plucking. After several different farm animals, zoo animals, and the whole family, Tommy ended the song. "Wow, that was a busy farm!"

Arthur laughed.

"Shall we sing something else? How about something new?" Arthur shook his head.

"You want me to stop playing?" Tommy teased.

"No, no!"

"I think you'll like this next one," Tommy said. "It's about a dragon!"

"Gon?" Arthur gasped.

"Yes, a dragon. Do you want me to sing it for you?" Tommy asked. He'd been practising the song for weeks in music class at school so that he could play it for Arthur.

Arthur nodded vigorously.

"Okay. I'm going to need sheet music for this one, though. It's a little more complicated than the others. You can't touch the papers or else I'll lose my place in the song. Do you understand?" Tommy asked, putting the music out between them.

"Tand!" Arthur agreed, and Tommy started to sing "Puff the Magic Dragon" by Peter, Paul, and Mary.

The little boy was entranced by the song, his eyes flicking between Tommy's face and fingers.

As the last chords faded away, Tommy heard applause from the doorway. He half turned to see his mother and Sarah standing in the hall.

"That was really good," said Sarah.

"Thanks," Tommy replied, blushing lightly. He still wasn't used to having an audience.

Something I'll have to deal with before the wedding, he thought absently.

His mother wiped a tear from her eye and sniffed. "That song always makes me cry. There's something so sad about growing up and leaving childhood behind."

"You're looking at it from the dragon's perspective," Tommy said. "But the dragon isn't real. Jackie *had* to grow up, and he'll get to experience so much more now that he's an adult."

"That's what *you* think," his mother said with a sniff. "It's dinnertime. Please wash your hands and come to the table."

"Oh, but I promised I'd let Arthur strum if he was good," Tommy protested.

"He did clean up," Sarah said, sticking up for him.

"Very well. Two minutes." His mother disappeared down the hall.

"Alright, Arthur, are you ready to strum?" Tommy asked. "Come sit closer to me, here, and gently run your hand over the strings… Perfect!" Tommy shifted his fingers through the chords of "Twinkle, Twinkle, Little Star" again, letting Arthur pet the strings to the tune. "Look at that! You're playing guitar!"

Arthur squealed with excitement and got up to run around the room, flinging his arms wide and spinning in a circle at the other end of the room before falling on his diaper-clad bum.

"I think that's plenty of music for today," Sarah said, heading for the little boy. "It's time to check your diaper, mister."

"No, no, no!" Arthur shrieked.

"Okay. Can you tell me if you've peed?"

"No…" Arthur didn't look at his mother.

"Then I need to check, please. It's not good for you to wear a wet diaper for a long time. It can hurt your skin," Sarah said calmly.

Arthur sighed heavily, and Tommy had to smother a chuckle. "'Kay."

Tommy put away his guitar, tidied up the music, and brought everything up to his room while Sarah quickly checked and then changed Arthur's diaper in the powder room just off the family room.

Tommy resisted the urge to refresh his inbox, but only because he would have had to wait for his laptop to reboot and reconnect to the internet.

He ate silently, his mind in too much of a turmoil over the impending test results to focus on the dinner chatter happening around him.

The phone rang while he was helping to clear the table for dessert and his mother answered.

"Hello? You are? Congratulations! No, he hasn't checked. Yes, I'll tell him. Thank you, Faith."

Tommy grabbed onto the edge of the kitchen table to steady himself. "Faith is in?" he gasped. "The results are out?"

"They are," his mother replied with a smile. "She's the junior replacement."

Tommy sank onto the bench. "What if I didn't get in? What if Paisley or a grade ten student beat me?"

"Then you'll help them prepare for the competition like the good sport you are and try harder next year." His mother hugged his head to her belly, and Tommy clung to her. "Not that I think you could have tried any harder. I'm so proud of you."

"Really?" Tommy felt his eyes water and pressed his face into her shirt. "Even if I didn't get in?" he asked, voice muffled.

"Even then. You worked hard these past two weeks to prepare for this test."

"Thanks, Mom."

"Now, are you going to go check your email?"

Tommy gave her a watery grin. "Will you come with me?"

His mother put a hand to her heart. "Alright then," she said, her voice raspy with what sounded suspiciously like tears.

She followed him up the stairs to his room and stood behind his chair as he booted up his computer.

Tommy pulled comfort from her closeness as he waited anxiously for the lines of code to end and thought about how, a month prior, he wanted her as far away from him as possible.

I wonder what changed? he thought.

But he knew the answer to that.

He had.

Somehow, over March Break, he'd managed to learn how to take the compliment and ignore the passive-aggressive comment that followed. He supposed it helped that he was now doing what she wanted him to do; focus on school and not hang around with Cindy Lou's gang.

Tommy connected to the internet with the usual screech and

whir of a dying robot. He looked forward to his parents getting high-speed Internet. He had gotten used to having it in Westmeath all too easily. "Finally!" he exclaimed when it connected.

Sure enough, there was an email from Mr. Travese.

Steeling himself, Tommy clicked on it. He scanned it quickly. "I did it! I'm in! I'm one of the junior competitors!"

"I knew you could do it, honey," his mother said, squeezing his shoulders. "Now you have to work even harder for the competition."

"Thanks, Mom," he said, brushing off the second half of her statement. He *would* have to work harder in the coming month. "I'm going to send off quick messages to Veronica, Carter, Elyse, Kennedy and Jason, and Faith before I head down for dessert, is that okay?"

"Make sure you thank Veronica for all her tutoring," his mother said as she left the room.

"Of course, Mom," Tommy replied, rolling his eyes because he knew she couldn't see them.

He read the email from his teacher more thoroughly first, in case there was more information he needed to know. It turned out that only fifty schools were allowed to compete. Mr. Travese had submitted all the tests to the STEM competition headquarters for grading, and only the top fifty were emailed a response.

"That explains why it took longer than I thought it would," Tommy said to himself. "Every school was graded at the same time."

Heart in his stomach, Tommy sent Carter a message first, half hoping that he'd be online by the time he finished notifying the others.

He was.

And he had good news as well.

"Looks like we'll see each other in a month! I'm the junior replacement!" CarterIsARockStar typed.

"Best birthday present ever!" MyNameIsNotTommy responded. "I have to go finish dessert with my family. I'll ttyl!"

"For sure. And hey! Congrats again!" CarterIsARockStar said.

"You too!" MyNameIsNotTommy ended the conversation.

Tommy hugged himself as he spun around in his desk chair. *I get to see my boyfriend again in a little over a month!*

WEDNESDAY THE 23RD OF APRIL, 2003 - PARRY SOUND, ONTARIO

"You know, I think I've figured something out," said Faith as they trudged up Tommy's long driveway through the leftover slushy snow that always seemed to stick around forever.

"Yeah? What's that?" Tommy asked absentmindedly, his mind still working through the particularly difficult problem Mr. Travese had set them at lunch that day.

"I've figured out why you never hit on me," Faith stated.

"Uh, because you've never shown interest, and I'm not a creep?" Tommy said.

"No. I mean, yes, you're not a creep. I had flirted a bit with you right after March Break, but you didn't respond," Faith said.

"Really?" Tommy stuffed his hands in his jacket pockets. "Sorry. I'm a bit oblivious to that sort of thing."

Faith chuckled. "Yeah. I've noticed. I've also noticed how you interact with your friends online. Or more specifically, one of them."

"We really bonded over the break," Tommy hedged.

"I'll say!"

"You don't hate me, do you?" Tommy asked hesitantly. "For not telling you?"

Faith scrunched up her face. "Why would I? It's not your fault you live so far away from her."

"*Her?*" Tommy blurted out, startled.

"Ah ha! I knew it!" Faith exclaimed, grinning. "You're—"

Tommy clapped a hand over her mouth and glanced around at the empty fields. "Alright, I'll admit it." He lowered his voice to a whisper. "I'm dating Carter. But my parents don't know I'm in a relationship. Carter understands. Please, you can't tell *anyone*, especially my parents!" he begged, hoping his friend would see his earnestness. He removed his hand from Faith's mouth, and they continued their walk to the house.

"I promise I won't say a word. Sooooo, Carter's your boyfriend?"

"Yeah," Tommy replied, feeling the corners of his mouth ticking up involuntarily. "He's pretty great."

Faith smirked. "You have to think so."

Tommy gave her a light shove. "If I didn't, I guess I wouldn't be dating him."

"No wonder you came home so different," Faith said thoughtfully. "You really had quite the time in Westmeath, didn't you?"

"You have no idea," Tommy agreed fervently.

He led the way into his house, and they took off their outdoor gear, putting it away in the front hall closet.

"Why don't you get settled in the living room, and I'll go get my laptop?"

"Welcome home," his mother said as he passed the kitchen. "Is Faith with you?"

"Yeah, she's in the living room," Tommy said, pausing to lean against the doorframe.

"You know, you *could* study in your room. Then you wouldn't be bothered by family members all the time," his mother suggested.

"Nah, that's alright. There's more space to spread out down here." Then a thought occurred to him. "Are we taking up too much space?"

"No, no, I just thought you'd want some privacy," his mother said, altogether too innocently.

Tommy narrowed his eyes and took a couple steps into the kitchen. "Why do you think we need privacy? We're on a video call with Carter and Elyse, sometimes Veronica, and occasionally Kennedy. We're studying for one of the most intense competitions I've ever seen—"

"Have you seen many competitions?" his mother interrupted with a smirk.

"I've seen the tests from the past few years," Tommy countered. "My point is, whatever you're implying is going on between me and Faith is not happening. We're friends."

"Mmhmm." His mother raised an eyebrow.

Tommy refused to be pulled into her game. "May we have a snack, please? Remember, Faith's allergic—"

"To chocolate. Don't worry, I won't poison your *friend*."

Tommy rolled his eyes. "I'm glad to hear it. Thanks, Mom."

He retrieved his laptop and the phone cable that would allow him to connect to the internet and set it up in the living room.

"It sucks you still have dial-up," Faith said, munching thoughtfully on an apple slice as they listened to the screech of a robot being tortured.

"Yeah, but at least we have two lines, so I'm not tying up the phone all evening." Tommy made a sandwich out of two apple slices around a piece of cheese. "We're making it work. There we go."

He texted the group chat to let the Westmeath duo know they were ready and opened the video chat program. "Let's get down to business."

The video chat program sprang to life, and Tommy accepted the call; Carter's smiling face simultaneously made his heart leap for joy and ache with longing.

Only a few more weeks and then we can hug again, he thought.

"How much homework have you got before we can start Veronica's stuff?" Elyse asked, flicking her pencil against her cheek.

"I've got a couple more math questions, some geography, and I have to write a poem for English. I think the poem will take me the longest."

"I've got math and science questions to answer," said Carter. "How about you two?"

"We've got a math test on Friday," Faith replied. "I just need to add today's stuff to my study notes. Science... What was the homework?" She reached for her agenda.

"Label animal and plant cells," Tommy said. "I finished that in class. But I have music to practise, so after I fix up my math study notes, I guess I'm serenading you as you work."

"Oh, sweet. I love to hear you play," Elyse said. "What are you working on today?"

"I've got a music test on the scale of F major tomorrow, so I'm going to practise that first. Then I'm going to work on the wedding song a bit. Try to get the rhythm for the chorus down," Tommy said, getting to his feet to get his guitar. "It'll be a lot of stopping and starting. Sorry."

"I can't wait to hear the finished product," Faith enthused. "The lyrics are beautiful. Your sister is going to cry."

Tommy grinned mischievously. "That's the goal."

Chapter 8

♥

Tommy woke up when his head banged against the window of the bus. He had been twisted sideways so that his back rested against the window. Faith was sitting between his legs, leaning against his chest, one of his arms wrapped around her waist to keep her from falling off the seat.

He craned his neck to see they were in the middle of nowhere before resettling, trying to find a comfortable position for his head.

Unfortunately, the bump had jostled him too far awake, and he couldn't fall back to sleep.

Faith turned her head and sighed in her sleep, a light snore escaping her lips.

Tommy smiled down at the top of her head and reached down for his bag, digging through the top layer for something to do. His fingers connected with the rigid plastic of the disposable digital camera his brother had given him the night before. He pulled it out and angled it to capture the image of Faith asleep on him. He checked it on the tiny screen to make sure he'd gotten the angle right. Phillip had explained that you could delete only the last picture taken, but you could scroll through and see all the pictures. Satisfied with the image, Tommy replaced the camera in his bag and pulled out his book.

He'd borrowed the second in the Everdome series, *The Children of Everdome*, from the library. He'd started the first one in

Westmeath, reading the well-loved copy that Jason owned, and finished with a library copy once he returned home. He hadn't thought he'd have any time to read, but now he was glad to have it.

A couple chapters in, the bus slowed and pulled off the highway. Signs on the side of the road read *Orillia,* and Tommy assumed they were collecting another set of students heading to the competition. The charter bus had started in Sudbury at five that morning, picked them up in Parry Sound just before seven, and now it was nearing eight o'clock.

The bus moved through the streets of the town until it reached a large high school, where it jerked to a stop.

Faith sat up with a start. "Are we there already?" she asked a bit sleepily.

"No, we're picking up more students."

"Really?" Faith leaned over Tommy to peer out the window. The driver was opening the storage under the bus for the newest passengers. "We're one of four schools on this bus."

"Four?" Tommy asked, surprised.

Faith smirked at him. "Didn't you do a headcount when we got on the bus? There were more than eight people already on board."

"I didn't," Tommy admitted. "I was up at the same time as Phillip this morning so that my dad could drive me into town. I picked a seat and sat."

"I wonder where the other group is from," she said.

"The Soo," said a boy from behind them.

They twisted around to look at the new face. "Hi."

"Sorry, I couldn't help overhearing your conversation," said the boy. "I'm Joel. The bus picked us up in Sault Ste. Marie last evening, we stayed at Hanmer in Sudbury last night, and then the Sudbury group joined us on the bus this morning."

"You slept in a school last night?" Tommy asked.

"Yeah, we camped out in their gym. It was like a big sleepover." Joel grinned. "How long have you two been together?"

"We're friends," replied Faith.

"*Close* friends," Joel said, raising an eyebrow.

"Yeah," Tommy said. "Feels like we've spent every waking moment together since the beginning of April, studying for this competition."

Joel's second eyebrow joined the first. "Are you replacements or competitors for your school?"

The bus dipped as the new passengers boarded.

"I'm a replacement," Faith said. "But I prepared just in case."

"Good idea. I'm one of the senior competitors from Korah Collegiate. This is my second year competing, although not in a row. I was the junior replacement in grade nine. We didn't score high enough the past two years. How many times has your school attended?"

"I think Mister Travese said that this was the first year he's even tried," Faith said.

"Hey, that's great! Good for you, getting in on your first attempt! You must have some impressive grade nines if he hadn't tried before," Joel said.

"Ummm," said Tommy, blushing slightly. "We *are* the grade nines."

Joel smiled. "Accidental compliment achieved. I thought you were seniors. Doesn't make what I said any less true. Enjoy your first STEM competition, kids!"

The doors closed, and the bus vibrated awake. Tommy and Faith turned to face the front again.

"Want to play Go Fish with me?" Faith asked. "I brought a pack of cards."

"Sounds fun," said Tommy.

One of the teachers from another school stood up at the front of the bus, holding onto the high seat backs. "We have no more pickups and should be arriving at the Burt Hotel and Conference Centre in about an hour and a half. Why don't we get to know one another?"

"Maybe we can play another time," Tommy whispered to Faith.

They played games and sang songs for the rest of the ride into downtown Toronto. By the time they arrived at the hotel, Tommy felt like he had travelled with old friends.

THURSDAY THE 8TH OF MAY, 2003 - TORONTO, ONTARIO (MORNING)

One teacher from each school entered the building to check in. Mr. Travese was the first teacher to return, so Tommy and his teammates got off the bus, found their bags underneath, and entered the hotel.

"Elevators this way," said Mr. Travese, and they filed after him, mouths agape at the splendour of the foyer.

The walls had dark wood accents against light cream. The light fixtures were golden candelabras that made Tommy think of Lumière from *Beauty and the Beast*. A fresco that reminded him of pictures he had seen of the Sistine Chapel sat in the centre of an otherwise mirrored ceiling, which made the whole foyer look taller than it was. The elevator bank was off to the right. The hallway continued through the elevator area and opened up to a large space that was filled with people.

"That's where the STEM competition is," Mr. Travese said, when he saw where the students were staring.

The elevator arrived and they were surprised at its size. Two adults and six students, with baggage, all fit comfortably.

"We're on the seventh floor. Let's say ten minutes in the rooms to unpack and use the toilets before meeting back at the elevator?"

Instead of the front doors, it was the back doors that opened, surprising them. There were two large, black leather couches opposite the elevator doors and the entire right wall was open to the conference foyer below.

Tommy resisted the draw of the balcony and followed the teachers down the hall to their rooms. The girls were first, the boys beside them, and the teachers were across the hall, sharing rooms with teachers from another school.

Tommy followed the two senior boys into the room that would be theirs for the next four days. The bathroom was right beside the main door, a closet beside it. The main part of the room had two beds and a sofa, a dresser with a TV, a desk, and one chair.

"Dibs on a bed," said Chris quickly. He was a tall blond who could have been mistaken for Tommy's brother.

"Dibs," echoed Tommy quickly.

"A pullout bed isn't so bad," Bryan said with a shrug. "You two need to be more well-rested than I do anyways."

Chris put his bag on the bed nearest to the bathroom, so Tommy claimed the other.

He opened his duffle and pulled out his dress shirts, surprised to see that there were no wrinkles. He hung them in the closet and dumped the rest of his clothes in the top drawer of the dresser in a clump.

"I'm going to head out to the elevators," he told the other two.

"Okay, go ahead," said Bryan, waving a hand. He had unfolded the couch and was setting up his bed.

Chris was lounging on his bed, playing with his phone and grunted acknowledgment without looking up.

Tommy made sure he had his camera and a copy of the room key in his pocket before leaving silently. He headed straight for the balcony and watched the tiny people move around six floors below him. He spotted what looked like the registration desk, swarming with people on both sides, volunteers running back and forth behind it and a line of contestants in front. He was interested to note that each contestant was receiving a bag after registering.

"I thought I might find you here," Faith said from behind him.

"We're going to get swag bags!" Tommy said excitedly. "Look!"

Faith joined him at the balcony. They watched some people pull dark grey shirts out of their bags after moving away from the table. "Cool! Any sign of them yet?"

Tommy blushed. "No, but it's hard to see from up here. We don't even know if they're here yet."

"Well, they were scheduled for pickup at six. Do you think they were the last to get on the bus?" Faith asked.

"Probably. Oldtown is close to the highway. *If* they left right away, they would get here at about eleven, *if* traffic was good." Tommy checked his watch. "It's just after ten now. We won't see them for another hour at least."

"Don't look so disappointed," Faith teased. "I'm sure we'll see them at the opening ceremony at one."

Tommy sucked in a breath between his teeth. "Yeah, we'll check everything out and then be able to tell them all about it."

"That's the spirit!" Faith linked her arm through his. "I know you're eager to see... them. We'll have all weekend."

"You're right."

The rest of their team joined them, and they took the elevator back down to the main floor. Tommy felt the energy from the other contestants, some of them bouncing a little in place, others talking too loudly, and tried to resist joining in. His stomach felt like it had butterflies flying around inside it, and he couldn't decide if he was excited or was going to throw up. He hoped it was the former.

They joined the line of teams at the registration desk, which moved quickly, despite its size.

"Parry Sound High School," Mr. Travese said, once they reached the organizer signing them in.

"First time attending?" the woman said in a bored tone of voice.

"Yes."

She signalled to a volunteer to join her. "The Parry Sound group, please," she said to the young man, who dashed off. To the group, she said, "Each welcome bag contains a list of rules and regulations. Read them, understand them, absorb them. If you have any questions, ask a volunteer. Once read, you must each sign them and return the signed portion before the opening ceremony." She gestured at a desk just inside the doors of the main conference hall.

"Disobey a rule, and you will be penalized. If it's serious

enough, you will be disqualified." She glared at each member of their team over her glasses. "No exceptions."

Tommy gulped and nodded vehemently. *I hope they're easy to remember, like 'no cheating' and 'no fighting,'* he thought to himself.

The woman smiled slightly. "Glad you understand. You've been assigned your seats in the opening ceremony according to your rank, decided by your written test scores. You will find the seating chart at the back of the room. Two schools per table. At the beginning of each day, your rank will be updated based on your performance the day prior, so keep an eye on the chart. Replacements and one supervisor are required to attend every event. Seating will be provided for those not competing. Do you have any questions?"

The volunteer returned at that moment, carrying a handful of drawstring bags.

Tommy timidly raised his hand. "On the website, it said there were booths somewhere?"

"Yes, the event booths are in the room beside the main conference hall. Walk through the far doors. You can't miss it."

Tommy nodded his understanding and raised his hand again. "Where will we be competing? In the main hall?"

"No, you'll be competing in one of the rooms above the main hall. The elevators for the conference centre are behind us," she gestured under the giant staircase that curled up the side of the building, "or you can take the stairs. Your room will be listed in the schedule. Any changes will be posted on the main wall on the competition floor." She smiled at Tommy. "Any further questions?"

He started to shake his head, but then nodded. Faith stifled a giggle beside him. "Can we see the competition rooms now or are they off limits?"

"They're setting up for the first event after the opening ceremony, so I'm afraid you can't see inside the rooms, but you can go up to the hall if you like."

"Thank you," Tommy said. He grinned at her. "No more questions."

"I have one," Mr. Travese jumped in. "It said that breakfast and lunch are provided each day. Where will we find that?"

"In the main conference hall. Food is buffet-style at the back of the hall." She glanced at her watch. "Lunch will start being served at eleven and continue until one. Breakfast starts at six and continues until eight. There'll be fruit and water available twenty-four seven in the main hall upstairs. You'll see where all the rooms are in the floor plan on the last page in your schedule."

She clapped her hands together. "Alright, each of you sign in, please, and then collect your welcome bag!"

Tommy let the others go first and, when it was his turn, he asked the woman quietly, "I know it's a long shot, but have any of the Westmeath teams checked in yet?"

"Westmeath?" she asked, surprised. "No, I don't believe we're expecting them for another half-hour. Do you know someone from there, Mister," she glanced at his name, "Fairfield? Hang on..."

She turned the sign-in sheet around and rifled through papers on her clipboard. "Any relation to MacKenzie Fairfield?"

Tommy was startled to hear his sister's name. "Yes, she's one of my older sisters. Why?"

"She's one of the judges."

"What? Really?" Tommy frowned, concerned. "Please tell me that doesn't disqualify me!"

The woman laughed. "Not at all! I take it she didn't tell you?"

"No. I had no idea. We're not exactly close."

"Then she didn't tutor you for this competition?"

Tommy felt like he was being tested. "No. Veronica Giles, from Westmeath Door Technology, and Kennedy Fairfield, one of my other sisters and an agricultural scientist, have been my tutors."

"Really?" The woman's eyebrows rose. "No wonder you did so well in your testing."

"What?" Tommy said as he grabbed the last welcome bag.

But the woman had greeted the next school behind him, and he was pushed off to the side.

Mr. Travese was waiting for him. "Everything alright?" he asked.

Tommy blinked a couple times. "My sister's one of the judges," he said, feeling like he was listening to someone else talk in his body. He squared off to face his teacher. "Do you know what my score was on my test?"

"No. We faxed the completed Scantron sheets directly to the competition and they scored them. They only told us who had the highest scores, not what they were. Why?"

"No reason," Tommy said, brushing off a sense of unease. She'd said he did well.

They joined the rest of the group in a corner where they sat and went through their welcome bags. Along with the bag and shirt he had seen from the seventh floor, there was a pen, pencil, eraser, pin, small flag, and a folded poster, all with this year's STEM competition logo emblazoned on them. The rules page was folded inside the schedule book. Tommy read it carefully and was happy to see that they were pretty standard, no curfew or rules against fraternizing with other schools.

He signed the bottom and tore it off before opening his schedule.

He examined the floor plan of the conference centre, noting the different rooms, and read about the events.

The opening ceremony was the first event at one o'clock, followed by optics on the second floor at two. There were five rooms listed, and Tommy wondered how they knew which room they were supposed to be in.

Flipping through the book, he found the group listings at the back. Each student was listed under their school and had a number next to their name. Perplexed, as the numbers seemed random, Tommy scanned through for either his school or Oldtown High and realized that the schools were arranged alphabetically. He found both schools in group four and silently cheered because that meant that he'd be seeing Carter every day of the competition.

"What do the numbers mean?" he asked the group.

"It's your score on the test," Faith said, pointing to a note at the back of the book.

Tommy flipped to the back and read it. "It's out of two hundred?"

"Holy shit, Tommy!"

"What?" Tommy looked up to see everyone staring at him. "What?"

"Look at your score," Faith said with a grin.

Tommy flipped back again. There was a *181* next to his name. He rubbed his eyes, and it was still there. "Whoa."

He glanced up the page, looking for Elyse's score. She had a *181* next to her name as well. Carter's was *162* and he felt a surge of pride in both of them. He looked back up at his classmates. "I wasn't the highest," he said. "Stop looking at me like that."

Everyone bent back over their programs, and Tommy scanned the numbers. There were other high scores, but mostly from seniors. Tommy gulped. He felt like he and Elyse had targets painted on their backs, and the competition hadn't even started yet!

He leaned over to Faith. "What if I don't live up to the expectations of the judges? Are they going to expect more from me during the practical challenges because of my high grade on the test?"

Faith shrugged. "If you keep thinking about it, you're going to stress yourself out. Just focus and do your best. That's all any of us can ask, judges included."

Tommy took a deep breath. "I might need you to repeat that a couple times throughout the weekend." He put everything away in his bag and pulled his camera out of his pocket. "Hey, can I get a picture of the group of us?" he asked.

After a chorus of 'yesses,' he turned around and held up the camera.

"Everyone say cheese!" He checked the mini screen and nodded happily. "Looks good. Thanks!"

"Everyone understand the rules? No questions?" asked Mr. Travese. "Great. Why don't we turn them in, figure out where we're sitting, and then go check out the event booths?"

Chapter 9

♥

THURSDAY THE 8TH OF MAY, 2003 -
TORONTO, ONTARIO (MORNING)

They each received a numbered ticket in exchange for their signed forms, which they were told to print their names on and not lose.

They were seated about midway through the room, slightly closer to the front than the back. Oldtown High was seated at the table in front of them, which made Tommy's heart leap in his chest. *At the very latest, I'll see Carter in,* he checked his watch, *two hours! It's eleven. He might be here now!*

He looked back out to the foyer, scanning the queue of people waiting for registration, hardly daring to hope he'd see a familiar face. But there were too many people now.

"The Toronto schools must have arrived," Faith said, joining him. "Come on, let's check out the event booths."

"You must think I'm so clingy," Tommy said with a sigh.

"No." Faith smirked. "I think you're lovesick."

Tommy stuck his tongue out at her and led the way to the event booth room. "I don't really know what love is yet. But I'm really excited to see... them... again." They crossed the threshold of the other room, and his jaw dropped. "Okay, this is seriously cool."

There were tables set up around the room with displays from various government organizations, universities, and private tech companies.

Tommy and Faith hovered at the edge of the groups listening to each booth's pitch.

"I feel like the seniors will get more out of this room than we will," Faith whispered to Tommy while they listened to the person from the University of Waterloo. "It's almost like they're recruiting."

Tommy nodded silently, and they moved on to the next booth, which was from Door Technology. "Oh, hey, I know this one!" he said excitedly. There was a woman with red hair talking quietly with the person at the booth. "Ms. Door?" he said aloud, surprised.

The woman turned around, and Tommy flushed.

"I'm sorry, I thought you were someone else. Please excuse me for interrupting," he stammered.

"But I *am* Ms. Door," she said with a smile. "Not the one you must have been expecting, though. You know my daughter, Ellen? Are you from Westmeath?"

"No, I'm not, but I attended her March Break camp a couple of months ago. It was incredible."

"I'm happy to hear that. I will pass on the compliment, Mister...?"

"Fairfield. I'm Tommy Fairfield," he managed to fill in for her. "And this is my friend Faith Roi."

"A pleasure," Ms. Door said politely. "Ellen mentioned you, the only student not from Westmeath. She doesn't usually accept students from outside the city, but she made an exception. From what I heard, you certainly were memorable."

Tommy opened and closed his mouth a couple times, searching for words. "Thank you, Ms. Door! I hope I was memorable in a good way."

"Highest scores across all lessons, excellent leadership skills," Ms. Door said, reciting from memory. "I am not at all surprised to see you here. I look forward to judging your entry."

"Oh!" squeaked Tommy. "You're one of the judges?" His voice only settled at the end of his question, to his embarrassment.

"I am, much to my honour." She gave a little bow.

"I look forward to seeing you during the events then," Tommy said politely, trying to not show his panic on his face.

"Enjoy the rest of the booths," Ms. Door said, in clear dismissal of them, and turned back to the person at Door Tech's booth.

Tommy walked the next few booths in a daze.

Faith finally noticed and dragged him back into the large main hall. "You're as white as a sheet. Did Ms. Door rattle you that much?"

"*Two* of the judges know me personally," Tommy hissed. "I'm feeling a little overwhelmed."

"Two? Who's the other—" Faith cut herself off, looking over Tommy's shoulder.

"My sister," Tommy said, ignoring her distraction. "It just feels like extra pressure to do well, you know?"

Faith put her hands on his shoulders, making sure he was looking directly at her. "You have already done very well just by being here. Focus on what you can control, which is what you do during your events, and ignore everything else." She grinned. "Except for that."

"Sorry, except for what?" Tommy said, just before he was tackle-hugged from the side. "Oof!" He looked into familiar grey eyes crinkled in a grin and hugged him back. "You're here!" he gasped, breathing in the scent of his boyfriend.

Carter pulled back just enough for Elyse to join the tight hug.

"You dyed your hair!" Tommy said to Elyse, brushing the streak of blonde in her wavy brown hair behind her ear. "It looks nice."

"Hey! Why aren't you running your fingers through *my* hair?" Carter teased.

Tommy let the corner of his mouth tick up in a smirk as he stared at his boyfriend. "Do you want me to?" he asked, voice huskier than he expected.

"Yeah," Carter replied, a light flush on his cheeks that Tommy could feel himself echoing.

"Okay, not to interrupt this little reunion, but I'd like to meet Faith in person," said Elyse, shoving their shoulders slightly to jar them from their intense focus on each other. "And by the way, not very subtle."

"Yeah," Tommy said, blinking and pulling back from the hug to drag Faith in. "You all know each other after a month of studying together. No intros needed."

"When did you have time to dye your hair? We saw you yesterday afternoon!" Faith asked Elyse. "It suits you."

"My sister Rachel came over for dinner and to spend some time with me in the evening. She did it for me," Elyse replied.

"Hey, what's with the hug-a-thon?" asked Bryan, the senior replacement from Tommy's school, as he came up behind Faith. "Is this an 'anyone can join' thing? Because I don't mind two pretty girls hugging me." He grinned at Elyse and ran a hand through his light brown hair. "Might I have the honour of knowing the name of the most beautiful girl in the room?" He glanced quickly at Faith. "Excepting yourself, of course, oh lovely Faith."

Carter let out a tiny chuckle, and Elyse sighed before smiling and introducing herself.

"And how do you know our Tommy?" Bryan asked. Chris, one of the other senior students from Tommy's school, came to join their group.

"These are my best friends," Tommy replied, indicating all three so that Faith wouldn't feel left out.

"You can't keep all the pretty girls for yourself, Tommy," Chris said. He held out a hand to Elyse, and when she put hers in it, he kissed the back of her hand.

"I'm not keeping them anywhere," Tommy protested. "We're just friends!"

"Uh huh," Bryan said, rolling his eyes. "We all saw Faith cuddled up to you on the bus this morning." He shot a glance at Elyse.

Tommy wondered if he was trying to make the girls jealous of each other by using him. He almost laughed at the absurdity of the situation. "Friends cuddle," he said aloud. To his friends, he added, "I got a super cute picture of it. I'll show you later."

"Boys and girls can't be friends," Bryan scoffed. "Not unless there's an ulterior motive."

"Man, are you missing out on some pretty great friends," Carter said, shaking his head. "What about bisexuals?"

"I meant you can't be friends with anyone you're attracted to," said Bryan.

"No. The best part about being in a relationship is hanging out with your best friend all the time. And I like looking at pretty people. Just because I like how they look doesn't mean I'm going to jump them." Carter chuckled, defusing the tension. "Remind me never to go to an art museum with you. That could get awkward." He gestured at the buffet tables. "I'm starving. Let's get lunch?"

"We're not at the same table, though," Faith said.

"Ah, nobody will notice if we eat fast enough," Carter said, brushing aside her concern. "Then you two can show us what you've seen so far!"

After lunch, which was full of laughter, and a tour of the booths, they checked out the second-floor hall, easily finding the room assigned to group four for their event that afternoon.

By the time they had finished their tour, it was almost time for the opening ceremony. They headed back down to the main hall and joined the rest of their teams at their tables.

Not long after they sat, the lights dimmed, and the stage at the far end was lit. A short woman with close-cropped grey curls stepped onto it and walked to the centre, where a podium was set.

"Welcome, students and advisors, to the two thousand and three STEM Competition!" The woman paused and everyone applauded politely. "My name is Nancy White and I'm the director of the competition. We have a packed schedule planned for you, so I hope you're ready to do some *science!*"

She cleared her throat. "I would like to introduce you to this year's panel of judges. First, we have Professor Joshua Adams from the University of Waterloo in electrical and computer engineering."

As she spoke, a nondescript white man with brown hair and glasses walked onto the stage behind her and gave a little wave at the room.

"Our second judge is Ms. Margery Door, the brilliant creative mind that started Door Technology Industries."

Ms. Door joined the professor on the stage, holding herself like a queen. Tommy was more than a little in awe of her.

"Third, we have Ms. MacKenzie Fairfield, lead researcher with Elmsley."

Tommy had never heard of Elmsley before and felt bad that he had never asked his sister about her work. He watched her walk out onto the stage, her long brown hair pulled back in a tight bun as stiffly formal as her attire. Her expression softened as she smiled at the audience, her eyes searching the faces. Tommy hoped she was looking for him, but she didn't find him before the woman began speaking again.

"Next is Ms. Samantha Franklin, Member of Parliament for Parry Sound—Muskoka." A short, impeccably dressed woman with a stern expression joined the other three on stage. She smiled, but it looked fake to Tommy, like one of Cindy Lou's smiles when she was uncomfortable.

"Last but certainly not least, Captain Mary Herrington of the Canadian Space Agency." The last woman entered the stage casually, smiling and waving at the cheers from the audience.

Faith squealed excitedly and bounced in her seat next to him, grabbing his arm and giving it a shake. "Oh my *God*, I *have* to meet her!" she whispered fiercely at him. "She is my *idol*!"

Tommy grinned at her enthusiasm. "I'm sure you'll get the chance. She'll be around all weekend."

"I'm not going to be able to say anything if I do!" she moaned. "She's the first Indigenous woman to even come close to going to space! I think I'm going to pass out just from being in the same room as her!"

Tommy grabbed her water glass and pressed it into her hands. "Breathe. Drink. Not at the same time," he teased. "She's human, just like the rest of us."

Ms. White had shaken the hands of each judge and returned to the podium. The judges exited the stage.

"You'll have a chance to corner them and pick their brains throughout the weekend," she said, smiling at the excited buzz in the room. "Does everyone have their tickets that you received when you handed in your signed forms?"

Several hands shot up in the air, waving their tickets. Tommy dug his out of his pocket.

"Excellent. We've got a couple door prizes to pull..." A volunteer walked out to her with a glass fishbowl full of tickets and placed it on the podium. "Thank you. First, for a digital microscope, generously donated by Celestron..."

She reached into the bowl and pulled out a ticket while another volunteer walked onto the stage holding the microscope box.

Tommy could hardly believe his ears. "A microscope?" he hissed at Faith. "What a prize!"

A student from the back of the room won the microscope and walked up to the stage to collect their prize.

"The next prize is a telescope, also generously donated by Celestron..." She read out the ticket number and a cheer went up from the other side of the room.

"The newest laptop by Door Technology, generously donated by Door Technology..."

Tommy smirked. Unless it had a touchscreen, it probably wasn't as good as his custom designed laptop.

Someone near the front of the room won the laptop.

Several more door prizes followed, including a Pentax digital camera and various cash prizes.

"Thank you to all our amazing sponsors!" Ms. White said after a volunteer had taken away the fishbowl. "And congratulations to the winners!" She clapped briefly.

"We have one last surprise for everyone. Don't throw away

your tickets, because starting *after* the first event today, you will be able to exchange them for Broadway tickets to see either *The Lion King* or *Mamma Mia* on Friday or Saturday evening!"

There was shocked silence for a second before the entire auditorium erupted in excited applause.

Tommy looked at Faith and they both said, *"Lion King!"* at the same time.

"I hope the others agree," Tommy said, looking in Carter and Elyse's direction.

Carter made a circle with his hands and lifted it up in the air toward them as if he were lifting Simba.

"I think they do," Faith said with a chuckle as they nodded vigorously in agreement.

"I'm glad you're excited," Ms. White said, amusement colouring her tone. "You have half an hour to chat and mingle before the first event. Remember to hang onto your tickets!"

The main lights in the room brightened and many students got to their feet, rushing to the booth room. Tommy assumed they were hoping to talk to the judges. He caught a glimpse of motion next to the stage and saw his sister peeking out at the room from behind the curtains hiding the backstage area.

"Hey, come with me. I want to introduce you to my sister," he said to Faith.

They collected Carter and Elyse as they surreptitiously made their way to the front of the room. By the time they'd reached the curtains, there were very few people left in the main hall.

MacKenzie held the curtain open for the small group and they joined her backstage. "I'm sorry I couldn't tell you sooner that I was a judge. My boss couldn't do it at the last minute, and he suggested I take his place." MacKenzie wrung her hands. "I'm a little nervous, to be honest."

"You'll be great," Tommy encouraged. "I'm really glad to see you."

"Yeah?" MacKenzie beamed at him. "I'm really proud of you for getting yourself here."

"Oh, introductions! These are my best friends and study companions," Tommy said, gesturing to each of his friends in turn.

MacKenzie shook hands with each teen. "I've heard about all of you from Mom. Actually, I have a message from our parents for you. She says, 'You are all winners in our eyes. Celebrate and have fun!'"

"Aww, that's sweet of them," said Elyse, smiling.

"That's not all. They said to keep Saturday evening free for a surprise. The last event ends at four, so be ready for five-thirty in the hotel lobby." MacKenzie grinned at them. "Don't worry, I'll get you tickets to the show you want on Friday evening. *Lion King*, I assume? Come with me." She peeked through the curtain again and held it open for them.

"I don't want you getting in trouble," Tommy said as they headed to the back of the room. "You're not supposed to play favourites."

MacKenzie brushed off his concern. "I'd be in more trouble with Mom if I don't do this," she joked. "Don't worry, little bro. The only strings I'm pulling are getting you tickets early."

Her conversation with the man in charge of the tickets was brief. Tommy was impressed with the ease with which she flirted with the man, getting his name and him to agree to exchange their tickets early. "Thank you, Lucas," she said, batting her eyelashes at him as he opened the folder containing the tickets to Friday night's *Lion King*.

Lucas checked that the tickets were all seated together and exchanged them. "The centre of the front row of the balcony," he said. "The best I can give you." He glanced at MacKenzie and blushed when he saw she was beaming at him.

"Thank you," Tommy and his friends said together.

"You're the best, Lucas," MacKenzie said, touching his arm lightly. "I won't forget it."

"No problem at all, Ms. Fairfield," Lucas stammered.

"Call me MacKenzie," she replied with a wink.

Tommy glanced at Carter, eyes wide.

"Come on, kids. How would you like to meet Captain Herrington?" MacKenzie said, leaving Lucas behind with a starry-eyed expression on his face.

"Eek!" squeaked Faith. "Is my hair alright? Do I have any food stuck between my teeth? Please tell me I don't smell!"

The three teens fussed over her, smoothing her hair down and making sure she was presentable.

"You look great," Elyse said, linking her arm through the other girl's. "Ready to meet your hero?"

Faith swallowed hard. "Yeah. I can do this."

"Do you have talking points ready?" asked Carter. "Like what influenced her to become an astronaut? Who her heroes are? Whether she's anxious about going to space after *Columbia* in February? That sort of thing?"

"Those sound good," Faith said, a panicked look crossing her face. "No way I'm bringing up *Columbia*, though!"

MacKenzie smiled gently. "It's intimidating to meet your heroes, and they're never what you expect them to be. Heroes make mistakes, too. They're not perfect, they're human." She chuckled. "They put on their pants one leg at a time just like the rest of us."

Tommy laughed. "I like that. You can do this, Faith."

She straightened her shoulders. "Yes, I can." She glanced at her friends. "You're coming with me, right?"

"We'll be right beside you," Elyse said, squeezing her arm. "Now let's get going before the event starts and she's busy judging!"

MacKenzie glanced at her watch. "Good point. We should get moving."

They left the main hall and headed up the stairs to the event rooms. There was a small room off to one side that Tommy had assumed was a storage closet but was quite spacious inside. The other four judges were there, making themselves coffee and sitting on the comfortable chairs.

"There you are!" said the captain. "Who are these young people?"

MacKenzie performed introductions, adding, "I thought they

might like to meet you before judging started, and then I discovered that Faith is a big fan of yours."

Captain Herrington smiled at them. "Always a pleasure to meet people who have heard of me. Are you enjoying yourselves so far?"

"Ngk," said Faith and flushed a violent red.

"Deep breaths," whispered Tommy to her. Louder, he said, "It's been great to meet so many like-minded kids my age."

The captain smiled at him. "This sort of environment is really exciting, isn't it?" She looked at Faith. "Why don't you join me for breakfast tomorrow in the main hall? You'll see that I add way too much sugar to my coffee to be intimidating. We'll say six-thirty?"

Faith nodded eagerly. "I would be honoured," she whispered.

"Let's hope you still feel that way that early in the morning!" laughed Ms. Door. "I plan to sleep until the last possible second."

"Have you four competed before?" asked Professor Adams.

"No, we're in grade nine," said Elyse.

"Faith and I are replacements," added Carter.

"Replacements this year, on the team next year?" the captain said with a wink.

"We'll certainly try!" said Faith with determination.

"Now shoo. We have to get ready before judging, and you need to find your teams. Good luck!" Captain Herrington said with a smile.

"Don't worry, they don't need luck," Carter said with a smirk.

Tommy hushed him and urged them to leave. He exchanged an anxious look with Elyse. Once they were in the hall and surrounded by people, he said, "I'm not making a big deal about my score. I don't want the judges to know in case they expect more from me because of it."

Carter nodded thoughtfully.

"Same," said Elyse. "I'm trying to focus on the competition and not have a past test score affect me, even if it is good."

Tommy noticed that the hall was much less full than it had been and checked his watch. "We have to go. Good luck, Elyse."

"You too."

The girls hugged, and Tommy pulled Carter into a tight embrace. "I'm expecting a kiss after the event," he whispered. "If you're okay with that, of course."

Carter smirked at him. "We'll find a quiet corner away from people. I've been saving them for you."

Tommy shivered. "Looking forward to it."

Chapter 10

♥

THURSDAY THE 8TH OF MAY, 2003 -
TORONTO, ONTARIO (AFTERNOON)

The little group entered room four and found their teams.

"Good luck," Carter said as Tommy and Faith continued walking, splitting their group.

Tommy joined Chris; Naomi, the other senior; and Sabrina, the other junior, at their table, which was covered with a cloth. There were two booklets on top of the cloth.

One of the judges that Tommy didn't know, Ms. Franklin, stepped up and tapped on a microphone, making it thump loudly throughout the room. "Everything you need is in front of you. You have two hours. And... Go!" She pressed a button on a stopwatch.

Tommy and Sabrina picked up the booklets, while Chris and Naomi pulled off the cloth. He examined the pieces on the table carefully, noting the different-sized lenses with tiny numbers on their edges, prisms, and colour filters. There was a stand with multiple slots for the lenses and a high-powered LED flashlight. Off to one side were four pieces of cardstock that looked splattered with random coloured dots.

"Are those hidden image pictures?" asked Chris.

"No, they look like Ishihara plates," said Naomi. When they looked at her with blank stares, she added, "My mom is colour blind, so I have to look at them when I go to the eye doctor. If you have issues with not seeing certain colours, then you can't see the number in the middle."

Underneath the cardstock was a flattened box. Pens, pencils, erasers, and a basic calculator were in a small box on the other side of the table.

The booklet in Tommy's hands contained an equation and blank pages at the back.

Chris had been studying the cards. "I have no colour vision issues, but I can't see a thing on these."

Sabrina picked one up and said, "Maybe you need to block out a colour, like the old 3D movies my dad loves. There are two images, one in green and one in red. When you put on the glasses, they block out their colour and create a 3D effect."

"Okay then, first thing we need to do is figure out which colour will work on these Ishihara plates," said Chris. "Sabrina, set up the black box so that we can differentiate between the colours."

Tommy showed them the equation, which was the basic speed of light.

"We know the speed of light in air. We need a wavelength or a frequency. I'm going to guess that the exact wavelength number will be the colour filters needed to look at the image on the Ishihara tests."

Naomi nodded, her black ringlets bouncing. "That makes sense because there are multiple frequencies that are the same. Red and orange, for example."

"Okay, so we need a quick test to find out which colour we need," said Chris.

"The prism." Tommy pointed one out. "If we disperse the light from the flashlight, we can scan the plates and find out which one shows the image. We won't be able to read it through the prism, but it'll give us something to go on."

Chris clapped his hands together. "Great. We'll each take a plate and give the prism trick a try. Tommy, why don't you go first?"

Heart thumping in his throat, Tommy bent over the box and set up the prism and flashlight so that the rainbow created was set widely apart, and then he scanned the Ishihara plate through the colours, taking his time in case he missed something.

After a couple minutes, he stood up. "I got nothing. Sabrina?"

By the time both girls had taken their turns and the group still had nothing to show for it, Tommy was second-guessing himself. What if this didn't work?

Thankfully, Chris's plate showed an image. "It's in the blue area," he whispered.

"Really?" Tommy glanced over the filters. "That seems too easy. Maybe cyan?"

Naomi nodded. "I'd be willing to try that. It's not hard to try blue first, but we'll get the green ready to go."

They put the card at the back of the box and set up the flashlight with the blue filter. Nothing appeared, so they added the green overtop.

"There we go," whispered Naomi, peeking in the box. "But that doesn't look like a single number. That looks like a random list of numbers."

"It's a blueprint!" gasped Sabrina.

"For something with the lenses," added Chris. "Tommy, can you read off the numbers to me, top to bottom?"

Slowly, Tommy read each one, with the others searching through the vast quantity of lenses for the correct ones. They lined them up in the stand.

"Okay, what are we supposed to look at?" Chris asked, once they had built their device.

"The Ishihara cards?" Tommy asked. "Why don't we start with the one that has the blueprint?"

"That's as good a place to start as any," agreed Naomi. "This is going to take a while."

They sat in a line next to their table, all focussed through the lenses as Chris moved the card around slowly, looking for a number amidst the now giant circles. After about fifteen minutes, Tommy was getting anxious again.

"There!" said Sabrina loudly, pointing. She lowered her voice. "It's really small, but I think it's there!"

Chris moved the card closer to the makeshift microscope, but it only got blurry. "Drat," he muttered, moving it back into focus. "Can any of you make it out?"

"It looks like 498," said Sabrina. "Tommy, second opinion?"

The girls moved away, and Tommy bent close. "I'm getting 499 I think," he said after a pause. He closed his eyes tightly and rubbed them before trying again. "Yeah. Naomi?"

Naomi agreed with him and then Chris tried. "I honestly can't make it out," he said at last. "Sabrina, did you want to take another peek before we go with 499?"

She shrugged. "I can see 499. We'll go with that."

"Naomi, you have the best writing. Can you fill out the equation, please?" asked Chris.

"Sure thing." She filled out what they knew, and Tommy handed her the calculator with the completed answer.

"Would someone check my math, just in case?" he said.

Chris took the calculator back and got the same answer.

"Does this mean we're done?" Tommy asked, looking down at their paper. "Should we write 'cyan' on there somewhere, like in a finishing statement or something?"

"Good idea," said Naomi, writing it out quickly. "Now what?"

"It's only been an hour. We're not missing something, are we?" asked Sabrina nervously.

They glanced at the other teams, who all seemed to still be working with the lenses. One team was staring at the cardstock intently and looked frustrated.

Tommy flipped through the booklet. "The equation was the only thing printed in here, and we solved it. I guess we raise our hands?"

They stood up and put everything back on the table before raising their hands, looking around the room for the judge, Ms. Franklin. She was walking around the tables, watching over the students. When she saw their hands, she headed over to them.

"Are you finished?" she asked.

"Yes," said Chris. As the oldest in their team, they had decided that he would speak for them if needed.

Ms. Franklin checked their booklet against something on her clipboard, checked her stopwatch, and wrote something down. "What is your school?" she asked.

"Parry Sound High School," replied Chris.

"You're in my riding," she said, smiling thinly. "Congratulations."

Tommy was unnerved by her smile. It didn't reach her eyes.

"Excuse me," she said, noticing that another team had their hands up.

Tommy saw that it was Oldtown High and crossed his fingers that they had succeeded as well. They joined their supervisor and replacements against the wall and watched as Oldtown was processed.

Carter gave Tommy a thumbs up and a smile that he returned wholeheartedly. When their group started to gather their things and leave quietly, Tommy's group did the same, meeting them in the hall.

"Congratulations," a tall boy with light brown hair said to them. Tommy wondered why he looked so familiar. "We weren't too far behind you."

"Then we're the team to beat," said Chris cockily.

Tommy rolled his eyes and turned to his friends. "Great work, Elyse. How do you feel about going for a swim before dinner?"

Carter shot him a sideways glance. "I was thinking we could swim after dinner, although I sink like a rock."

Elyse started coughing.

"Are you alright?" asked Faith, concerned. "There's water over here by the balcony." She led Elyse over to the table with the water pitchers and glasses.

The rest of their groups had already headed down the stairs, leaving the grade nine boys by themselves.

Carter wrapped an arm around Tommy's neck, bringing his mouth close to Tommy's ear. "Since we've got some extra time before dinner, I was thinking we could find a quiet place, just the two of us? Watching you get your science on is super hot. I'd forgotten just how hot."

Tommy blushed. "Weren't you supposed to be watching your own team in case you had to replace them?"

"I couldn't help myself," Carter said huskily. "So? Quiet, alone? Whatever could we get up to?"

"Do you think your room will be empty?" Tommy asked shyly.

"Why, Mister Fairfield! That sounds an awful lot like a proposition." Carter's eyes twinkled with mischief. "I'm sure I could find out. Let's try to catch up with my team."

With the girls trailing behind them, they made their way down the stairs. Both teams were talking quietly in the conference lobby. They split up and checked in with their teams to find out what the plan was.

Mr. Travese was telling the team that they could all go out for dinner together, or they could find their own way around. "Just don't get lost and please get to bed at a reasonable time. The next event is tomorrow at eight in the morning."

"Faith and I are going to stick with Elyse and Carter from Old-town," said Tommy.

"We are?" Faith asked, smirking.

"Well, you can go with the others if you want to, of course," Tommy said. "Sorry, I didn't mean to presume on your behalf."

"No, no, I'll definitely be sticking with Elyse. And you guys."

Tommy resisted the blush that threatened to creep up at her slight pause. "Great. Is that alright, Mister Travese? We'll be coming back after dinner and going to the pool."

"That's just fine, Tommy."

Tommy listened carefully as the others made their plans. It looked like the seniors were all heading out right away, Sabrina tagging along with them after a lingering glance at Tommy. He shifted uncomfortably. "We all did a great job today. We worked well together," he said before they split up.

The rest of the team agreed, happily thumping each other on their backs or giving hugs.

Once the older students and supervisors had headed into the main hall to exchange their tickets, the four grade nine students headed for the elevators.

Elyse rolled her eyes as Tommy and Carter both bounced a little while they waited for the ride up. "How long do you think you'll be?" she asked them.

Tommy checked his watch. "Well, it's just after three. We should try to get to a restaurant by five, and we need to decide on which one, so I guess we should meet up at four?"

"Four-fifteen," said Carter seriously. They got on the elevator, and Carter immediately took Tommy's hand in his, pulling out his cell phone and fiddling with it with his other hand. "We have almost two months to make up for."

Faith shrugged. "That gives us an hour to get ready."

"Makeovers?" suggested Elyse.

Tommy lost track of the girls' conversation; all his attention focussed on Carter's hand in his. He was starting to feel a little dizzy. "Your room or mine?" Tommy whispered.

"Mine." Carter's gaze intensified somehow. "I want the scent of your shampoo on my pillows, so it feels like you're with me tonight."

Tommy's jaw dropped and then he swallowed hard. "'Kay," he squeaked.

Faith heard and smirked at him. "Keep it in your pants until you get to a room, Fairfield," she teased.

Tommy flushed and cast a sideways glance at Carter, who was just as red. "We should have a quick chat about things before going to the room."

"Kissing, no further," Carter said bluntly. "I don't want to wait a single second longer than I have to before I taste your lips."

The girls blushed at his candour.

"Or you could talk about it here," Elyse said sarcastically.

"It's better than them making out in front of us," Faith pointed out.

"I'm not ready to go further than kissing either," Tommy said quietly.

"Still on the same page," Carter said, the corner of his mouth quirking up.

Tommy's knees felt weak. "Yeah."

The elevator doors opened on the ninth floor, and Carter pulled Tommy out. "Meet you back here in an hour. I've set an alarm on my phone, so we'll be ready." He took off at a slow jog until Tommy got his feet underneath him. Then they ran together down the hallway until they got to Carter's door. He unlocked it and pushed the door open, the two of them stumbling inside.

Carter pushed Tommy hard against the wall, one hand cushioning his head, and pressed their foreheads together. "We have been in the same room for five hours now, and I've been wanting to kiss you since the second I saw you," Carter breathed against Tommy's lips.

"Then what are you waiting for?" Tommy whispered back, his hands fisting in Carter's shirt at his waist.

"I'm nervous," Carter admitted. "What if the spark is gone because we've spent so much time apart?"

Tommy chuckled and shifted his hips slightly. "It's not gone on my end, and we've barely touched."

Carter's eyes widened at Tommy's admission. "Okay, same." He cleared his throat. "What if my kissing skills are rusty and I'm not good at it anymore?"

Smirking, Tommy pushed on Carter's hips, backing him up until he hit the wall on the other side of the entry. "You're stalling. I thought you said you couldn't wait to taste me?" Tommy's lips brushed Carter's as he spoke, but he pulled back slightly, rather than pushing his advantage.

A whimper escaped Carter. "Tommy, kiss me already." His hands twitched against Tommy's sides.

"If you insist." Tommy ran his hands up his boyfriend's body to his face. He traced sharp cheekbones with the pads of his thumbs and then the defined jawline with his fingers. "You're so gorgeous," he breathed. "I'm so lucky I get to hold you like this."

Carter shivered and tilted his head slightly, eyes half-closed. "You even get to kiss me," he hinted.

Tommy hummed his agreement, thinking his boyfriend looked like a cat who enjoyed being petted and was about to purr any second. He buried his fingers in wavy curls, the way he'd wanted to for over a month, and pressed their lips together.

Oh yes! Tommy thought, head spinning as their kiss immediately deepened. He pressed his body harder against Carter's, relishing in the hard planes and wiry strength against him.

He felt warm hands draw up his shirt and run gently over his back. Pulling away a little, Tommy whispered, "I can take my shirt off if you want?"

Carter grinned. "Yeah? I can take mine off too."

Tommy nodded vigorously. "Probably a good idea for the first time we see each other shirtless to be private instead of in public at the pool."

"Anything to justify getting me half-naked, eh?" Carter teased.

"And yet you're still dressed," Tommy said, raising an eyebrow.

"So are you."

Tommy stepped back and tugged his shirt over his head. "There."

Carter's jaw dropped. "Damn, have you been working out?" He reached out to touch Tommy's bicep. "I thought you felt more solid than the last time I held you."

Tommy's flush started in his cheeks and spread down his chest. Carter's eyes dropped to track the colour. "Yeah, I was helping my family build Phillip and Sarah's house on weekend mornings. Lots of heavy lifting and repetitive motions. I'm nowhere near Jason, though."

"He didn't look like that at fifteen either," Carter said absent-mindedly, his fingers stroking over the newly revealed skin, goosebumps following in their wake. "I had no idea how much I'd appreciate you with muscles."

"Yeah?" Tommy smirked and flexed his arm under Carter's fingers. "You want me to toss you on the bed?"

Carter blushed, eyes fixed on the toned swell of muscle. "You can try. I'm a black belt, remember. I might throw you instead."

"Show me what you got, Karate Kid," Tommy teased.

Chuckling, Carter removed his shirt as well. "You don't want to mess with me, boy," he sneered playfully.

"Oh, yes, I do," Tommy breathed, eyeing his boyfriend appreciatively. "Which bed is yours?"

Carter pointed to the one closest to the bathroom.

"Great." Tommy kicked off his shoes, climbed on the bed, and rubbed his head on one of the pillows before flopping onto his back. "Shampoo on your pillows. Check." He grinned. "Unless you want me to go buy a bottle of my shampoo and dump it onto your pillow," he said with a chuckle.

"How are you so cute?" Carter murmured, removing his shoes before crawling onto the bed and up Tommy's body on all fours.

Every nerve on edge, Tommy maintained eye contact as Carter hovered over him. "How are *you* so hot?" he asked in return. "Are you going to kiss me, or am I going to have to flip you over and take control again?"

"No, I've got you right where I want you," Carter said, lowering his body and touching from hip to chest. "Ohh," he gasped. "That's... That's a lot."

Tommy's hands hovered in the air, about to hold his boyfriend. "Is it too much?"

"No, no, I just..." Carter closed his eyes and took a deep breath. "I wasn't expecting skin to skin to feel this good."

"Can I touch your back?" Tommy asked quietly. Getting a nod, he placed his hands firmly on Carter's lower back and rubbed them up and down. He could feel tension in the muscles under his palms. "You can relax. You're not going to crush me."

Carter huffed a laugh and shifted his knees up to bear his weight better. "Not so sure about that," he muttered.

"What do you—"

But then Carter was kissing him. Really kissing, tongue inside his mouth, dancing with his. Groans vibrated in his chest and Tommy echoed him, fingers dancing over smooth muscle that shifted under his touch. He brushed the waistband of Carter's jeans with his knuckles and slid over them, sliding his hands into the back pockets. He pressed down at the same time as he lifted his hips.

Carter pulled back from the kiss, pupils wide with desire. "Yeah?" he asked, breathing hard.

"If I put my legs around your waist, it might be a better angle," Tommy said, cheeks flushing.

"You've thought about this a lot, haven't you?" Carter smirked.

"Hard not to," Tommy admitted.

"A little past kissing then?"

"Only if you're okay with it too."

"Tell me when to stop," Carter said, shifting one knee up and then the other so that Tommy could move his trapped legs.

"You too," Tommy replied, wrapping his legs around Carter's hips. "Kiss me?"

Carter did as he asked, fusing their mouths together as he rolled his hips down against Tommy's.

Tommy saw stars and broke from the kiss with a groan. "Oh my *God*, do that again!" he begged. Foreheads pressed together, heat built between them. The two boys gasped as pressure and pleasure rose higher and higher.

"Tommy," Carter moaned. "I can't..."

"Yeah, me too. I don't think..." Tommy closed his eyes tightly and whimpered when Carter stopped moving. "Why'd you stop?"

"I'm not ready for that," Carter said quietly.

Tommy opened his eyes to meet his boyfriend's, both of them breathing hard. Carter was flushed from arousal and embarrassment. Tommy brushed their noses together lightly. "I guess I'm not either. That feels like a big step. So... what now?"

"I don't want to stop kissing you." Carter nuzzled into the crook of Tommy's neck.

Tommy tilted his head to offer better access. "*Please* don't stop kissing me." He skated his fingers up Carter's back to press his head tighter against him. His legs fell to the sides as Carter kissed and nipped his way up the column of his throat. "That feels *really* good," he moaned. "Can we... Can you lie beside me instead of on top of me?" Tommy asked apologetically. "It's a little *too* good, if you know what I mean." He clenched his jaw.

Carter smoothly slid the lower half of his body onto the mattress, mouth still connected to Tommy's skin. He worked his way down to the collarbone and bit at the meat behind it.

Tommy whimpered wordlessly, squirming and drawing his knees up. His fingers tightened in Carter's curls but didn't pull him away. "Carter, I don't think it was you being on top of me."

"You want me to stop?" Carter asked, his breath tickling Tommy's wet skin.

"*Want* is not the right word," gasped Tommy. "Probably best, though."

Carter propped himself up on his elbows and looked down at his boyfriend.

"Sorry," Tommy apologized.

"What for?"

"For suggesting that we... And then stopping... And stopping again..." Tommy stumbled over his words. "You wanted to kiss, and I feel like we've barely done that."

Carter smiled. "I've been having a lot of fun. I don't see anything to apologize for. Do you?"

"No," Tommy agreed shyly.

"I was a little too enthusiastic here. Should be covered by your shirt." Carter pressed a finger to Tommy's trapezius muscle, where it wrapped around his shoulder to join just above the clavicle.

"You gave me a hickey?" Tommy thrilled at the idea that his boyfriend was so into him that he didn't notice he was bruising his skin. "The girls are going to tease us when we go swimming."

Carter's eyes widened. "Oops, sorry. What are you going to do if there are other students there?"

Tommy shrugged. "I'm not going to borrow trouble." He cupped Carter's cheek. "You promised me kisses. Come here." He lifted his head off the pillow and brushed Carter's lips with his own.

Carter followed him back down to the bed. "Not going to argue with you there," he murmured into Tommy's mouth.

Chapter 11

♥

Tommy woke up early on the second day of the competition. He tiptoed around the room, grabbing his clothes and going into the bathroom to wash and change for the day. He slipped his room key into his pocket and checked that he had his camera in the bag provided by the competition before slipping out the door into the brightly lit hallway.

He stood there for a few seconds, blinking as his eyes adjusted, and then headed for the elevators.

He took one down to the main floor and walked slowly toward the main conference hall where breakfast was served.

Checking the seating chart before collecting a plate, he was surprised to see that both his and Carter's schools had moved up quite a bit. They still weren't seated together.

Looks like we both passed the optics event with flying colours, he thought, smirking to himself at his pun.

He filled his plate, taking his time to look over the variety of food available, since he was the only person in the huge room. He made himself a waffle using the waffle maker in a corner and topped it with whipped cream and fruit. He put several slices of bacon on the side and grabbed a circle of pineapple to eat on the way to his chair.

"Looks good enough to eat!" Carter's voice came from behind him and echoed through the empty room.

Tommy swallowed his bite of pineapple. "I can show you how to use the waffle maker if you like?"

"Mmmm, pretty sure I'm not talking about the waffles." Carter swooped in for a kiss that Tommy happily returned, despite having no hands free.

A shuffle of feet came from the main doors and the boys sprang apart.

Nobody was there.

"I'll meet you at your table?" Carter said huskily.

"Hurry or I'll be done before you get there. I'm starving." Tommy turned to go to his table. "Oh, and we're quite a bit further up than yesterday."

"Hey! Go us!" cheered Carter. "I'll hurry."

Tommy put his plate down and realized he had no drink. On his way to the back of the room, MacKenzie walked in.

"Mind if I eat with you?" she asked Tommy. "Or am I interrupting?"

"What would you be interrupting?" Tommy asked, not looking at her as he carefully poured himself a glass of apple juice. "Hey, Carter, what do you want to drink?"

"OJ, please!"

"Gotcha!"

MacKenzie gripped his chin in her perfectly manicured hand before he could pick up the glasses, turning him to meet her gaze. "If that's how you want to play it, then I didn't see anything. But if you're trying to hide it, maybe don't kiss in the middle of a public space."

Tommy blushed. "Please don't tell Mom!" he begged.

"Why?" MacKenzie stared at him. "What could she possibly have against Carter? From what I've heard, she loves him."

"I'm just not ready to tell them yet. I will when we go to Westmeath for the wedding. I want to introduce them to Carter properly."

"I think they'll be sad you've kept your first boyfriend a secret from them," MacKenzie said softly. She released his chin. "I'm sorry that I walked in on you instead of giving you the chance to tell me about him on your own."

Tommy hugged her quickly. "Do you want to have breakfast with us? Get to know my boyfriend a bit better?"

MacKenzie checked her watch. "Probably not a good idea. I don't want to show favouritism, especially since you're my brother."

Tommy's smile fell.

"Don't look so sad. I'll have plenty of time on Saturday evening. Um, if you're willing to tell Eliza, that is. If not, then I'll get to know him as your friend. No pressure," MacKenzie added.

"I'll think about it." Tommy knew how difficult it was for her to keep secrets from her twin. "Thanks." He picked up the glasses.

"Hey, what are sisters for, if not hiding secret boyfriends from Mom and Dad?" MacKenzie teased.

Tommy laughed. "You're good for more than that!"

"I'm glad you think so."

Tommy joined up with Carter and they headed to the table together. "My food is going to be cold," Tommy said with a pout.

"Really, you're talking about food right now?" Carter said incredulously. "She saw us, didn't she? Are you mad at me?"

"Definitely not," Tommy reassured him. "She won't tell Mom. I'm thinking about telling Eliza on Saturday."

"Serious?" Carter heaved a sigh of relief. "That would be cool."

"Yeah, it would be," Tommy said, biting into a slice of bacon. "What do you think the electrical challenge will be this morning?"

"Good morning, students and supervisors!" said MacKenzie, standing at the front of group four's event room. "This morning you'll be building something to help you 'clean up' the competition." She paused for effect and a couple students chuckled.

Tommy groaned and laughed. *I wonder if she went off script for that pun,* he thought fondly.

"Before you remove the covers, I have a few rules for you to follow, so please listen carefully. There are tools on your table. You may *not* take *these* tools apart and must put *all* of them back neatly on the table before scoring. When using these tools, proper safety measures must be taken. Failure to do either of these will result in docked points."

MacKenzie paused to look sternly around the room to make sure everyone was paying attention. "There is a bin of upcycled materials beside your table. Feel free to use any of those in any way you see fit, including taking them apart."

Brief chuckles met this statement.

"Safety goggles have been provided for each of you. Please wear them and please be careful when using the tools. You don't want to get sent to the hospital and be replaced. Although your replacements might want that." She smiled at the nervous laughter that rippled through the room. "All your instructions are in the booklet on your table, including an image of your table with every tool labelled and instruction manuals for the more unusual tools. You have three hours. Your time starts... *Now!*"

Tommy and his teammates scooped up their goggles and the booklet before carefully lifting the covers off the table and bin.

"Whoa," said Tommy, looking over the tools. "These are fancy."

"These objects are so random," said Sabrina, peering into the bin, her long brown hair falling over her shoulder and hiding her face. "Sheets of metal, empty bottles, a drill, a toy car? I don't get what all of these have to do with each other." When she stood upright again, she pulled her hair back with an elastic that had been around her wrist.

"Focus. Let's read the question first," Chris said, drawing their attention to the booklet in his hands. He put it on the table, and they all leaned closer to read it together.

Build a vacuum cleaner. Draw a sketch of it and write out relevant details in the following pages.

"That is so cool!" breathed Naomi. "It's like *Junkyard Wars!*"

"Brainstorming," said Chris. "A mini vacuum? We can use

water bottles, a smaller one inside a larger for containment of the dirt."

"Hang on," said Tommy, getting excited. He lowered his voice. "When I was studying, Veronica had us study the plans for this new vacuum, an automated one, and then we had to explain it in simple terms. I'm fairly sure I remember how it worked and how to modify it for upcycled parts."

"An automated vacuum?" Chris said. "That's pretty cool. And I doubt anyone else will think of that."

"Well..." Tommy shifted in place. "Elyse might. She was in my study group."

Chris sighed and blew a strand of his shaggy blond hair out of his eyes. "Of course. Okay, why don't you start by sketching it out? When you get to a part, the rest of us will scavenge the bin. Is that alright with you, girls?"

Naomi and Sabrina nodded, so Tommy picked up a pencil from the table and bent over the paper. "We're going to need batteries, a fan, a motor, filter, wheels... Hang on, Sabrina, did you say there was a toy car in the bin?"

"Yeah, here." She rolled the car down the table to him, and Tommy picked it up.

There was a switch on the bottom of the hand-sized car. Tommy flicked it on and put it on the table. It rolled toward the tools, bumped into them, and changed direction. He scooped it up again and turned it off. "This is perfect. We can take off the top and front bumper. We only need the base."

"How's this for the main container?" asked Naomi, holding up a large translucent plastic tub with a screw-on lid.

"Perfect. We'll need to use a water bottle to create a shield for the fan. And we also need something to shield the car base. Any Tupperware in there?" Tommy continued sketching. "Any luck on the motor or fan yet?"

"What about the old, corded drill in the box?" suggested Chris. "It's not on the table, so we can take it apart and use the motor inside it. I'm sure it can be modified to run on a powerful enough battery."

"That's brilliant!" Tommy said, and Chris started taking apart the drill.

"I don't see anything that can be used as a fan, though," said Sabrina, looking at the scattered pieces that were in the bin.

"You said a sheet of metal earlier," said Naomi. "And they gave us metal cutters in the tools. I can make us a fan."

"Hold off on that until we know the diameter of the bottle for the shield." Tommy sketched out what the motor part would look like in more detail. "Think you can do this part?"

"I'll start right away by cutting the bottle."

"Tell me the diameter and height once you know it, and I'll mark it down," Tommy said to her.

"I'm not sure how much space the fan will need, so I'm going to start with way too much room and then cut it down," Naomi said.

"Good idea. I'll drill holes through the plastic to create air vents," said Chris, picking up the new drill from the table. "Where do you think would be best?"

Together, they studied Tommy's sketch. "Behind the fan, so that they're under the fan shield," Chris said at last. "I'll measure the diameter of the motor and make a hole slightly smaller than that first, so it doesn't fall in, and then add smaller holes around it."

Tommy drew in little holes and wrote down the numbers that Chris and Naomi gave him. "We'll need a switch to turn it on, too."

"I'll find one," said Sabrina.

"Okay, I guess I'll dismantle the car," Tommy said, looking around at his busy teammates.

It took less than a minute to take the colourful plastic off the top of the car, exposing the mechanism inside. He used the box cutter to cut off the front bumper and then used the ruler to get the dimensions of the stripped-down car, writing them on the paper.

"How's this switch?" Sabrina asked, showing him an electric toothbrush.

"That's great! Not too big, so it'll fit on the lid. Take it apart. How's your electrical work?" Tommy asked.

"I'm not sure," Sabrina hesitated.

"No worries. One of us can help you."

"I'm so glad we're not doing this by ourselves," Sabrina confided. "I'd be so lost in this challenge."

"What do you feel is your strength?" Tommy asked.

"Coding, math, forces, that sort of thing," Sabrina said as she took apart the toothbrush.

"I'm sure you'll get a chance to shine later. Like in robotics this afternoon?"

Sabrina smiled at him. "As long as it's not building a robot, I'll be fine."

"Even if it's building, coding will be required, I'm sure."

"Okay, I've got the fan," said Naomi. "How do we attach it to the lid?"

"We need a flat surface to glue to the lid," Tommy said thoughtfully. "Another piece of metal, I guess?"

"No, use plastic," Chris said firmly. "We don't want the metal fan to scrape against metal."

"Good call. How about we use the plastic from the bottom, where the car will go?" Tommy suggested.

"I can cut that out," offered Sabrina. She squinted at the sketch. "Off-centred?"

"Yeah, because we want the vacuum opening to be as close to the ground as possible."

"Okay. Here." She gave Tommy the switch and picked up the ruler and a marker. "The exact size of your numbers?"

"Please."

Tommy joined the other two working on the motor portion. "We should test the motor before we glue anything down."

"Sounds good. You want to run the wires?" Chris asked.

"Sure." Tommy bit his lip. "I'm going to be honest here; electrical trips me up sometimes. If it doesn't work, it's probably because I got my wires crossed."

"Hey, no worries." Chris slapped him on the back. "It's nice to know that you're not perfect all the time."

Tommy stuck his tongue out at him and then focussed on the wires. "Positive to switch to motor, negative to motor?" Tommy muttered to himself, running his finger along the wires. "Is this right, Chris?"

"One way to find out!" Chris tossed him a battery to put in the chamber.

He made sure the switch was off, popped the lithium-ion battery in, crossed his fingers, and pressed the switch. The motor hummed to life, spinning in the direction they wanted.

His teammates cheered, and he blushed. "I'm going to draw the wiring out. It feels important in an electrical event."

The other three chuckled. Then they added the plastic and the fan to test again, with great success.

"Okay, let's get this motor put together!" Chris made a hole for the switch and left the wires hanging under the lid, keeping the battery on the outside, away from the dirt.

Naomi speared a hole through the plastic for the motor and glued it to the lid, then glued the fan to the tip of the motor spindle. She measured the distance from lid to fan and cut her bottle down to the right size. "Can I get a hole in the bottom of the bottle and the filter glued over it, please?" she asked.

Sabrina eagerly agreed and dealt with that, while Tommy calculated the height necessary to cut the large clear tub, marking it down on the paper.

"One hour is up, you have two hours left," MacKenzie said into the microphone.

"We're doing great on time," Naomi said happily.

Tommy drew a line in marker around the bottle and grabbed the box cutter again. "We really are," he agreed.

"What needs to be done?" asked Chris.

"Find a Tupperware that fits over the car. If it's too tall, cut it down. Measure it, and I'll cut the bottom off this." Tommy didn't move his eyes from the sharp blade in his hands.

"Shall I glue the fan shield to the lid?" asked Naomi once he was finished.

"Yeah, use the hot glue gun. Make sure there are no holes. Then we're going to need the car cover done, and then the top of the tub glued to the bottom."

Tommy drew a line at the bottom a little taller than the height Chris measured for him.

"Home stretch, team!"

"Hang on, we need the vacuum hole!" exclaimed Sabrina.

Tommy paled. *Holy shit! I can't believe I forgot about that!* he thought, panicked.

"Good catch, Sabrina," said Chris. He looked as relieved as Tommy felt.

Once he'd cut off the bottom, Tommy tossed it to Chris, who melted a thin line through the plastic.

"That should be good," Chris said. "Who wants to glue the car cover in place?"

"I'll do it," Sabrina offered and took the glue gun from Naomi.

Tommy took the time to look over the sketch and numbers with Chris, double-checking to make sure they hadn't missed anything else. "We need to measure the width and length of the vacuum hole to include in the diagram, the diameter and height of the entire vacuum, and I think that's it?"

"I think so." Chris slapped him on the back. "You did a fantastic job leading the team on this one. You should be proud of yourself."

"Thanks. I am." Tommy beamed at him.

"Tommy, you want the honours?" Sabrina said, offering him the glue gun.

Using it to seal the vacuum, Tommy thought, *I can't believe we built an automated vacuum in just over an hour! Who else can say that they can do that?*

"We should probably let it dry a bit," Chris said. "We don't want dirt sticking to wet glue."

The team agreed, and they tidied up their station. They then added notes and measurements to the booklet diagram, and checked that they had put everything back where it belonged.

Sabrina assessed the glue on the outside and declared it dry.

"Shall we do a test run?" asked Tommy anxiously.

"Sure." Chris dropped some torn bits of paper in front of the vacuum; Tommy turned on the car and then turned on the vacuum.

The group watched as the vacuum trundled off in the opposite direction, and Sabrina hurriedly stepped in front of it. The vacuum hit her feet, paused, and turned in another direction. They guided it over to their garbage pile and held their breath as it finally drove over it.

The pile of paper bounced around inside the clear container and they cheered, relieved.

While Tommy, Sabrina, and Chris raised their hands to call MacKenzie over, Naomi turned off their project.

MacKenzie hadn't even reached them before Oldtown raised their hands.

"You *had* to study with another team," Chris grumbled to Tommy.

"If I hadn't, Elyse would have still studied with Veronica, and then I wouldn't know how to build an automated vacuum and she would," Tommy hissed back. "Isn't the secondary goal of these sorts of competitions to promote inter-school co-operation? You're going to university next year. Do you really think that you won't make friends with students from other high schools at Laurentian?"

Chris looked sheepish. "Yeah, good point."

"What we're going to have to watch out for is if their junior replacement gets called in. Carter thinks differently than the rest of our study group, and not only do his ideas work, but they're usually better."

"Why isn't he on the team, then?" Chris had to whisper because MacKenzie had arrived.

"I'm going to mark down your time and then go get theirs before I evaluate your project," MacKenzie said cheerfully. She wrote something down quickly. "Be right back."

"Because two others got higher test scores," Tommy replied to Chris. "He still got 162. That's incredibly high." *Higher than almost everybody else on this team,* he thought, but didn't say aloud. Chris would know that he was thinking it.

"Alright, let's take a look at your vacuum!" MacKenzie was back. "Can you put it on the table, please?"

She examined their project from every angle, making notes on her clipboard every so often. She took a quick glance at the tools and then read the booklet, making some more notes.

"Okay, can you vacuum this up, please?" She took a film canister out of the fanny pack she was wearing and dumped it on the floor. There were pieces of confetti, small pieces of rock, sand, and two feathers.

Naomi turned on the car, made sure it was pointing the right direction, put their vacuum back on the floor, and turned on the motor.

The vacuum headed straight for the pile of dirt, much to Tommy's relief. After one pass, it sucked up most of the confetti, sand, and one of the feathers. The second pass, once they had convinced it to turn around, got the rest except for the rocks, which stayed on the floor.

MacKenzie nodded and made another note. "Congratulations on completing this event. You may exit the room." She left them.

The team looked at each other, blinking at the abruptness of MacKenzie's departure.

Tommy followed his team to the door, keeping an eye on the Oldtown team as MacKenzie evaluated their vacuum. He had been right; they had built a similar sort of automated vacuum.

From his angle, it looked square instead of round as it trundled around on the ground.

Strange that I only feel proud of my friend, not competitive toward her team. I certainly want to beat all the other teams! Tommy shrugged and left the room.

He was greeted by a tight hug from Faith. "That was amazing!" she exclaimed.

"But it didn't suck up the rocks," Tommy said with a pout. "We didn't make the opening large enough for them."

"You got all the grit. Rocks are easily picked up by hand. I can't imagine that would be a big penalty," Faith tried to reassure him.

"I'm sorry I didn't make the hole bigger," Chris said, frowning.

"It's not your fault. None of us thought it should be made bigger," Naomi said, shaking her head.

"There's no guarantee that a hand-held vacuum would provide enough suction or would be big enough to get the rocks either," Sabrina pointed out. "I'm really proud of what we accomplished this morning."

"You did a fantastic job communicating with each other and you built an incredible design," Mr. Travese said. "You should *all* be proud of yourselves. You've earned a rest. Why don't you go for a swim, take a nap, see the event booths, or something until noon? We'll meet up for lunch in the main conference hall before the robotics event at one."

"There's a games room on the second floor next to the pool," suggested Faith. "We spotted it last night when we went swimming. It looked like they had pool tables, table tennis, and several arcade-type games. Why don't we challenge Oldtown to a little friendly competition?"

The door to group four's room opened at that moment, the Oldtown group exiting.

Everyone went downstairs in case their voices carried, and Chris laid out the challenge.

"You're on!" replied George, a muscled Black senior. "Get ready to get your asses kicked!"

"I didn't hear that," Ms. Rubens, Oldtown's supervisor, said mildly. "I am going to go and have a nap."

"That sounds like an excellent idea," Mr. Travese agreed, much to the delight of the students.

"Ooooh!" they all said at the same time, making both teachers blush.

"There's nothing you can say now that will make us think anything but the worst," Bryan teased. "You two go 'nap' and we'll have some fun."

"I hate you all," Mr. Travese said, resigned.

"Play fair and be safe," Ms. Rubens told them.

"*You* be safe!" joked another senior from Oldtown named Alicia, flipping her long, wavy black hair over her shoulder.

Chapter 12

♥

"Now that we've organized how to keep score, we'll randomly split into groups of four, with one senior and one junior from each team. Then we can cycle through the three types of games and have a partner for each." Alicia's reddish-brown skin darkened as she flushed with excitement. She seemed like a take-charge kind of person.

I wonder how she's handling being a replacement instead of a contestant, Tommy thought to himself.

"Juniors, print your names on these papers. Seniors, draw a name."

Tommy crossed his fingers, hoping for Naomi, but Chris pulled his name instead. He gave their team leader a tentative smile that was returned.

"Okay, to pick your opposing players, one junior from each team will draw a name."

Tommy went first, drawing out the folded paper. "Carter," he read, beaming at his boyfriend.

Carter's teammate was a tall, pale boy with light brown hair and oddly pointy ears. He reminded Tommy of someone, but he couldn't quite put his finger on who.

"Adrien," he said, introducing himself. "Grade thirteen."

"Me too," said Chris. "The oldest and the youngest boys. Should be entertaining."

"Pool to start?" suggested Tommy.

"One person from each team will pick their starting activity," said Alicia.

"Maybe not," muttered Tommy, feeling pleased with himself when Carter chuckled beside him.

Their team was to start with the arcade games.

"*Dance Dance Revolution*?" Carter said eagerly, pointing at the machine.

"Of *course,* you'd pick that one," Tommy said with a sigh. "You're a great dancer."

"*DDR* is more about rhythm than moves," Carter countered. "You're taking music this semester. You should find this a breeze."

"Coordinating fingers is not the same thing as coordinating feet," Tommy grumbled, following Carter over to the machine.

"We'll play the shooter game," said Chris. "Once you've had your turns, we'll switch."

"Yeah, sounds good," said Carter. To Tommy, he added, "Want to go first?"

"I've never played this. Why don't you go first so I have an idea of how it works?"

Carter smirked. "Don't get too intimidated by how amazing I am," he teased as he stepped onto the platform.

Tommy watched how he scrolled through the music selections.

"We should both play the same song so that the scoring is fair," said Carter. "The higher the difficulty, the more points you can score. You don't have to play at the same level of difficulty as me. Ah, this one is perfect." He selected "Cartoon Heroes (Speedy Mix)" by Barbie Young and increased the difficulty level to Heavy, the highest.

"You've *got* to be kidding me," muttered Tommy. Louder, he said, "How have you had time to play *DDR* so often while we've been studying practically every waking moment?"

"Jason had one put in at The Hawaiian in one of the community hangout rooms," Carter told him, one foot hovering over the start button. "I'd go work up a sweat after studying so that my brain would relax, and I could sleep."

"Nice that you had that outlet," said Tommy.

"Yeah. At first, I'd practise my Katas, but that wasn't enough. I needed to fully exhaust myself. Are you ready for this?" Carter grinned at him.

"No, but go ahead." Tommy dug his camera out of his bag and snapped a picture of Carter at the beginning of the song, his jaw dropping as Carter smoothly transitioned through the complex stepping patterns.

When there was a hold, Carter rocked his hips to the beat, getting his arms into the dance. The pace picked up again, Carter not missing a step, even with half-steps being thrown into the mix. At the end, he had a combo score over four hundred and Tommy wanted to pin him against the wall.

"Oh my *God*," gasped Tommy, feeling like he had been the one dancing with the speed his heart was racing.

"You liked that?" Carter said, grinning and swinging himself down off the platform.

"Words cannot express how much I liked that," Tommy said breathlessly. He noted the glisten of sweat across Carter's brow and had the inexplicable urge to lean close and lick him. He gave himself a shake and noticed that he was still holding his camera.

Carter lifted his shirt to wipe his face on the hem, and Tommy swallowed hard, eyes fixed on the light trail of hair below his belly button.

"You're distracting me on purpose," Tommy complained. "I'm already at a disadvantage!"

"How am I distracting you?" Carter asked, lowering his shirt. "Oh." He grinned unabashedly. "Sorry, didn't mean to. You going to be alright to have a go?"

Tommy stuffed the camera back in the bag. "I'll manage." He placed the bag at the edge of the platform and climbed on. The metal rocked a bit under his feet, and he tensed, anxious about trying something new.

"The song is already selected, so step on it to activate," encouraged Carter from the side. "You should lower the setting, especially for your first attempt."

Tommy followed Carter's suggestion, lowering the setting to Light. "Okay, let's give this a shot," he muttered to himself.

The arrows came faster than he expected, and he stumbled a bit at the beginning, getting used to the footwork. After a few bars, he caught onto the rhythm and managed to get a short combo before he missed another arrow.

"Just relax. Flow with the rhythm," said Carter.

"I'm not a river," Tommy snarked back. He took a breath and focussed on the arrows, getting the hang of the timing by the end, and finished with a combo of fifteen. He watched the screen give him his score, chest heaving from exertion.

"That was so much fun," he said at last, turning to Carter. "That was probably boring for you, watching me go so slowly and constantly making mistakes."

"Don't put words in my mouth," Carter said. "You got a good score for your first try. I don't remember *mine*, but it was comparable."

Tommy chuckled. "Thanks for trying to make me feel better."

"Did you have fun?"

"Yeah, I really did."

"That's what's important. The score is just for the silly competition between our schools." Carter bent to pick up Tommy's bag and returned it to him. "Shooting game next?"

"I suppose you have a lot of experience with that, too?" Tommy said as they headed over to where the senior boys were shouting at the digital screen of the co-operative shooting game called *Mulciber*. "I mean, you throw knives. Isn't it a similar concept?"

Carter snorted. "They're nothing alike. Haven't you shot a gun before? I think you've got more of an advantage this time."

"I mean, yeah, I've used a gun. I wouldn't say I'm a great shot though."

"Don't worry, kids. You point and click," said Adrien, demonstrating. He ruffled Carter's hair as they moved out of their way. "Did you have fun dancing?"

"He destroyed it!" exclaimed Tommy enthusiastically. "It was on the highest level, and he made it look like it was the easiest dance in the world!"

"And you?" asked Chris.

"I had fun on my first attempt at the game. I wouldn't say I did very well, though," said Tommy apologetically.

"Hey, this is just for fun, right?" Chris said cheerfully, clapping Tommy on the shoulder. "The real competition is happening next door."

"Right." Tommy smiled gratefully as he settled in front of the shooting screen. "Although I'm still going to appreciate the successes of my friends."

"Nobody said you shouldn't," Carter said, shoulder bumping him. "Are you ready to fight monsters?"

Tommy rolled his shoulders back and picked up the gun, aiming it at the screen. "So ready."

"Okay, kinda seeing what you mean by distracting," murmured Carter, picking up his own gun. "You've got this intense thing going on that's super hot."

Tommy smirked. "Should I pick up skeet shooting or something?"

"If you want to. There are tons of other ways you look hot."

The game started then. It was a co-operative game, but they were scored separately.

"On your right," said Carter, pointing out a monster that Tommy hadn't seen.

"In that tree," said Tommy as he took down the monster.

They moved quickly through the scenario, taking out the monsters that attacked them. The big bad guy at the end was a giant steel serpent, and Tommy was worried that they wouldn't defeat it. Carter pointed out the weak point, distracted the monster, and Tommy took the kill shot. They ended with a complete kill score, with Tommy having slightly more points than Carter. Giving each other high-fives, they turned to the rest of the room, checking to see how the other groups were doing.

"I think we might have time for another dance off," Carter said, a twinkle in his eye.

"What song are you going to pick this time?" Tommy asked.

"There's a pretty awesome remix of 'In the Navy,'" Carter said with a smirk.

"You're just picking all the queer-coded songs, aren't you?" Tommy said with a laugh.

"Every song can be queer-coded if you try hard enough." Carter leaped onto the platform. He scrolled through the songs. "Ooh wait, no! I'm going to do this one!"

Tommy leaned over to read the screen. "'Sexy Planet' by Crystal Aliens?" he asked.

"Because I'm so sexy that I need the whole planet to know it," Carter said with a wink and a wiggle of his hips.

"Can't argue with you about the level of sexy," said Tommy admiringly, looking forward to watching his boyfriend dance again. "You know, if you want to dance, I'm sure we can convince the rest of the group to turn this room into a dance floor."

Carter chuckled. "I'm sure we could. Why would you want to do that?"

"Because when you're dancing up there, you're not dancing with me."

Carter smiled. "Ooh, good line."

The look Carter shot at him had heat curling low in Tommy's belly, and he shivered. "Any chance we could sneak away at some point?" Tommy asked quietly.

Carter turned away from the screen and leaned on the back bar. "We can go now."

"You don't want to do your dance first?"

"I can play this any time I want at home." Carter glanced around the room. "I only get to be with you for a short time. I'm going to make the most of every second, and if you want to sneak away, then we'll figure out a way."

At that moment, the door to the room opened and a few more students wandered in.

"The more people that come in, the less likely we are to be noticed when we leave. Come on." Carter stepped off the platform and grabbed Tommy's hand, pulling him toward the door.

"I wondered when I was going to run into you, Yee-haw," said a familiar voice, and Tommy's stomach sank.

"Nice to see you, Greg," said Tommy, turning around to face the bully. "How's your hand?"

Greg flexed his left hand gently. "The bones have healed, but it's going to take some time before I get full strength back," he grunted. "That was a lucky duck on your part."

"Not going to argue with you there," Tommy said lightly.

"Still together, then?" Greg said, nodding at them. "I didn't think it'd last, you living so far apart and all."

"Yeah, we are," Tommy said, gripping Carter's hand tightly.

"Good for you." Greg nodded. "Going to take advantage of an empty hotel room?"

"Maybe we were." Tommy sighed. "Guess we should stick around now that more people are coming in."

"I suppose we should be sociable," Carter agreed amenably. "Does your team want to join our friendly competition?"

"Nah, we're just here to hang out," Greg said. "Maybe try to convince the bartender to serve us alcohol."

Tommy's eyebrows rose. "Good luck with that."

The three groups met up again in the middle of the room.

"The place is a little more crowded now," Alicia said. "Obviously, there's nothing keeping you from mingling with other teams other than forfeiting the game!" She held the aloof glare for all of two seconds before George guffawed loudly and she cracked a smile. "Just kidding. We're not offended if you go talk to other teams now that they're here."

Chris nudged Bryan and nodded over to a group of senior competitors. "We're heading over there. Talk to you later."

Adrien and George frowned as they watched them leave.

"Is everything okay?" Carter asked them.

"It's nothing, I think," Adrien said. "Hey, Tommy, are you okay in the room with them?"

"Yeah. Why wouldn't I be?" Tommy answered, confused.

"They were asking Adrien and I some odd questions," George put in.

Tommy blinked. "About me?"

"No, not about you. Not directly, anyway. Bryan was saying something about getting hold of alcohol for a party in their room later." Adrien's brow furrowed in concern. "They invited us, but we both turned them down. Is drinking a big thing in Parry Sound? I thought that was something that only happened on TV."

"There have been underaged drinking parties," Tommy acknowledged guiltily. "I went to one, back when I was part of Cindy Lou's group." Belatedly, he remembered that Bryan was Cindy Lou's older brother. They were so different in so many ways. *Maybe not as much as I had thought.*

"I'm more concerned about their drinking hurting your abilities as a team," George said, crossing his arms. "If you're in their room, and they're partying all night, not only will Chris be dealing with a hangover, but you'll have a crappy night's sleep."

Tommy bit his lip. "Maybe we can convince them not to do it? If we get both teams together?"

"It's worth a shot," Carter said. "And if not, you can always come sleep in our room."

Adrien and George exchanged glances.

"What?" Tommy asked.

"That creates a whole host of problems," George began.

"But he's a Fairfield. We could probably bypass a lot of the problems just because of that," Adrien argued.

"What does my family have to do with anything?"

It looked like the three Oldtown boys had a silent discussion just by frowning and raising their eyebrows.

"Your sister is pretty popular in Oldtown," Adrien finally said. "Gabrielle speaks very highly of her."

"How do you know Gabrielle?" Tommy was surprised to hear her name dropped in the conversation.

"She's *my* older sister," Adrien said with a wink.

Tommy gaped at him. "No wonder you look so familiar! But..." He frowned. "What problems need to be bypassed, and how does Kennedy help?"

"Problem number one," George said, lifting a finger. "You can't just switch rooms like that. There are protocols. Your supervisor needs to know where you are."

"Problem number two," Adrien added. "You're a minor. Parents need to be notified."

"Which brings us to problem number three," George said. "Your parents don't know that you're dating our roommate."

Tommy startled and glanced at Carter, who shrugged. "I talk about you a lot. I can't help myself."

Adrien chuckled. "I get it. I talk about Ariel all the time too."

"And Kennedy...?" Tommy asked.

"Our supervisors know Kennedy and Jason really well. They might be willing to pass it by them instead of your parents if we explain the situation to them. And they could talk your supervisors around as well." George spread his hands wide. "It's worth a shot, if we need to move your room."

"Let's gather the others and let them know what's going on," Adrien suggested.

Naomi in particular was incensed. "What are they *thinking*?" she hissed, glaring daggers at the unsuspecting boys across the room. "Not only is it illegal, but it might get our team disqualified!" She pushed up her sleeves past her elbows. "I'll go knock some sense into them!"

Alicia grabbed her hand before she could take a step. "Let's not make a scene, if there's a chance they could get you disqualified. Keep it low-key."

Naomi's nostrils flared, but she nodded and let the older boys lead the way.

"We would like to talk to you two," Adrien said.

Chris and Bryan looked up from their conversation with a group of boys. "Yeah? Come to join us?"

"No," Naomi said flatly. "We've come to stop you."

"Is this an intervention?" Bryan sneered. He looked from face to face, settling on Tommy's. "Cindy Lou said you'd gotten boring. I see what she meant."

Tommy rolled his eyes. "It's not boring to want to remain in the competition and do well. I really don't want to be associated with alcohol. My parents would kill me."

"You don't have to drink," Bryan said with a roll of his eyes. "We don't do peer pressure." He nudged Chris sharply.

Naomi growled under her breath. "You're underage at a competition that requires your whole brain. If you touch a drop of alcohol, I'm informing on both of you, and we'll use Faith as the replacement."

Chris sighed and stood up. "If you feel that strongly about it—"

"I do," Naomi interrupted, followed by a chorus of agreement from the rest of the group.

"Fine," Bryan snapped, standing as well. "We'll still have fun but skip the alcohol."

"You don't need alcohol to have fun," Tommy muttered under his breath.

Carter grinned at him.

"I haven't changed my mind," George said suddenly. "I still think Tommy should room with us."

"Worth a shot, if Tommy wants to," Adrien agreed.

Chris frowned. "He barely knows you guys!"

Tommy cleared his throat. "Um, that's not exactly true."

A slow smile spread over Carter's face, and Tommy's heart skipped a beat.

"Carter's been my boyfriend since March Break," Tommy finished.

Bryan scowled. "Is that why you broke up with Cindy Lou?"

"I was never dating her!" Tommy exclaimed, exasperated. "She kissed me *once*! I broke up with the group because they were only interested in drinking parties and smoking and all that stuff. It had nothing to do with dating Carter and everything to do with a newfound love for science."

"But she doesn't know you got yourself a boyfriend," Bryan pointed out.

"No. It's none of her business, and I would like to keep it that way." Tommy sighed heavily.

With a roll of his eyes, Brian walked away, taking Chris with him.

Waiting until they were out of earshot, Tommy said, "Yes, Adrien, I would like to see if I can switch rooms. I don't like this talk of 'fun'."

"No time like the present!" Adrien and George flanked Tommy and led him out of the room, Carter trailing behind.

"We'll ask permission from our supervisors first," said Adrien. "I'm not too worried. Ms. Rubens and Mister Coolidge are pretty great."

"Aren't you worried about waking Ms. Rubens? She said she was going to take a nap," Tommy asked.

"This is more important. She'll understand." George brushed off Tommy's worries as they entered the elevator.

Ms. Rubens answered the door and the older boys explained that Tommy was concerned about sharing a room with his teammates.

"That's an unusual request. I need to discuss this with Mister Coolidge." She knocked on the door next to hers, and the boys re-explained once the second teacher opened it.

"I don't know if they'll stick to their promise of not drinking," Tommy said apologetically.

"Tommy doesn't want to disqualify his own teammate," said George.

Mr. Coolidge nodded thoughtfully. "Are you sure you boys don't mind sharing? You barely know each other."

Tommy cleared his throat. "Carter's my boyfriend. We shared

back in Westmeath when I was staying with Jason and Kennedy, over March Break."

"Your parents are okay with you sharing a bed with your boyfriend?" Ms. Rubens said, frowning. "Maybe we should call..."

"Your last name is Fairfield?" Mr. Coolidge said suddenly. He glanced sharply at Carter, who nodded, grinning slightly. Then the teachers had a whispered conversation that Tommy couldn't quite make out.

"Actually, I don't mind calling my mom," Tommy interrupted them. "She knows Carter and Gabrielle, Adrien's sister. There shouldn't be a problem."

"You can use my phone," Carter said, fishing it out of his pocket.

"Thanks."

His mom picked up on the second ring. "Tommy! How is the competition going? Is everything okay?"

"We're working really well as a team," Tommy said. "But I'm not comfortable staying with the guys on my team. They were talking about bringing alcohol to the room."

"I'm not sure I like the idea of you sharing with the girls," his mom said hesitantly. "Although I'm very proud of you for being so responsible."

"Actually, Adrien, Gabrielle's brother, suggested I stay with them. Carter's in their room too," Tommy said.

"That's a wonderful idea!" his mother said brightly. "Who do I need to give my permission to?"

"Both sets of teachers, probably," Tommy said. "Here's Mister Coolidge, from Oldtown."

It took no time at all to grant permission to the Oldtown teachers, and then the entire group went to find the Parry Sound teachers.

Mr. Travese was more concerned about the talk of alcohol than he was with Tommy changing rooms, once he understood that the Fairfields were fine with the move.

"I don't care if they promised they weren't going to drink. The fact that they had originally planned to do it is a problem," Mr. Travese said, frowning.

"I don't want them getting in trouble," Tommy said. "They haven't done anything wrong yet."

"That's true," the teacher replied, rubbing his chin. "There won't be a punishment. But I still would like to have a chat with them, maybe get their parents involved."

Tommy sighed with relief. "Thank you."

"Of course. We want you to feel safe." Mr. Travese cleared his throat. "They're down in the games room, you said?"

"They were when we left them."

"I'll go see them now."

"Carter, you help Tommy with his things," suggested Adrien. "We're heading back to the games room until lunch. See you in the main hall?" He winked.

Carter nodded and gave a salute. "Don't worry, I won't leave Tommy's side."

"It's nice that you have such great friends from other schools, Tommy," said Mr. Travese, clapping him on the shoulder.

Ms. Rubens raised an eyebrow at Carter, who grinned innocently at her. "Behave," she whispered and followed the boys and teacher down the hall.

"Let's get you packed up and moved," said Carter.

Tommy led him into his old room and pulled out his duffel. "My clothes are in the top drawer. I'll grab my dress shirts from the closet and kit from the bathroom." He also snagged his bathing suit where it was drying on the shower rod and returned to the main room.

It took less than five minutes for the two boys to clear the room of Tommy's things.

"What should I do with my key?" he asked uncertainly.

"Give it to your supervisor at lunch," suggested Carter. "You won't need one for your new room because you won't be going anywhere without me."

Tommy smiled shyly. "I like the sound of that."

They returned to the ninth floor and their room, where Tommy unpacked for the second day in a row. He tossed his clothes in the same drawer as Carter's, rehung his shirts, and put his toothbrush next to his boyfriend's on the counter.

"You were looking for some alone time," Carter said, smirking and wiggling his eyebrows. "We've got about an hour. Whatever are we going to do with ourselves?" He shook his phone in the air. "Timer is set. Want to nap?"

"Napping couldn't be further from my thoughts," Tommy said, stepping into Carter's personal space. "Although I would like to be horizontal with you."

"It's like you're reading my mind," Carter replied, sticking his fingers through Tommy's belt loops. He stepped back, pulling Tommy with him, until his calf muscles hit the bed. "And look at that! We're next to *our* bed."

Tommy made a noise deep in his chest that could only be described as a growl and gave Carter's shoulders a light push. "Take off your shirt and get on the bed," he ordered.

Carter obeyed, cheeks dark with a blush.

"I want to kiss you everywhere," Tommy said, and climbed onto the bed to do just that.

Chapter 13

♥

FRIDAY THE 9TH OF MAY, 2003 -
TORONTO, ONTARIO (AFTERNOON)

They did end up napping for a short while, Tommy waking up groggy with sleep at the sound of the alarm.

"We gotta go," he muttered, running a hand through his mussed-up hair before shaking Carter awake. "Come on, lunch."

Carter groaned and pulled Tommy tighter against him. "Fine. But only because of the competition. One of these days, we'll wake up in bed and not have to do anything or go anywhere."

Tommy chuckled. "Yeah? When will that be? Even the week of the wedding, we'll have things to do every day."

"Leave me to my wishful thinking," Carter said and released him.

Tommy got out of bed and tossed Carter's shirt at him, finding his own on the next bed over. They got dressed and hurried to the elevators.

"You look like you just had a nice roll in the hay," Carter smirked, trying to arrange Tommy's hair.

"So do you," Tommy said, eyeing Carter's curls. He had shaved the sides sometime after March Break but kept the curls on the top. "Looks good on you."

"We're not hiding anymore?" Carter asked, one eyebrow raised.

"Nope. There's no point. My team won't tell my ex-friends how happy you make me. I want to walk in that room holding your hand and have everyone know what we were just up to." Tommy grinned as Carter's jaw dropped. "That okay with you?"

"Can I kiss you 'good luck' before you start each event?" Carter asked. At Tommy's answering nod, Carter beamed. "'I like you' doesn't even begin to cover how I feel about you right now."

"*Je t'aime?*" Tommy suggested. "It covers a wider range of feelings."

"*Je t'aime,*" whispered Carter as they walked hand in hand through the convention centre foyer.

Tommy shivered. "*Je t'aime aussi.*"

They smiled shyly at each other.

Lunch was arranged on the back tables, as usual. There were a few stragglers, but most of the attendees were already sitting at the tables and eating.

Tommy didn't let go of Carter's hand as they got themselves plates and chose their food.

Showing affection in public feels different than I'd expected, he thought, glancing at Carter, who gave his hand a reassuring squeeze. *It's a good different. I like it.*

They headed for their tables, reaching Tommy's first. Carter tugged on his hand, eyebrows rising in question. Tommy leaned in and pecked Carter on the lips. He pulled away, Carter's shy smile echoing his own, before he sat next to Faith at the table.

"Look at you, acting all innocent in public when you have obvious sex hair," Faith teased, trying to straighten it for him.

Tommy blushed and batted her hand away. "It's mostly nap hair, actually."

"Uh huh." She winked.

"Ugh, can you be a little less obvious?" snarked Bryan.

It seemed from the glares levelled at him from both boys, that neither were happy he'd told the teachers about the alcohol thing. *Oh well. Nothing I can do about it now,* Tommy thought.

"Bryan..." warned Mr. Travese.

"I believe I saw you making out with your girlfriend in the hallway at school on Wednesday," Naomi said to Bryan. She made a face. "I could see your *tongue. This* was cute. Little innocent kisses," she cooed.

Tommy smirked into his sandwich. "Only because we're in public," he said before taking a bite.

Faith elbowed him in the ribs.

"Judge alert!" hissed one of the students from the other school sitting with them, and they all sat up straighter.

"Ms. Door!" said Ms. Daguerre, the alternate supervisor for Parry Sound. "To what do we owe the pleasure?"

"I wanted to come over and say how impressed I am with the team from Parry Sound. You've moved up in the ranks more than any other team, with one notable exception.

"Oldtown," Tommy said with certainty.

Ms. Door's lips twitched. "Possibly. I wanted to let the students from your school know that my summer camp through Door Technology in Westmeath is open to all students in Ontario. You should seriously consider applying."

"No way!" Bryan shouted in excitement.

"Thank you for the information," Naomi said politely, her eyes sparkling.

Ms. Door inclined her head in acknowledgement and then smiled gently at Tommy. "You remind me of a very dear friend. She was cautious with her love, but once she loved you, she was fiercely loyal."

"What happened to her?" Tommy asked.

"We lost touch not long after my daughter was born," Ms. Door said sadly.

"I'm sorry." Tommy didn't know what else to say.

Ms. Door gave herself a little shake. "Don't be. It was a long time ago." She clapped her hands together. "I look forward to judging your team this afternoon. Have a nice lunch."

After she walked away, Faith and Tommy looked at each other.

"Did she just invite us to her summer camp?" Faith asked.

"It certainly sounded that way." Tommy was having a hard time getting over his shock that Ms. Door had opened up to him like that. "Although it's probably similar to the March Break camp. I had to do a test in order to get in."

"You also probably have to behave yourself," Mr. Travese said pointedly at the two older boys.

Bryan rolled his eyes. "Yeah, yeah, I get what you're trying to say." At a hand motion from Mr. Travese, he continued through gritted teeth to Tommy, "I'm sorry I made you feel unsafe in the room with us."

"I accept your apology," Tommy said graciously. He took the card key out of his pocket. "Speaking of the room, I didn't know what to do with this."

"I'll return it to the front desk while you're at the next event," Ms. Daguerre said, taking it from him.

"Are you four going to be able to work together for this event?" Mr. Travese asked, looking at each of them in turn. "None of this nonsense will affect your trust in each other's abilities?"

"No, Mister Travese," the four of them chorused.

"Good." Their supervisor checked his watch. "We've got about fifteen minutes. I'll meet you there."

Carter and Elyse met Tommy and Faith as they stood up to take their dishes to the back of the room. Tommy's hand immediately found Carter's.

"How are you feeling about this event?" Elyse asked Tommy.

"Robotics." Tommy shuddered. "You know programming is my weakest skill. It's a good thing we're not on our own or else I'd be in trouble."

"It's definitely not one of my strengths either," Elyse acknowledged. "Fortunately, George is brilliant at it, so I assume he'll take the lead."

"Sabrina told me this is her forte, so I'll be encouraging her to do the same," Tommy said. "Hopefully we won't run into a problem because of the whole alcohol thing."

Faith patted his shoulder. "Naomi's got your back, Chris seems to be acting a little more mature about it now that he's over his snit, and Sabrina..." Faith trailed off and looked uncomfortable.

"What?" Tommy's stomach rebelled, eager to rid itself of his lunch. "I thought she seemed quiet. Is she..."

Faith shook her head. "No, nothing like that. You have to promise me you won't tell her I told you."

"Okay?"

"She has a crush on you. Had, I guess. She's a little disappointed that you're not available," Faith blurted out.

"Oh." Tommy blushed. "I had no idea. Don't worry, I won't say anything. That would make things awkward for everyone."

"Wow, an older woman," Carter teased. "Should I be jealous?"

"Nah, it just means you got the cream of the crop," Tommy said nonchalantly, making them all giggle.

"Good luck," Elyse said, waving to Tommy as she headed for their station.

"Good luck," he and Faith replied.

Carter brushed his lips lightly over Tommy's, making them tingle. "Go be a leader. You already know I'll follow you anywhere."

A goofy smile spread across Tommy's face. "I'll do my best."

Carter winked and squeezed his hand before letting him go.

"You two are going to give me a cavity," Faith said as they headed for their own station. "You're too sweet."

Tommy shrugged. "Can't help it. I'm just doing what feels natural."

He joined the other contestants in front of the table as they waited for their judge to give the instructions.

"Good afternoon," Ms. Door said. "This event is all about robotics. Today, you will build and program a robot. Tomorrow morning, those of you that successfully completed your robots will get to see them attempt a maze."

"An A star search algorithm," Sabrina muttered beside Tommy. "No, a depth-first graph traversal search."

"Every group has been provided with a single-board microcontroller, donated by my company, Door Technology, that you will program using our proprietary modules. You will build your robot and install the microcontroller in the three hours you have been given today. I will be judging you on your building skills and teamwork. Tomorrow, your programming will speak for itself. Good luck to all!"

It took a moment for the students to realize that was their cue to start, but when they did, they leaped for the booklet and cover on the table.

They had been given several boxes of various parts; wheels, treads, and metal bars were in one; an array of batteries and electronics, including what Tommy recognized as several types of sensors, were in another; and screws and bolts were in a third. Beside these were the microcontroller, a tablet, several tools, and a thick book that read *Door Technology: Codes and Syntax*.

Tommy whistled. "Alright, Sabrina. What do you need me to do?"

"Me?" She looked startled.

"You're the programmer. I'll follow your lead." He walked around the table and pulled out a chair.

"Um. Okay. I think I should be the one to figure out the programming language. A depth-first search for the mapping algorithm would be fastest for a maze. And we'll need to set up if-then programming for when the robot comes to a wall so that it knows what to do." Sabrina bit her lip anxiously. "I'm not sure if I can do all that by myself. Are any of you good at programming, too?"

"I can help," Chris said.

"I'm pretty sure I can build a robot," Tommy said. "But I would definitely appreciate a collaborator."

"I've built a robot before," Naomi said. "I was obsessed with *Robot Wars*, and I made one that did a chopping motion with an arm."

"Okay, so I'll be helping *you* build the robot," Tommy said with a laugh.

"There are some specifics that you need to know about the design in the booklet," said Chris, handing it to Naomi. "Keep those in mind while you build."

"Got it." She joined Tommy on the far side of the table and showed him the dimensions of the maze.

He nodded thoughtfully.

"We want speed, good manoeuvrability, and stability. It would suck if our robot fell over on the first turn, or if it couldn't make the turn," Naomi said.

"Four small wheels, a robot that's not too tall, with a touch sensor sticking out the front like an antenna," Tommy enumerated. "Like an ant."

"Ooooh," Naomi said, pulling the booklet toward her and grabbing a pencil. "We can put each wheel on its own articulated axle to decrease the turning radius."

Tommy dug through the parts bin and pulled out round balls. "What about these? They're tracker balls, like in a computer mouse. If we can mount them properly and have a sensor on each side of the robot, we wouldn't need a turning radius at all!"

"But computer mice aren't self-propelled," Naomi pointed out. "How would we tell the wheels to move?"

"Oh." Tommy blushed. "Right."

"It was a good idea," Naomi reassured him. "But I like your ant one better."

She sketched out a basic design and tapped her lip with the pencil. "Hey, Chris, can we get your eyes on this?"

"Yeah? What's up?" He leaned across the table and Naomi flipped the sketch around so he could see it. "That looks good."

"Thanks. I'm worried about what would happen if the robot didn't manage to make a complete turn at a corner."

Tommy frowned. "You mean if one wheel got stuck against the wall, but the touch sensor doesn't register it as a wall?"

"That's it exactly." Naomi furrowed her brow. "The robot would just keep trying to go forward until it ran out of batteries."

"What if you rigged up the touch sensor to a bumper?" Chris suggested.

"I suppose that could work," Naomi said. "But how would the robot know that it missed a turn rather than hitting a full wall?"

Tommy was digging through the second box containing the sensors. "We've got two of them here. What if we put one over each wheel with a separate bumper for each? Can the robot be programmed to tell that if only one gets hit, it's a corner?"

Chris nodded slowly. "Yes, I think I can figure that out."

Naomi pulled the booklet back toward her and erased part of the sketch to add their latest ideas. "Shall we start building?" she asked Tommy.

"Chris, I think I've got the start down. Can you check it, please?" Sabrina asked.

"Yeah, be right there. We're going to add some modifications to the if-then programming to account for two sensors instead of one," Chris said, sitting back down again. "How are you finding the IDE? Easy to work with?"

Sabrina nodded and tapped on the tablet with a stylus. "It's pretty intuitive, thankfully, because the coding is taking all my brain power."

Half an hour later, Tommy was arranging the left sensor when he paused. "What happens if there's an opening in the middle of a wall, not at the end?" he asked Naomi. "How would the sensors find it?"

"Shit," Naomi whispered, pulling her hands back from what she was doing. "Team meeting," she called.

The other pair stopped working.

"Tommy just brought up a good point. What if there's a T-junction?" Naomi said.

Sabrina paled. "I didn't think of that. I'm a terrible leader."

"You're allowed to make mistakes," Tommy said reassuringly. "You're not alone in this. Deep breath, we'll solve it together."

"What if we followed a wall?" Chris suggested. "Pick a side and put a light sensor. If it sees a wall, it keeps going. If it sees open space, it turns. It'll take a while, unless we guess where the exit will be, but it'll get there eventually."

"Will we have to worry about the bumper thing if we're sensing for a lack of wall?" Tommy asked.

The group all thought about that for a second.

"Yes," Naomi said finally. "Because we're going to bump into a corner eventually, and if there's no turn, then the robot has to know to turn away from the light sensor somehow. Touch sensors on the front make the most sense."

"We need to make sure the robot can turn one-eighty in a small space," Tommy said. "We might want to consider one wheel in the front to improve the turning radius. We don't want it getting stuck and doing a fifty-point turn."

Naomi shuddered. "Flashbacks to driving lessons," she said when they all looked at her.

Chris groaned. "The worst!"

"I think that if we don't make the robot too long, four wheels will be fine. We'll test it once we put the two halves together," Naomi continued.

"Big question," Sabrina jumped in. "Light sensor to follow the right or the left wall?"

"Don't they say that if you're lost in a maze, always turn right?" Chris said. "Anyone disagree?"

"Right it is," said Naomi, picking through the electronics box until she found a light sensor to attach to the front-right section of the robot she was holding. "Let me see that microcontroller again? I want to make sure this is going in the right place."

Together, Naomi and Tommy built the robot and then tested its turning radius on a marked paper.

"Glad that works," Tommy said with relief. "We've got just under an hour left before we have to attach the microcontroller to the robot body. What can we do to help?"

Chris glanced up from the syntax book. "Write down all the commands you think could be important. I'll make sure they're included."

Naomi nodded. "We can do that."

The time flew by. They attached the microcontroller to the robot with ten minutes to spare and flicked the ON switch. Tommy pushed the boxes to form a simple maze, and they shifted boxes around to make a dead end to try to trap the robot. The little robot did exactly what they wanted it to do, and they sighed with relief when they turned it off.

"Put everything down, turn your robots and tablets off, and step away from your tables, please," Ms. Door said. "I will be going table by table to evaluate your robots. Please stay until after I'm finished at your table and then your team may leave the room quietly."

Tommy glanced around the room. Nobody had left before their time was up.

"We should name it," Sabrina murmured, looking at their little robot.

"Great idea," said Naomi. "What about Asimov?"

"Nice. What about after the father of science fiction, H. G. Wells?" suggested Chris.

"Mary Shelley did more for science fiction than he did," scoffed Naomi.

"Sure, but *Frankenstein* didn't have robots," Chris pointed out.

"What about a pun?" Tommy suggested quietly. "We used Door Tech to program it. Why not Key, or the French word, *Clé*?"

"Robo-*clé*?" Sabrina said. "*Clé*-bot?"

"I like *Clé*-bot," Chris said with a chuckle. "Nice work, team."

Ms. Door had reached the team before theirs, and they watched anxiously as she made notes on her clipboard. She touched their robot a couple times, even picking it up once. Finally, she put it down and said something to the team that made them lower their heads.

"Oh, I don't think their robot worked," Naomi whispered to the others. "That's too bad."

Tommy agreed. *What a letdown that must be,* he thought.

"Hello, Parry Sound High School," Ms. Door said.

"Hello," Chris replied. "This is *Clé*-bot."

Ms. Door chuckled. "I do appreciate a good pun." She made a tiny note before starting her examination of their robot. She turned it on and off again, made some more notes, and tore off the bottom of the page.

"Please secure this to your robot. It will be moved to storage overnight and placed in the maze tomorrow morning by volunteers. Please be ready by nine a.m. sharp to watch all the runs. There is no planned order, so yours might be first."

They nodded their understanding.

"Thank you, Ms. Door," Chris said, and she moved on to the next table.

Chris carefully secured the paper to the top of the robot using a piece of string and then their group left the room.

Chapter 14

♥

***FRIDAY THE 9TH OF MAY, 2003 -
TORONTO, ONTARIO (EVENING)***

Oldtown was waiting for them in the hall.

"Did you pass?" Alicia asked eagerly.

"We did!" Chris replied with a smile. "You too?"

Adrien patted George on the back. "He did some masterful coding."

Sabrina gave a little whimper.

"Hey," Tommy whispered to her. "You did really well. We tested it a bit, remember? You should be super proud of yourself for learning a new language and coding a new piece of tech in under three hours."

Chris patted her on the back. "Tommy's right. Don't compare yourself to other teams. You did a fantastic job no matter what happens tomorrow."

George held out his hand to her. "I don't think I could have done this when I was in grade ten. Kudos to you, Sabrina."

Sabrina shook hands with him with wide eyes. "Thank you," she whispered, her cheeks flushing.

Mr. Coolidge clapped his hands together, and both teams turned to look at him. "Who has tickets for tonight's plays?" he asked.

Every hand went up.

"You'll be happy to hear that the competition has arranged for shuttles to bring you to and from the theatres. There are two shuttles for each, and I have the times listed here." He held up two pieces of paper. "You can eat dinner here or there. Personally, I would suggest there, in case of traffic."

Tommy nodded his agreement.

Mr. Coolidge gave one paper to Ms. Daguerre, who had been standing beside him, although Tommy hadn't noticed her thanks to her short stature. "I've got the times for *The Lion King*, Ms. Daguerre has *Mamma Mia*."

It turned out that everyone was going to see *The Lion King*, and Ms. Daguerre laughed. "Guess you didn't need the other times," she said to Mr. Coolidge, who shrugged.

"We've got about an hour," said Adrien, checking his watch. "Come on, boys, we should wash up and get changed. We'll meet the rest of you in the main lobby at ten to five."

Everyone agreed, and they all headed down the stairs to the elevators, piling into one when it arrived.

"How will we all have time to wash up?" Tommy asked anxiously as they neared their room.

"We all shower together," replied George with a straight face.

Tommy turned bright red. "Ummm..."

Carter laughed. "Don't tease him. He's not used to your humour." To Tommy, he said, "It's a quick wash, not a long pondering soak. I only need about four minutes. Then I leave the bathroom to get dressed in the bedroom part, and someone else takes over."

"Okay," Tommy said, impressed that his voice didn't squeak at the thought of Carter in just a towel, dripping wet. *I just won't look at him at all,* he thought.

"Who takes the longest to get ready?" Adrien asked.

"You do," said George. "You take forever with your hair."

"Then I'll go first," Adrien replied cheerfully. "Carter, you next, then Tommy, then George because you don't have to do anything with your cornrows."

They all agreed, and Tommy found that it wasn't as awkward as he had feared. They each wore their old boxers into the bathroom and brought a fresh pair to put on afterward, and other than the brief glimpse as they passed each other in the bathroom doorway, Tommy didn't really see Carter half-naked at all. He wasn't sure if he was disappointed or not.

"You look really great in this colour," Carter said, brushing the arm of Tommy's turquoise sleeve. His eyes widened. "Is this Seams Likeable work?"

Tommy nodded. "Thanks. You do, too. Jason bought three for me when I was there. I won't wear any other dress shirts if I can help it."

"Yeah, I know. I've got several, too." Carter adjusted the rolled sleeve of his royal blue shirt. "Need some help?"

Tommy stopped trying to roll his sleeve and held out his arm. "Please."

"It works better if you roll them *before* you put the shirt on," Adrien offered helpfully.

Tommy smirked up at him. "But then my boyfriend doesn't get to touch me."

"Excellent point." Adrien took over styling everyone's hair once he was done with his own, and they were ready in the lobby with five minutes to spare.

"I'll be right back," Carter said to them, heading over to the information desk.

Before Tommy could sit down, the Parry Sound girls arrived.

"Can I talk to you for a second, please?" Sabrina asked him, blushing slightly. "Alone?"

"Yeah." Tommy followed her across the lobby. "Are you still worried about the robotics event? Try to have fun tonight."

Sabrina shook her head. "It's not about that. I was wondering..." she trailed off and looked at her feet. "Has George mentioned me at all? Or if he has a girlfriend back home?"

"George?" Tommy asked, surprised. "We haven't had much time to talk, to be honest. But he's a nice guy. What's the worst-case scenario?"

"He's not interested."

Tommy shrugged. "That's not so bad, right? He'd be gentle in letting you down, and you probably won't see him again after this weekend."

Sabrina chuckled. "Yeah, that's true."

"You good?" Tommy asked, noticing that Carter had rejoined the others.

"Yeah, I'm good. Thanks."

"No problem. Good luck." Tommy smiled.

"Hey," Carter said when they returned. "I'm taking you on a date for dinner."

"You are?" Tommy couldn't stop the grin that spread across his face. "Where are we going?"

"I got the hotel to get us reservations at a Mexican restaurant right nearby. They know we've got to eat quickly because of the theatre tickets." Carter gave a half smile. "Apparently, they're used to that. Happy birthday!"

"It's your birthday?" chorused half a dozen voices.

Tommy jumped, startled. "On Sunday," he elaborated.

"We should do something special as a group tomorrow night to celebrate," suggested Adrien.

"Oh, actually, my sisters have something planned for the study group," Tommy said. "Sorry."

"No worries. We'll figure something out." George grinned mischievously.

Tommy narrowed his eyes, unsure if he should be worried or not.

"The shuttle's here," announced Alicia. "Let's go!"

Tommy noticed Sabrina and George were hanging back and crossed his fingers for his friend. She seemed shy at first but was smiling by the time they got on the bus.

"Alicia, Naomi, mind sitting together so I can sit with Sabrina?" George asked when they got on the bus.

"Ooooh!" everyone said in chorus.

"Stuff it," George replied cheerfully and gestured to Sabrina to slide in first once Alicia had moved.

"Was that what Sabrina was talking to you about?" Carter asked quietly after the shuttle started up.

"Yeah." Tommy glanced at the new pair. "I'm glad it worked out."

"Long distance is hard, though. And he's going to uni next year," Carter said.

"That's their business." Tommy squeezed Carter's hand. "Long distance can work."

"It's only been two months without you, and I'm dreading Sunday night," Carter said sadly.

"So am I." They sat in relative silence for a moment. "Silver lining, our video chats mean I know you pretty well now."

"This is true," Carter said. "But I can't bring you with me to dances, plays, babysitting, or hangouts. I also can't kiss you whenever I feel like it."

"Major downside," Tommy said. He smirked. "I guess you don't feel like kissing me right now?"

"A little PDA?" Carter asked slyly, sliding one hand behind Tommy's head to play with the hair at the back of his neck.

"If you're okay with that," Tommy said breathlessly, leaning forward.

"We're going to get teased." Carter's voice was husky.

"I really don't care," Tommy replied, brushing his nose against Carter's. He tilted his head slightly in anticipation.

"Just checking," murmured Carter. He pressed their lips together, hand tightening in Tommy's hair.

Tommy closed his eyes and inhaled through his nose, Carter's freshly clean scent mixed with the hotel soap and shampoo, filling his senses and making him dizzy. He hummed happily and scooted closer, copying Carter's grip on the back of his head. The sounds around them faded to background noise, his heartbeat thudding loudly in his ears.

The bus turned and Tommy swayed backward, Carter catching them against the window with a hand, protecting his head from banging against it with the other. They pulled apart just far enough to rub the tips of their noses together.

"Good?" Carter breathed, eyes dark.

"Very," responded Tommy, tilting his head and capturing Carter's lips again.

"Guys, come on, we're here," said Elyse, interrupting them with a tap on both their heads. "You don't want to go back to the hotel with the shuttle, do you?"

"Come on," Carter said, getting to his feet and helping Tommy up. "We've got a date!"

"I think this is our first actual date," Tommy said thoughtfully as they followed the rest of the group off the shuttle. "I suppose we could count the dance at the end of March Break as one, but there were other people there."

Carter opened and closed his mouth a couple times. "Other than virtual dates, yeah, I guess you're right. Well then." He smirked. "I can't believe I kissed you before our first date!"

George chuckled. "And you're going to bed together tonight!" He winked as they blushed.

"Okay, people," Alicia said, taking charge. "This is our theatre. We'll meet inside, at our seats. Try to be there no later than ten minutes to curtain. Boys, enjoy your date. The rest of you, let's go scavenge some food!"

Carter pulled a piece of paper out of his pocket and flipped it, squinting at it. "If this is the theatre," he said, turning himself around, "then we need to go—"

"That way?" Tommy asked, pointing at a sign down the street.

"Yeah, that's it," Carter said with a chuckle. He stuffed the paper back in his pocket. "They said it was close, but I didn't expect it to be within eyesight!"

The hotel had been right about their efficiency as well; they were served within five minutes of ordering and were able to take their time eating, returning to the theatre with time to spare.

"The Princess of Wales theatre is amazing!" Tommy exclaimed. "Have you ever been to a show like this before?"

"No, never. We went to Westmeath Little Theatre last year for graduation, and that was great, really, but it wasn't *Broadway*." They stopped in front of a sign for *The Lion King*. "We should get a picture of us!"

After posing for both camera and phone, they headed up the stairs to the balcony of the auditorium.

"Oh no! One of the girls must have the seat between us!" Tommy said, comparing their tickets. "I've got seat five, and you've got seat seven!"

An usher directed them to the right side of the balcony, and they started walking along the edge, Tommy holding tightly to the railing. "This feels awfully high up," he said breathlessly. They squeezed past a couple, who stood up so the boys could get by. "Sorry, thank you," they said.

"Oh, hey, the seats are all odd," Carter said suddenly, pointing at the numbers. "We are sitting beside each other."

"Oh, that's alright then," Tommy said, relieved. They got to the centre and sat, then leaned forward to look down at the main auditorium far below them and the people moving along the aisles and into their seats. "This is so exciting! I can't believe I'm here!"

"You and me both," Carter said. "Look at that stage!"

They were distracted by the arrival of the rest of the group. Faith and Elyse were sitting beside them, in seats one and three, and the rest of the group spread out on Carter's other side.

After talking and laughing with their friends for a few minutes, three notes sounded out, and the lights dimmed. The play began!

"I don't think I've *ever* seen *anything* as *amazing* as that!" exclaimed Carter excitedly.

"At first, I was having trouble visualizing the animals beyond the dancers, but by the end of 'Circle of Life,' I was completely sold that the entire cast were animals," George said. He picked up Sabrina under the arms and started singing the opening song, pretending she was Simba.

"*George!* Put me down before you drop me!" she shrieked.

The rest of the group joined in the song, pretending to be different animals as they pranced along the sidewalk to where the shuttle had dropped them off before the show.

When the song ended, and Sabrina had been returned to earth, Carter started up the next song, "Just Can't Wait to be King," Tommy joining in, and Chris interjecting as Zazu.

Adrien and George took over next as Timon and Pumbaa, and Naomi added her voice as Simba for "Hakuna Matata." They continued into the love song, this time Faith and Elyse taking over for the ballad. Carter grabbed Tommy's arm and spun him around in a slow waltz to their song, several others joining them.

"You're all forgetting the best villain song ever," said Alicia, smirking widely as she started it, the rest of the group backing her up and leaping around, pretending to be hyenas.

"Oh my God, that was amazing," Naomi said at last. "I don't think I've ever had this much fun in my life."

"I don't think I've ever acted like this in public," Sabrina said, blushing.

A couple walked past them and smiled knowingly.

"I love that all of us know all the songs," Lauryn said shyly. "It means nobody feels left out."

"You know what song I want to hear now?" Carter said, looking at Tommy mischievously.

Tommy started shaking his head, but the others jumped on Carter's question. "What song?"

"I want to hear the one Tommy wrote for me," Carter replied, smirking. "It's been so long since I heard it last."

"I wrote that in like, half an hour," Tommy protested. "And you won't let me change it to tighten up the verses or fix up the rhymes!"

"You wrote him a song?" Faith asked. "Please, can we hear it?"

"I'm not even sure I remember it," Tommy hedged.

"If you're not comfortable, that's okay," Carter said, noticing Tommy's awkwardness. "I know it's personal. I shouldn't have asked."

"I was just caught by surprise." Tommy cleared his throat and fixed his gaze on Carter, ignoring everyone else and the blush on his cheeks. "It sounds better with accompaniment, but here goes…"

Tommy cut off the last note as abruptly as he had the end of the other choruses, and there was silence for a moment.

"Damn," George said with a whistle. "I'd get on my knees if I was sung to like that."

Adrien smacked him across the head, and Carter flushed.

"You'd propose?" Sabrina asked, brow furrowed in confusion.

"Aren't you cute," George said, cupping her chin in a large hand.

"But…" Her eyes widened. "Oh!" She blushed. "Forget I said that."

"Never," George said with a chuckle, giving her a hug. "That was adorable."

"That's how you told him you were into him?" Elyse asked Tommy. "That's so sweet!"

"So romantic!" cooed Alicia.

"What did you mean, lethal grace?" Chris asked.

"Oh, I had just watched Carter throw knives for the first time. He has five custom blades, and every one of them hit the bullseye." Tommy's throat went dry just thinking about it. "That's when I finally accepted that I wanted to be more than just his friend."

"He throws *knives*?" squeaked Bryan.

"A man of many talents," Adrien said with a smirk, dropping one arm around each boy. "And look at that. Our shuttle's coming."

"Were we the only ones to go to this show tonight?" Tommy asked, looking around for more students. "Wasn't the shuttle more crowded on the way here?"

"We didn't take the first shuttle back," Chris said. "I guess everyone else took it."

"What time is it?"

"Almost midnight," Adrien said, looking at his watch.

"Good thing we've got an extra hour to sleep in tomorrow morning," Naomi said. "Or else we'd all be zombies!"

"Come on, kids." Adrien herded them onto the shuttle. "Let's serenade our driver the whole way home, shall we?"

Chapter 15

**SATURDAY THE 10TH OF MAY, 2003 -
TORONTO, ONTARIO (MORNING)**

Tommy woke up to a gentle shaking of his shoulder.

"Time to get up," Adrien said. "You've got forty-five minutes to get dressed and eat before the maze."

Tommy groaned and buried his face deeper into the hard pillow he was wrapped around.

A hard pillow that shifted underneath him.

Blearily opening his eyes, Tommy was confronted by the soft grey tank of his boyfriend. "Time's it?" he rasped.

Adrien chuckled. "Eight-fifteen. We all missed breakfast. Good thing there's fruit out in the second-floor hall."

Just then, a knock sounded on the door. George went to answer it. Tommy could hear quiet murmuring and then there were more people in the room.

"We brought you guys bagels, since you didn't show up for breakfast," Faith said.

"With peanut butter," added Sabrina.

"You girls are lifesavers," George enthused, swiping a bagel.

"We can't let our teammate go hungry," Sabrina said with a smirk. "And it seemed cruel to only bring *him* food."

"You wound me!" George exclaimed dramatically, grasping at his well-defined bare chest with one hand. "I'm an afterthought!"

Tommy snickered into Carter's shirt.

"Too much noise," Carter complained. "Five more minutes?"

"Aren't you two sweet, all cuddled up together," cooed Elyse.

From the corner of his eye, Tommy watched her walk around the bed to where Carter had plugged in his cell phone the night before. She picked it up and unlocked it quickly.

"One picture of the cuteness, and then you're waking up," she said, and the phone clicked.

"Tommy, you want one on your camera, too?" Sabrina asked.

Tommy sat up quickly at that.

"No!" Carter said emphatically. "He hasn't told his parents."

"Oh." Sabrina looked apologetic and put the camera back down on the dresser. "Sorry. I forgot."

Tommy winced and rubbed sleep from his eyes. "It's not that I don't trust you. You know that, right? My mom is super overbearing, and she's definitely going to look at these."

Sabrina played with her shirt hem. "I understand. My mom starts the whole diabetic speech every time I even *look* at candy."

Tommy inclined his head in acknowledgement and took the bagel Faith handed to him. "I'm still shocked she let me switch rooms. The mention of alcohol was definitely a tipping point. Even though the guys are mad at me, I'm glad it worked out this way."

"We get to cuddle together at night!" Carter said happily.

"That's a definite plus!" Tommy agreed exuberantly, making everyone chuckle.

The girls left after that, letting the boys eat and get dressed.

Tommy cuddled up to Carter as they leaned against the headboard, munching on their breakfast.

"If we leave you two alone, will you make it on time for the event?" Adrien asked once he was dressed, hands on his hips.

"Have we been late for anything yet?" Carter snarked. "This is kinda important. We'll be there."

"Okay, okay." Adrien raised his hands.

"Thought you might want some privacy to take care of things," George said pointedly.

"Oh my God," muttered Tommy, hiding his face in his hands.

"Yeah, right, because waking up to a room full of people isn't a mood killer," Carter said, raising an eyebrow.

"Just saying. We've all woken up with a—"

"They get the idea, George," Adrien cut him off with a grin. "Come on, let's go terrorize some other people."

"Please!" begged Tommy.

The minute the door closed behind the older boys, Carter murmured, "Well, that wasn't embarrassing at all."

"I wished I could melt into the mattress," agreed Tommy.

"Elyse got a good picture, at least," Carter said, showing Tommy the picture on his phone.

"I'm really clinging onto you, aren't I?" Tommy said, scrutinizing the image.

"No less than me to you," Carter said, shrugging. "I think I'm going to need a body pillow when I get home. I don't think I've slept so well since March!"

"Even once you've exhausted yourself playing *DDR* after studying?" Tommy teased.

"A sleep of exhaustion is not the same thing as a good sleep," Carter said seriously, running his fingers along Tommy's forearm.

Tommy shivered. "I thought we weren't supposed to get distracted?"

Carter wiggled his phone. "I set an alarm. We've got ten minutes."

"That's not nearly enough time to kiss you, but we'll make it work," Tommy said, climbing onto Carter's lap and spearing his fingers through his hair.

"Oh, I like this," Carter said breathlessly, gripping Tommy's hips. "Why haven't we done this before?"

"No time?" Tommy suggested. "Which we're running low on right now."

"Then kiss me already!"

There were five minutes to spare when they reached the event room. Their teams were sitting together against the wall. The centre of the room had a large maze.

"I wasn't worried," Chris said when they arrived. His blond hair was standing on end.

"He's lying," Faith stage whispered.

"Ms. Door isn't even here yet!" protested Carter. "We're early!"

"He was pacing the floor," said Adrien, a mischievous gleam in his eyes.

"I thought we'd have to restrain him from running off to find you," George teased.

Tommy shuddered. "I'm glad it didn't come to that."

"Can I talk to you?" Chris asked. "Alone?"

Tommy nodded, and Chris put an arm around his shoulders, leading him a short distance away from the others.

"I wanted to apologize about the whole alcohol thing. When Bryan suggested it, I was excited. It's the first time I'm old enough to buy alcohol legally, and we're away from home... I got carried away. I didn't think about my actions and how they would affect the team. Or you. I hope you can forgive me."

"Thanks for that. I'm glad we found out about it before you did it. I'm sorry for telling the teacher and getting you in trouble with your parents," Tommy said.

Chris grinned. "I didn't get in too much trouble. And Bryan will be able to talk his parents around. They're pushovers."

Tommy rolled his eyes. "I believe it. I think they bought the beer for Cindy Lou's party."

"Gross." Chris wrinkled his nose. "You're a good kid." He clapped Tommy on the shoulder as they headed back to the group.

"Good morning!" The microphone squealed, everyone covered their ears, and Ms. Door stepped back quickly. More cautiously, she approached the mic stand again. "Now that we're all suffi-ciently awake..."

There were scattered chuckles and Ms. Door smiled.

"Let us bring out the first robot. When your school is called, please step forward so that you can watch your robot's progress in the maze. When your turn is complete, please leave the room."

The first team was Nepean High School, from Ottawa.

Tommy held Carter's hand tightly as they watched from a distance. They couldn't really see what was going on inside the maze as the walls were too high, but they watched the reactions of the team. It didn't take long for them to droop with dejection.

"I wonder what happened," Carter whispered.

Tommy shrugged and watched as Ms. Door made some notes on her clipboard before dismissing the team. His gut clenched with anxiety, but another school was called, and then another, and another, until they were the last two.

"Oldtown High School."

"Excuse me, Ms. Door," said Adrien. "But could Parry Sound watch with us? We've become close, and we'd really appreciate the support."

Ms. Door smiled and winked at Tommy and Carter. "Of course."

"Can Oldtown stick around for ours, too?" Chris said.

"Why do you think I left you two for last?" Ms. Door said with a knowing look.

They all stepped forward and the volunteer placed the first robot into the maze.

"Ready and... *mark*!" said Ms. Door, pressing a button on her stopwatch.

The volunteer turned on the robot at the same time and the little device leaped forward.

Tommy studied it carefully. The robot seemed to be built the same way as theirs, with the light sensor on the side. It detected the first opening halfway down the initial path and turned right.

"Excellent," said Ms. Door. "First one to detect that opening."

"Nice work, George!" exclaimed Adrien.

"Nah, that was you suggesting a light sensor," said George.

Tommy traced the maze with his eyes, looking to see how many wrong turns their robot would take before it found the exit.

The maze wasn't too complicated; the T-junction in the initial path and a Y-junction that was coming up. Tommy held his breath as the robot approached it, squeezing Carter's hand tightly.

The robot turned right with no problem, adjusting course when it bumped into the wall slightly from turning too far.

"Now *that* was your code," said Adrien, jostling George.

"Yeah, I know I'm good," George said haughtily, cracking a grin afterward.

Sabrina looked ready to throw up her breakfast as she watched the robot near the dead end. It would have to do a complete turn, travel back up the right arm of the Y, and make a sharp turn into the left arm to reach the exit.

The little robot managed it all, bumping the walls a few times, but eventually navigating its way out of the maze. It kept going, to the cheers of both groups, following the right wall until the volunteer chasing it managed to catch it and turn it off.

"Very good," said Ms. Door. "Now, Parry Sound."

"Sabrina, you okay?" asked Alicia, giving the girl a concerned look. "Can we get some water over here? And a chair?"

"Breathe, sweetheart, breathe," said George, turning her away from the maze. He pushed her into the chair when Mr. Travese brought it and took the water from Ms. Rubens, kneeling on the floor in front of her. He leaned in close, whispering something that nobody else could hear.

Sabrina nodded a couple times and took sips of water. "Okay, I'm ready. Sorry for wasting everybody's time."

"We're still on schedule. No time has been wasted." Ms. Door smiled gently. "Your little robot did very well."

Sabrina looked down at Parry Sound's robot. "*Clé*-bot is mine," she said.

Ms. Door's smile widened. "I see. Shall we?" At Sabrina's nod, she said, "Ready and mark," and their little robot started on its way.

The T-junction was solved easily, and Tommy watched Sabrina sigh with relief. He did too since they would have been stuck going back and forth if he hadn't noticed the problem of only using touch sensors at the front. Their robot reacted the same way as Oldtown's before them, and after passing through both arms of the Y, their robot left by the exit to cheers from the room.

"You did it!" exclaimed Carter.

"We both did!" Tommy replied excitedly.

"Well done," said Ms. Door. "Good luck this afternoon." She made another note on her clipboard and left the room.

"Is that it?" Sabrina asked.

"It's more feedback than we got at other events," said Lauryn softly. "More than the other teams got from her today."

"That's true," said Chris. "What should we do for the next," he checked his watch, "three hours before the afternoon event?"

"Personally, I'm dying to check out the pool," said George.

"It's nice and warm," said Elyse. "I wouldn't mind another dip."

Everyone else eagerly agreed, and they hurried off to their rooms.

"There's a hot tub and a sauna," Carter told the older boys as they headed to their room. "And they have towels down there, so we don't have to worry about bringing the ones from our room."

The room had been tidied in the brief time they had been gone, beds made and towels replaced with fresh ones.

"They're ninjas," George said, impressed.

The other three laughed.

They got changed quickly and headed for the pool on the second floor. There were already several teams in the water, and they joined them, jumping into the deep end with giant splashes.

"Hello," Adrien said to one of the other people. "Oldtown, Westmeath." He gestured at Tommy. "Parry Sound. Mind if we join you?"

"Sir Arthur Conan Doyle, Baker. We've also got Westmeath Prep and Korah Collegiate from the Soo in here right now," said the boy. "I'm Trevor."

The four boys introduced themselves.

"Oh, hey, Tommy!" a boy said, swimming over to the little

group. "I wondered when I'd bump into you again. How's it going?"

Tommy squinted at the boy, trying to remember his name from the bus. "Joel?"

"You remembered my name," Joel teased. "Good on you."

"It's going pretty great," Tommy said. "We've completed all the events so far. This last one was intense, eh?"

"Ugh, I know what you mean! Our robot couldn't see the T-junction, so it kept going back and forth." Joel shook his head. "I can't believe we didn't think of that."

"Lots of people didn't think of that, from what I saw," said Trevor. "Lots of disappointed teams."

"Well, at least we're in good company," Joel said with a half-hearted chuckle. "And we made it to the maze."

Tommy shifted restlessly in the water, uncomfortable with discussing the events in so much detail. "Why don't we all play a game?"

"Great idea," said George.

"How about Kelpie?" suggested Carter.

The non-Westmeath boys looked at him oddly. "What's that?" asked Joel.

"It's like Marco Polo, but with none of the historical baggage," Adrien said with a chuckle. "The seeker calls out 'kelpie' and the response is 'neigh.'"

"Seems easy enough," said Trevor. "I'll grab a couple others before we start."

"As long as the seeker doesn't drag the person they capture under the water to drown, I'm good to play," said Tommy with a chuckle.

"Yeah, that's never a fun time," Carter said seriously. "Don't get on a strange horse near a body of water."

Tommy laughed. "I really don't plan on it."

George cracked his knuckles. "I'm 'it' so you two should move away now." He closed his eyes and Tommy and Carter quickly swam away in opposite directions. "Kelpie!"

"Neigh!"

When the rest of their group arrived, the Westmeath group filled in the Parry Sound students, and they joined in the game.

George caught a girl from Westmeath Prep quickly, and the game continued, getting more difficult as more people jumped into the pool to play with them.

Tommy was finally caught, and he swished through the water slowly, trying to corner a victim. He heard a quiet inhale and splash and then the water between his legs shifted as if a person was swimming between them. He closed them, his ankles catching on someone who surfaced with a gasp.

"How'd you know it was me?" Carter said, wiping water from his face.

"Who would think to swim between my legs?" Tommy said with a smirk. "Anyone else would've stayed in the corner. You must have wanted to get caught by me." He winked.

"Maybe I did," Carter said, moving closer.

"Hey, stop flirting in the middle of the game!" someone shouted, prompting chuckles from the rest of the players.

"Shut up, Greg," Carter called over his shoulder, not even looking at the speaker. "Just for that, you're 'it.' Tommy and I are taking a break."

"Hot tub?" Tommy questioned, ignoring the catcalls.

"Sauna," Carter said decisively. "Less towelling off before we get back in our clothes for lunch."

"Showers after the event this afternoon?" Tommy said as they hoisted themselves out of the pool.

Nodding in agreement, Carter said, "I'm excited to see where your sisters are taking us. Any hints?"

Tommy shrugged. "I haven't had any further chance to talk to MacKenzie since yesterday at breakfast. We'll just have to wait and see."

"I can be patient," Carter said, opening the sauna door for Tommy. There was no one else inside. "Let's make out."

Tommy chuckled. "I knew you were going to say that." He

pulled Carter inside and closed the door behind him. "Your turn to sit on *my* lap."

The rest of the morning passed in a happy blur of kisses, enjoyable conversation, and lunch. By the time the afternoon event was scheduled to start, Tommy was ready to go.

SATURDAY THE 10TH OF MAY, 2003 - TORONTO, ONTARIO (AFTERNOON)

"What have we got now?" Tommy asked nobody in particular while they were waiting for their room to be unlocked.

"Civil engineering," said Alicia.

"Really? I wonder if we'll have to design or build something." Tommy glanced at his watch. "I don't think they've ever let us in so late. What's going on?" He stood on his tiptoes to try to see ahead of them.

"The other rooms are locked, too," said Adrien, who was the tallest of the group. "They must not be able to cover everything, so they're having us wait outside to be fair."

"A big build, most likely," said Tommy. "This should be interesting."

Just then, the doors were opened, and they filed into their room.

"Good guess," said Chris, nudging Tommy's arm with his elbow. "How are you with a hammer?"

The centre of the room was filled with lumber and woodworking equipment.

"I've been helping my brother build his house for the past month. I'm unlikely to smash a finger."

"Good."

Carter gave Tommy a quick kiss for luck before the teams separated to wait quietly at their stations.

Professor Adams was their judge for this event. He eyed the microphone and clapped his hands together to get everyone's attention. "Everything you need to know is in your booklet. You have three hours. Good luck."

"Not one for speaking much, is he?" muttered Naomi.

Chris picked up the booklet and flipped it open. "Looks like we're building a footbridge. There are a bunch of specs here, max dimensions, required weight load, that sort of thing. And it looks like they gave us tensile and compression strengths for assorted designs. Who wants to draw, and who wants to math?"

Tommy chuckled. "I'll math."

"I'll draw." Naomi raised her hand.

"Sabrina and I will double-check both," Chris said.

Tommy quickly worked up the math for the designs. "It's looking like equilateral triangles are the best choice," he said at last.

"Warren-style trusses then," Chris said.

"You know a lot about building a bridge," Sabrina said in awe. "I have no idea what that means. Other than the *truss* part, of course."

"This is what I'm going to university to learn how to do on a larger scale," Chris said absentmindedly. "The sides are equilateral triangles. We should figure out how many we need for each side to make the bridge the dimensions required." He glanced at Naomi's sketch. "Yes, that's it."

Tommy looked over her shoulder. "I can do the math for that." His pencil was already flying over his page. "Okay, we want each side of the triangle to be this long, and we'll need this many triangles. Times two, for the other side of the bridge, of course." Tommy pointed to the two numbers, and Naomi added them to her sketch.

Chris gestured to the shared pile of lumber in the middle of the room and the shielded power tools. "Let's get a move on, then!"

Their two posts were provided for them; they just had to build the bridge across them. With Chris guiding them, the team measured twice and cut once for every piece of wood they needed. Tommy oversaw the construction, taking care to follow his mother's advice on how to properly use a hammer so he wouldn't hurt himself.

At the end of a very sweaty two and a half hours, they stepped back and admired their bridge.

"Shall we test it?" asked Sabrina.

"What if it breaks under our weight?" Tommy asked hesitantly.

"Do you doubt your math?" Chris asked, one eyebrow raised. "I don't."

Tommy smiled. "Well, you did double-check it for me, just in case."

"There is that," Chris said with a chuckle. "Come on."

He stepped onto the bridge and held out his hand for Tommy to step up beside him. Naomi was next, followed by Sabrina. They grinned at each other as they leaned on the railing and then raised their hands in the air to call the judge over.

Professor Adams examined their bridge from all angles, testing the stability of their joints and the angles of their cuts. "Thank you. Your bridge will be evaluated for maximum capacity after the event is over. You may leave."

I must be getting used to abrupt dismissals from the judges, Tommy thought as he gathered his bag.

Faith handed him his camera. "I got a picture of the four of you on the bridge. I hope you don't mind," she said quietly.

Tommy beamed at her. "Thank you." He took a detour to grab the room key from Carter before he left. Oldtown looked close to done, but he hoped he could shower before they returned.

Chapter 16

***SATURDAY THE 10TH OF MAY, 2003 -
TORONTO, ONTARIO (EVENING)***

Tommy took a little extra time in the shower to really get the chlorine out of his hair, using two rounds of shampoo and scrubbing the rest of his body thoroughly with the hotel soap.

Carter was lying on their bed, playing on his phone, when Tommy exited the bathroom in his boxers. Carter's phone dropped onto his chest, and he whistled appreciatively. "Now that's a view I could get used to seeing."

Tommy blushed. "Where are the others? How did your event go?"

"They're hanging out in the games room with the group." Carter got to his feet and walked closer to Tommy. "The event went well, although not quite as fast as yours." He ghosted his fingers up Tommy's arms. "I very much enjoyed watching you get your builder on. Super sexy."

"It was all for you, naturally," Tommy replied playfully. "I was hoping to get a kiss or two out of it."

"Hmm," Carter hummed, brushing their noses together. "One now, one after my shower?"

"One now, one after you're undressed, one after your shower," Tommy countered, slipping his fingers under the soft material of Carter's T-shirt.

"How can I refuse?" Carter murmured, tilting his head to the side to gain access to Tommy's lips.

Tommy's skin tingled everywhere Carter touched. He dragged

his boyfriend's shirt up and over his head, only separating for the brief moment required. "Can I...?" Tommy mumbled, hands questing downward.

"Yeah, take them off," Carter gasped in reply.

Tommy fumbled with the button on the jeans, half his concentration focussed on kissing, and then it was open, zipper down, and he pushed them over Carter's hips.

Carter groaned, breathing heavily and breaking the kiss. They stared into each other's eyes for a moment, grey and green swallowed by the dark pupils. "One day, I promise."

Tommy shivered. "One day sounds good."

Visibly swallowing, Carter said, "Maybe the after-shower kiss should be after I'm dressed."

"Not dripping wet in just a towel?" Tommy teased, trying to break the tension.

"You just want me for my body!" Carter said dramatically, kicking off his jeans. "Is that all I am to you?"

"Go shower," Tommy said, rolling his eyes. "We don't want to be late."

Carter grabbed a clean pair of boxers and disappeared into the bathroom.

Tommy threw himself onto the bed on his back, gazing unseeing at the ceiling with a wide grin on his face. He was trying to ignore his body's response to his boyfriend and failing. The tissue box on the little table between the beds caught his eye and he sighed. He buried his face in Carter's pillow, overwhelming his senses with his scent. He wondered if Carter was thinking about him too.

Tommy got dressed, choosing the emerald green dress shirt to wear with his jeans tonight.

Carter exited the bathroom while Tommy was fighting with his sleeves. "I should make you do those by yourself just so you can learn," Carter teased, walking over to help.

"But I like having your help," Tommy replied with a pout. He watched Carter's fingers to avoid looking at his bare chest, but he could feel the heat in his cheeks.

"You're adorable," Carter said once he was done. *Je t'aime.*

Tommy's breath caught in his throat at the endearment, and he looked up from his sleeves to Carter's smiling eyes. *Je t'aime aussi.*

Carter got dressed quickly, putting on his purple dress shirt, and drew Tommy close with one hand on the small of his back. "I believe I promised you a kiss once I was dressed," he murmured.

"Does it count as being dressed if your shirt isn't done up?" Tommy asked, his hands slipping under the open shirt.

Carter shivered. "Sure does."

"Awesome," Tommy said and mentally berated himself for his nonsense reply even as he joined their lips.

A knock on the door made them jump, banging their noses together. Tommy went to answer, rubbing his face and trying to pull himself together.

"Hey, you boys ready to go?" asked Elyse, peering past Tommy at Carter, who was rolling up his sleeves, buttons still undone.

Faith raised an eyebrow. "I heard the shower stop twenty minutes ago. What have you guys been up to that you're not dressed yet?"

Tommy smirked and Elyse elbowed him. "You two are..." She paused, searching for the right words.

"Super cute?" Tommy suggested with a grin.

"Polite to keep it behind closed doors?" Carter said, raising an eyebrow and doing up the last couple buttons.

"Yeah, I think we'll leave it at that," Faith said. "Do you have your room key? Camera? Wallet?"

Tommy grabbed his bag. "Camera and wallet, check." He took a moment to really look at the girls. "You two look beautiful," he said.

Faith was wearing an orange dress with a slim skirt, cap sleeves, and high neck. Elyse had on a red peasant blouse, white layered skirt, and a thick black belt.

"Oh, you noticed!" Faith teased. "Elyse thought you'd be too distracted by Carter to say anything."

"I'll admit he has most of my attention," Tommy said, blushing lightly. "But I *am* aware of my surroundings."

"Mmhmm," Elyse said skeptically.

"Room key, check," said Carter. "I left George's on the dresser for him. I think he's taking Sabrina out for a dinner date." He wiggled his eyebrows.

"Oh, poor Adrien will be alone tonight," said Faith as they walked to the elevators.

"Nah, he said he was going to hang with the rest of the group." Carter ran his fingers through his curls, checking his reflection in the mirrored doors of the elevator.

"Does anyone else find it funny that our two teams bonded together because of our little study group?" Elyse said with a giggle. "Like, Carter just referenced 'the group' and he meant both teams. I love it." They stepped into the elevator.

Faith smiled. "I'm ever so glad Tommy invited me to join you, even though I'm just a replacement. I feel like I learned so much from our study sessions, on top of keeping up with my classwork."

"We should keep it up," suggested Tommy.

"You sure you want us horning in on your time with Carter?" Elyse asked.

"We have to do homework anyways." Carter shrugged. "Besides, if you're there, it'll keep us from getting too distracted." He winked at Tommy.

The girls made faces at each other. "Are we your chaperones?" Faith teased.

The boys protested as they got off the elevator and headed for the lobby. MacKenzie stood up and greeted them.

"Wow, don't you look glamorous," said Carter with a whistle. She was wearing a royal blue dress with silvery embroidery on the low neckline. "Is Lucas coming too?"

"Who?" asked Tommy while MacKenzie blushed.

"No, he is not," MacKenzie said firmly. "Tonight is for you four. Also, Eliza and I get to celebrate Tommy's birthday in person for the first time in years. Ready to go?" She didn't wait for their answer before heading to the shuttle desk and handing over her ID. "Five to *Knights of Everdome*, scheduled on the five-thirty shuttle."

The man behind the desk marked something on his papers. "Right this way, please." He led them out the back of the hotel to a small shuttle. "You're the only ones attending today, so you get the shuttle to yourselves. The standard pickup time is at ten. Would you like to make any amendments to that?"

"Yes please, eleven would be better for us," MacKenzie said.

The man bowed. "Very good, my lady."

The moment they boarded, they bombarded MacKenzie with questions.

"What is *Knights of Everdome*?"

"Why the late return?"

"Who is Lucas?"

MacKenzie held up her hand for silence.

"Lucas isn't important," she said to Tommy.

"He's the guy who got us *Lion King* tickets early because MacKenzie was flirting with him," Carter said. "I've seen them together a couple times since then, and they looked rather cozy," he teased.

"You don't have to come," MacKenzie said, glaring at him.

Carter raised his hands. "Hey, I'm all for you having fun. He's cute."

MacKenzie rolled her eyes. "The reason for the delay is because we don't want to have to rush after the show."

"We're going to see a show?"

"It's dinner theatre, actually." MacKenzie grinned at the excited faces.

"I'm sorry, I must have heard you wrong," Tommy said, rubbing his ears dramatically. "There's a show called *Knights of*

Everdome, and the first time I'm hearing about this is from you and not from Jason, the self-proclaimed Everdome fanatic?"

MacKenzie shrugged. "Yes, I guess so."

Tommy turned to Carter. "We need to take *so many* pictures for him!"

Carter nodded vigorously.

"After the show, there's a dance, but Eliza said that we should be able to get backstage to see the actors and horses," MacKenzie continued.

"Horses!?" squeaked Faith. She gripped Elyse's arm excitedly. "Did you hear that? Horses!"

MacKenzie laughed. "Horses that are extremely familiar with Eliza because she's their vet. She'll be on call during the show, but she'll be able to sit with us unless something happens."

"That is so cool!" Faith looked awestruck.

"How haven't I heard about this from Jason, though?" Carter demanded.

"It's new. Only a couple of weeks old." MacKenzie grinned. "They're talking about doing a big marketing push in a week or so."

"When is the story set?" Carter wanted to know.

"I'm not sure," MacKenzie said.

The shuttle driver glanced back. "It's set in the year 1285, Post-Cataclysm."

"Nice," said Carter. "Good time to set it." The others all looked at him blankly. "The books are a decade before that, but the game coming out this summer is set about then. I guess the story told in the show will be unrelated to the game."

"You are correct, this show is based on the books, but not officially canon. We're here," said the driver, and they all climbed out.

The entrance to the parking lot was designed to look like castle walls and they had driven through the open gate. The building itself had a castle facade on the front with large letters proclaiming *Knights of Everdome* over the wooden main doors, which were open.

"Eliza said she'd meet us inside," said MacKenzie, leading the way.

"Ooooh!" all four teenagers exclaimed the moment they stepped through the doors.

The walls were stone with wooden beams and ceiling. There were colourful banners hanging on the walls and flags stuck in every post. There was merchandise everywhere, including an entire wall of weapons, both training and metal.

Tommy hardly knew where to look first, one thing and then another catching his eyes.

"Hey, kid," said a familiar voice, and Tommy turned to see Eliza, MacKenzie's twin. She was dressed simply in jeans and a flowy black shirt. *Probably in case she needs to work tonight*, Tommy thought as he gave her a hug.

"This is such a nice surprise!" he said excitedly. "I had no idea you worked somewhere this cool!"

Eliza chuckled. "I was hired just after New Year's. I've been alternating between the horse farm and the training yard for the past four months, but now I get to be at the shows, too. It's super cool. You kids are going to *love* it."

"Oh, these are my friends, Faith and Elyse," Tommy said, his heart thumping in his stomach. "And my boyfriend, Carter."

"Excuse me?" Eliza asked, blinking rapidly. "Boyfriend?"

"Yup." Tommy twisted his hands together until Carter took one in his.

Eliza glared at MacKenzie. "*Both* our younger siblings have boyfriends before us?"

MacKenzie chuckled. "Appears so."

"Ugh. Not fair." Eliza smiled at Carter. "What do you do?"

"I'm in grade nine at Oldtown in Westmeath—"

"What do they put in the water there?" Eliza interrupted him. "Sorry, continue."

"And I do Kung Fu with Kennedy and Jason."

"Beauty, brawn, *and* brains," Eliza said. "You'll do. You've got good taste," she said to Tommy. "Mom and Dad will love him."

"Ah—" Tommy started to say.

"Secret boyfriend?"

Tommy nodded. "For now. I'll tell them when we go the week before the wedding."

"Yeah, good plan." Eliza turned back to Carter. "Now I place the name. You're one of Kennedy's attendants."

"I am."

"I'll see you again at the wedding." Eliza clapped her hands together. "The most important thing to do before the show is get a picture with King Pincas in front of our feature wall. Come, I'll introduce you!"

They dutifully followed as she led the way to where a man with a salt-and-pepper beard in rich burgundy clothing was lounging on a throne.

"Ah! Esteemed guests!" The man leaped to his feet and adjusted his gold and silver crown. "Welcome! We are honoured by your presence in our Pakaha Castle!" He gave a short bow. "Horse mistress Eliza, would you perform the introductions?"

"Certainly, Your Highness. This is my womb-sister, Lady MacKenzie, and our youngest brother, Lord Thomas. His partner, Lord Carter, and their friends, the Ladies Faith and Elyse."

"Welcome, welcome!" the king said jovially. "I hope you are looking forward to tonight's tournament and feasting as much as we are."

The teenagers nodded vigorously.

"We very much are, Your Highness," said Elyse, gracefully sinking into a curtsy. "Thank you for the chance to watch such a spectacular event."

"Well!" exclaimed the king after recovering from his surprise. "It is I who thank you, for what would a tournament be without spectators?"

"A very quiet affair, Your Highness," said Faith mischievously, wobbling a bit on her curtsy.

The king roared with laughter. "Quiet in cheering only. The clash of swords is loud enough in its own right. Do you lords know much about swordsmanship?"

"No, Your Highness," replied Tommy, bowing. "I can shoot an arrow, but not very well."

"Archery is an excellent sport that requires much practise. And you?" The king looked last at Carter.

"I have never held a sword, Your Highness, but I know a thing or two about fighting," Carter replied with a grin.

"Oh ho, you do, do you?" the king replied, smiling. "Good for you, good for you."

"They were hoping you'd agree to a portrait?" Eliza said, and Tommy noticed that people had started to gather around, eager to listen to their conversation with the king.

"Of course, of course! Gather round, after you hand your devices to my attendant." The king indicated a young man in burgundy livery with a silver and gold crown on his chest.

Carter handed him his phone and Tommy his camera, and then the group posed with the king.

"Thank you very much for your time, Your Highness," said MacKenzie, curtsying with almost as much grace as Elyse as they left.

Faith turned to the rest of the group with wide eyes. "I feel like I'm actually in a castle! That was so ridiculously exciting!"

Eliza grinned. "I thought you'd like that. Want to try out the training weapons now?"

"Yes!"

All six of them had fun waving the wooden training swords around, pretending to fight each other in the ring set aside for the weapons to be tested out before purchasing.

"You don't want to get one of these," Eliza whispered to Tommy when they returned them. "The balance is all off."

He nodded as if he understood what that meant.

They looked at the real weapons next, and Carter salivated over the set of ten throwing knives.

"Didn't your dads have your set custom-made for you?" Elyse reminded him.

"Yeah, but these are carbon steel," gushed Carter.

"And?"

"And they're supposed to be the best!"

An attendant overheard the conversation. "Would you like to try them out?"

"Can I?" breathed Carter. He looked back at MacKenzie for confirmation.

"You sure you know how to handle these?" she asked with a frown.

"I've been training with knives since September. I know how to be careful," he replied.

"There's a target back this way," said the attendant. "Everyone is welcome."

He picked up the case of knives and walked them out the back of the hall, where there were several targets set up. There were some guests trying archery at one, and another set trying spear throwing at another. The attendant put the knives down at the centre target. "You can adjust the position of the target with the switch on the wall, here. Once you're finished, I can open the gate and collect the knives."

"Thank you," said Carter, picking up a knife and balancing it gently on one finger.

Tommy watched his boyfriend avidly; he hadn't seen him throw knives since the day he'd blurted out his affection. He watched Carter nod to himself, square his shoulders to the target, and let the knife fly. It sank directly into the centre of the target and Tommy let out a whoop.

He glanced at his sisters and the attendant, whose jaws had dropped in astonishment, and smirked. *Yeah, that's my badass boyfriend*, he thought proudly.

Carter worked his way through all ten knives, each of them hitting the target in a cluster in the centre, and then thanked the attendant. "They were beautiful to throw."

"It was an honour to watch you throw them," the attendant replied, more than a little taken aback.

When they returned to the main room, Tommy noticed the attendant whispering to another, who nodded and ran off.

I wonder what that's about? he thought, but then was distracted by his friends calling him over to a carved stone chess set.

After some more time admiring the various souvenirs, Eliza suggested they find their seats.

An attendant, again in burgundy with a silver and gold crown emblem, took their tickets and led them to their seats, one row back in the centre of the arena.

Tommy had to take a moment to look around; the arena was huge, with five rows of spectators encircling it. There was a raised dais at one end and large wooden doors at the other.

"Is this a repurposed skating arena?" Elyse asked Eliza.

"It is!" Eliza beamed. "It had fallen into disrepair and had been sitting unused for several years, so the Burt family bought it at a steal."

"Burt?" Faith asked. "Isn't that the name of the hotel where we're staying?"

"It is. They recently branched out into theme parks, and this was a nice little first step for a potential Everdome theme park," said MacKenzie.

"That's so cool!" exclaimed Carter. "An Everdome theme park? Soon, I hope?"

"Maybe one day."

"*So* cool," Tommy heard Carter mutter.

Tommy continued examining the arena. The large oval "stage" had a sandy floor. Above it were several riggings for use during the show. The audience were seated at long tables covered with burgundy tablecloths.

"I'm going to guess that Pakaha Castle's colour is burgundy?" Tommy asked.

"You are most correct, my lord," said a young blonde woman. She was holding menus and had an apron over her burgundy dress. "Burgundy with a silver and gold crown emblem is the symbol of the central castle of Pakaha, the High-King's residence. Burgundy with a white tower emblem belongs to the Dome of Pakaha." She lifted the menus in her arms. "My name is Daria, and I'm your server for tonight." She handed out the menus to each member of the group. "If you have any questions, please don't hesitate to raise your hand to call for me."

"Thank you, Daria," said MacKenzie.

"There are no prices," Tommy noted, opening the menu.

"The cost of the meal was included in the ticket," Eliza said. "You choose one option from each heading."

"Oh, I see," said Elyse.

"Wow, we have to thank your parents," Faith said, eyes wide. "This is incredible!"

"You four have worked really hard to get into the competition," MacKenzie said. "And a little bird told me that you're doing really well, too." She winked.

"I thought you weren't supposed to talk about your judging," Eliza said, one eyebrow raised.

MacKenzie shrugged. "I'm not! I'm commenting on the fully visible seating chart at the back of the main hall. Both teams have consistently been moving up. There are still a handful or so ahead of them, but they are doing incredibly well and I'm incredibly proud and impressed by both their teamwork and individual abilities." She smiled at Tommy, who basked in his older sister's praise.

"I'll be right back," said Carter suddenly, putting his menu down.

"You okay?" Tommy asked, concerned.

"Yeah, I just want to make a visit. Can you tell Daria what I want to eat, please?" He pointed at each item and then got to his feet. "You won't even notice I'm gone," he teased.

"Sure I will. My hand will get cold," Tommy joked back.

Carter returned just before the show started. "Sorry, my dads called," he said breathlessly. "They're really proud of all of us and want to wish you happy birthday, Tommy."

The lights went out, leaving them in complete darkness.

"Welcome to Castle Pakaha and the *Knights of Everdome!*" boomed the king's voice throughout the arena. "May you enjoy tonight's feasting and revelry!"

A bright flash appeared in the centre of the ring, followed by a billow of smoke, and suddenly three figures were standing in the middle of the arena, lit by spotlights.

"How did they get there?" gasped Tommy, blinking the spots away from his eyes.

"Magic!" said Carter, waving his hands dramatically.

At the end of the show, the High-King said grandly, "Now we drink and dance! All courtesy of the new queen!"

Everyone in the audience laughed.

"The attendants will lead you to the ballroom. Please do not leave anything behind," the king continued. "Make merry and have a wonderful evening!"

The attendants headed down the aisles, leading people out the door.

Carter bowed low to Tommy, flourishing the cape he had been given while participating in the show on stage. "Will you accompany me to the dance, my lord?"

Tommy immediately took his hand. "It would give me great pleasure to dance with you, my knight," he said, allowing himself to be pulled to his feet.

They tried to follow the attendants but kept being interrupted by other guests.

"Did you know that you were going to be called up on stage?"

"Yes, I had to sign a form before I could," Carter answered.

"How did you do the knife throwing trick?"

"It wasn't a trick. I've been training," Carter said.

"How did you plan out the fight choreography?"

Carter sighed. "I listened to the cues from the experienced actor and stunt choreographer, who was talking in my ear. Do you mind if I..." He gestured to Tommy, whose hand he was holding.

That brought the attention to Tommy. "How did you feel when he gave you the rose?"

"Happy?" Tommy twisted the stem of the rose in his free hand, confused by the question.

"Were you expecting to be given it?"

Tommy smirked. "I would have been offended if he hadn't."

The people around them looked confused.

Carter laughed and pulled Tommy closer, wrapping his arm around his waist. "This is my boyfriend, and he deserves more than a single rose. I want to give him the world. Now, if you'll excuse us, we're here to have fun and dance. No more questions."

MacKenzie and Eliza had moved closer to the large group of people. "Alright, leave the teenagers alone," Eliza said, pushing through the group. "Go to the ballroom, please."

Slowly, the group dispersed out of the arena, leaving the twins with the teenagers.

"You two okay?" MacKenzie asked the young couple.

"Yeah, we're fine," Tommy said, although he knew his grip was too tight on Carter's hand.

"You sure?" Carter looked concerned.

Tommy relaxed. "With you by my side, my knight, I can face anything."

Carter grinned and kissed the back of Tommy's hand. "My lord, you do flatter me."

"I could flatter you even more," Tommy said shyly. "You're beautiful. Your eyes twinkle when you laugh. You're highly intelligent. Your skills with a blade make me want to kiss you against a wall until I can't breathe."

"And that's our cue," MacKenzie said, blushing and taking Eliza's elbow.

Eliza said, "I was going to ask you if you wanted to come backstage and meet the actors and horses—"

"Yes!" both boys enthusiastically replied.

Eliza smiled. "Wait a moment and then follow me." She held them back until the rest of the audience had left for the ballroom.

"You really think all that?" Carter asked quietly.

"Every word and more," Tommy said earnestly.

"Darn it, I want to kiss you now," Carter said.

Tommy flushed. "I take it you don't mean a quick kiss?"

Carter leaned in close to Tommy's ear. "What do you think?"

Tommy shivered at the heat in his tone.

"Come on, time to go," Eliza said.

"Ugh, they're doing that lovey-dovey thing again where they gaze into each other's eyes and make me wish they were alone in a room somewhere," said Elyse, making a face.

Faith chuckled. "Horses, boys. And Carter, I know you already got up close and personal, but *I* want to meet the actors."

"Seriously, you two are almost as bad as Jason and Kennedy," Elyse said, rolling her eyes.

MacKenzie made a face. "I hope not. Hearing *them* at Christmas was almost scarring."

Tommy's jaw dropped. "I lived with them for a week and didn't hear a peep."

"Ah, but they knew *you* were there," Eliza said darkly. "Come on, this way." She led them in the opposite direction of the music pouring out from the ballroom.

They walked down a hall and ducked behind a thick wooden door that read *Employees Only*. The hallway beyond the door was vastly different from the rest of the building they had seen so far, with bland concrete walls.

"We're going to the common room first," said Eliza. "I told the actors that I was bringing my brother and his friends tonight, so they'll be hanging out after they get out of costume."

"Did they pick Carter to go up on stage because he was with you?" Tommy asked.

"Not likely. The people at the front don't know me. They're told to look out for people with athletic, cheerful, and enthusiastic characteristics. They haven't picked a kid in the past couple of weeks. They must have been really excited about you, Carter." Eliza grinned at him.

"I called my dads to let them know and signed some paperwork," Carter said. "Then they ran through the basics of what I'd be doing. They mostly said to have fun. Did I ever!"

"And you looked amazing at the same time," Faith said.

"You have quite the flair for the dramatic," Elyse added. "You're doing the fight choreography for the play at school, right?"

Carter nodded.

"Ooh, what's the play?" MacKenzie asked.

"*Romeo and Juliet*," Carter replied. "I'm doing the wrestling portions, and someone else is doing the sword fighting. It looks pretty great."

"I wish I could see it," Tommy said sadly. "But I'll be arriving a week too late."

"Speaking of arriving, we're here," said Eliza, opening the door of a room. The noise spilled out into the hall as they entered. "Hello everyone, this is the birthday boy. I believe you've already met his boyfriend, the knight who almost bested Roger?"

Loud cheers and catcalls greeted this statement, and the teenagers were pulled into the party.

"Best birthday *ever*!" Tommy whispered to his sisters at one point. "Thank you so much."

"Thank Mom and Dad," said Eliza. "I only get two comped tickets. They paid for the rest of you."

"I will."

Chapter 17

♥

SUNDAY THE 11TH OF MAY, 2003 -
TORONTO, ONTARIO (MORNING)

Tommy woke up before the alarm went off, nerves fizzing with excitement. *It's my birthday today!* He squeezed Carter a little tighter as his mood soured. *I have to say goodbye to him tonight.*

"Morning, birthday boy," Carter mumbled. "You're up early."

"Just want to soak up as much time with you as I can," Tommy whispered.

"I'm all for that." Carter sounded a little bit more awake now. "Morning kisses?"

"Oh, I don't know, your breath isn't so fresh in the morning," Tommy teased before pressing their lips together chastely.

"Right, because yours smells like roses," Carter pulled back far enough to reply sarcastically.

They were startled apart by Adrien jumping out of bed and running, stumbling for the bathroom, holding his stomach. Tommy and Carter stared at each other, eyes wide, as they heard the unmistakable sounds of sick hitting the toilet bowl.

George sat up in bed, rubbing his eyes. "What's going on?" Then, when more sounds reached his ears, "Oh shit, Adrien!" He half fell out of bed and ran to the bathroom.

The young teens sat on the edge of their bed, concerned but not sure what to do.

There was a hushed conversation going on in the bathroom and then George reappeared. "Carter, go tell Mister Coolidge that we've got a problem, please? And you two might want to get dressed for the day. The alarm's about to go off."

Carter hurriedly pulled on his jeans and dashed out the door.

Tommy changed his boxers first but got dressed just as quickly.

Mr. Coolidge was with Carter when he returned. "Lauryn's sick too. Ms. Rubens is with her. We think it's food poisoning. What did you eat last night?"

"We went to a little hole-in-the-wall place. I don't remember the name," Adrien said hoarsely. "Most of us had the chicken."

"*Most* of you?" Tommy paled. "Oh no."

"We should run down and see Chris and Faith," Carter said grimly. "Find out how your team is doing." He finished getting dressed. "See you at breakfast, George."

Rather than wait for the elevator, the boys dashed down the two flights of stairs. Faith was leaving her room with Sabrina.

"Naomi's really sick," Faith said, looking shaken. "Ms. Daguerre is with her, but I think Bryan's going to have to take her place."

"How's Chris?"

"I'm fine," Chris croaked, opening his door.

"You look like death," Sabrina informed him.

"I have to be fine. We need two seniors." He tottered down the hall toward the elevators, holding onto the wall with one hand.

Bryan exited the room. "I'm fine, thanks for asking."

"You are?" Tommy asked, relieved. "Good." He turned to Carter. "Can I borrow your phone? I'd like to call my mom."

"Of course."

"Mommy's boy," sneered Bryan.

Tommy ignored him. The phone was picked up on the second ring.

"Hi, Mom."

"Tommy, darling! Happy birthday! How is the competition? Are you having fun?"

Tommy couldn't help his smile, despite his worries. "Thanks, Mom. Happy Mother's Day. I'm having so much fun. Thanks for the tickets last night. The show was spectacular! As for the competition, that's what I'm calling about. A bunch of the other kids on both my team and Carter's got food poisoning or something last night. How can I help them?"

"Oh no! That's terrible! Are the teachers with them?"

"Yeah, Mom."

"Good. They need to stay on the BRAT diet. Banana, rice, applesauce, toast. Little sips of water. Nothing until at *least* half an hour after vomiting. Do *not* fill the stomach. Eat just enough to give strength."

Tommy relayed all that to the others. "Thanks, Mom. Wish us luck on our last event! Love you." He handed the phone back to Carter. "Okay, Carter, bring food to Adrien and Lauryn. Sabrina, you've got Naomi. I'll try to deal with Chris. Faith, Bryan, I think I'm going to need all the help I can get."

They found Chris sprawled on one of the couches in front of the elevators. "Come on, we've got you," Tommy said, as he and Bryan got their teammate to his feet. "You sure you can manage this?"

"I'm sure," Chris said, gritting his teeth.

They managed to get him down to breakfast and sat him at their table. As they were walking back to get the food, Tommy turned to Bryan. "You're the most senior person here. I need you to find someone who knows what's going on and ask them if three juniors and one senior are allowed to compete as a team."

Bryan raised an eyebrow. "You don't think Chris will make it."

It wasn't a question, but Tommy shook his head anyway. "I'm surprised he's still upright, to be honest."

They both glanced back at the table and winced as Chris swayed in his seat before pitching forward, the *thunk* of his forehead hitting the table loud in the otherwise quiet room.

"Yeah, I'll find out," Bryan said.

Tommy watched Bryan leave the room behind Carter and Sabrina. He took the plate from Faith. "Get yourself something to eat. I'll start helping Chris."

Chris did not want to eat.

"You need your strength," Tommy practically begged. "Even one bite of banana?"

Chris weakly pushed the tray away with one hand.

"What are we going to do?" Faith whispered when she arrived with her food.

"Sit far from me with all that gross-smelling food," croaked Chris.

Faith immediately moved to another table, Tommy following her. "I think you're going to be competing this morning," Tommy said quietly.

Faith looked at him in panic, her eyes wide.

"You'll be fine. You've trained for this. You're not alone." He grinned. "Now I'm going to leave you alone and go get my own breakfast."

He chose bland foods for himself so that he could sit with Chris, worried about leaving him alone for too long.

Carter returned, ashen faced, before Tommy had finished eating. "Lauryn can't move from the toilet. Neither can Adrien. Alicia's okay, she's a vegetarian and didn't eat the chicken so she can replace Adrien, but that means I have to replace Lauryn! I don't know if I can do this!" Carter said, voice rising in panic.

Chris raised his head slightly. "You know what Tommy said the morning of our second day? We were talking about how close our two teams were in the ranking. And he said... Tommy said..."

He put his head back down on the table, making Tommy look at him with alarm. Chris turned his head, but kept his eyes closed. "Tommy said that we might be even with Oldtown then, but that we had to worry if *you* were called in as a replacement. I didn't understand why, 'cause your score was lower than Lauryn's. Wouldn't that mean that she was better?"

Chris smiled and winced. "Tommy said no, that you thought about things differently and that you were Oldtown's secret weapon."

"I didn't say that," Tommy protested.

"It was implied. Don't argue with me." Chris took a deep breath and clenched his fist on the table. "Point is, we didn't know you were dating yet. Everything he said must have been true. Tommy—" Chris's eyes popped open. "I don't feel so good."

"Hang on!" Carter dashed to the wall, grabbed a garbage can, and brought it back just in time.

"Okay, you're going back to bed," Tommy said, concerned. "Come on."

He and Carter managed to deliver Chris back to his room and then notified Mr. Travese.

Fortunately, Ms. Daguerre had enough Pepto-Bismol for all four sick students.

"Did you really say that?" Carter asked Tommy on the way back down to breakfast.

"I was bragging about you a bit," Tommy said sheepishly. "But it's all true."

"You're the best boyfriend," Carter said shyly, stealing a kiss. "*Je t'aime.*"

The remnants of the two teams gathered to eat their breakfast in silence. Finally, Bryan joined them.

"I found Ms. White, the director, after asking several volunteers who didn't know." He took a bite of peanut butter-covered bagel and talked around his mouthful. "She said that we can definitely have three juniors, especially since it's an emergency."

"Why are you fine?" Elyse asked. "Didn't you go with the others?"

"I had the fish. I don't like chicken." Bryan shrugged. "Good thing, or you'd be a team of three today."

"What's the event?" Carter asked.

"Mystery," Alicia replied immediately. "The program didn't give any more information than that."

"That's not nerve-wracking at all," muttered Faith.

"I'm not concerned," Tommy said.

The others looked at him, eyes wide.

"I'm worried about our friends, obviously, but the competition? We'll be fine. We didn't know what we were going to get any other time, and we did really well. Look at our standings! You're tenth, we're ninth. Out of *fifty*! We each started halfway through the pack. I know how each of you works," he gestured at his study group, "and we all work well together. Add in our teammates, and our teams are forces to be reckoned with! We're going to do really well, and we're going to go home proud of our accomplishments."

"A rousing speech," Bryan said dryly.

"If you don't have anything positive to contribute, keep your mouth shut," Alicia growled.

"At least you have two seniors on your team," Bryan muttered.

"I'm sorry, did we not write the same test to qualify?" Faith demanded. "Both Sabrina and I got higher scores than you did. *We're* not going to hold the team back."

"Nobody's holding the team back," Tommy said firmly. "We're going to work together, just like we did for the rest of the competition. We're going to play to our strengths, double-check each other's work, and ask for help when we need it, just like we did on the other events. We are not competing individually but as a team."

"I'm with you," said Sabrina. "We can do this."

"I'll follow your lead," said Faith.

"You really think we'll be okay?" Bryan asked.

"I know we will. We can work together, right?" Tommy asked, looking at the girls for confirmation.

They nodded. He pinned Bryan with his eyes.

"Will *you*?"

Bryan fiddled with his napkin. "Are you going to take over the leadership role?"

"If you have a problem with that, work it out now," said Sabrina. "He and Chris were both leading the team, in case you hadn't noticed. Tommy did an excellent job."

Bryan sighed. "Alright. I can accept your leadership."

Tommy relaxed, relieved. Bryan was the person on their team

he knew the least. Add in the tension between them over the whole alcohol thing...

Bryan is our *wild card. I just wish I knew whether that's a good thing or not*, Tommy thought.

Mr. Travese approached the group. "The four sick kids are sleeping. They're hopefully going to be able to travel home today. How are you holding up? Are you prepared for the event this morning?"

"We're as ready as we'll ever be," replied Tommy.

"Good to go, sir," said George.

"Don't let your worries about your teammates distract you from your goals. Ms. Daguerre and Mister Coolidge have everything under control upstairs. Ms. Rubens and I will be with you in the room. You've got this." Mr. Travese cleared his throat. "I speak on behalf of all four of us when I say that we are all proud and impressed by your accomplishments thus far and your maturity in the face of the competition. The close friendship between our schools is what other schools should strive for."

"Oh, stop it, you're making me blush!" George exclaimed, over-acting shyness and making Sabrina giggle.

Mr. Travese smiled. "Perhaps next year, we can arrange an exchange of some sort between the two schools to continue to foster this friendship."

"I know two alumni who would love to see that," said Tommy, smirking at Carter.

"You're right!" Carter snapped his fingers.

"Who?" everyone else said.

"My sister Kennedy and her fiancé Jason went to these schools." Tommy grinned. "You can't get any closer than those two!"

"I didn't teach your sister," said Mr. Travese thoughtfully. "But if you think that they might be willing to speak to the schools, I can reach out to them."

"Jason's all about sponsoring youth," said Carter confidently. "I'll give him your email when we get home."

"We should head up to the room," Alicia interrupted. "We've got ten minutes."

Tommy stuffed the last bite of pancake into his mouth and took his dishes to the back of the room with the others.

Before the two teams separated in the room, they gave each other hugs or handshakes.

"You've got this," Tommy whispered to Carter. They shared a quick kiss and then took their places, one table separating them.

"Good morning!" Captain Mary Herrington said into the microphone. "Welcome to the last event of the competition."

"Eep, it's *her*!" Faith whispered in Tommy's ear. Her hands shook as she played with the hem of her shirt. "I *can't*—"

"You can and you will," Tommy said fiercely.

"This event is a little different. I'm sure all of you were confused by the description 'mystery.' That's because this last event *is* a mystery... A *murder* mystery!"

The captain paused for the low murmur of excited voices to quiet down. "You have been given the files provided by the forensic specialists and the notes made by the investigators, along with head shots of key witnesses and prime suspects. Your job is to find three pieces of incontrovertible physical evidence and the one witness testimony that will solve the case. You have three hours. Good luck."

"No pressure," Bryan muttered.

"Come on, this sounds like fun!" Tommy said cheerfully. "It's like Clue without the dice rolling."

"And a lot more reading," Sabrina said, lifting the thick binder off the table. "We should probably split this up to make it easier to go through."

"Let's find out how it's organized first, and then we'll split it up," Faith said. "We don't want to miss a relevant piece of evidence because it's in two places."

They both turned to Tommy for the final decision.

He scratched his head. "I think one person should pay attention to everything. They'll be the coordinator. When we find something that needs to be looked at in more detail, we'll assign someone to it. Is everyone okay with that?"

"I suppose you think that *you* should be the coordinator?" Bryan sneered.

"Get your head out of your ass," Faith growled. "You said you were okay with him being the leader, and he's the best person for the job."

"Actually, I thought Sabrina would be good at that," Tommy said. "She's used to keeping a lot of information in her head at once with coding."

Sabrina looked taken aback. "Alright. I'll try." She opened the binder, and they started flipping through it.

"I think a timeline might be useful to have," said Faith after a moment. "These witness testimonies are all over the place."

"Excellent idea," Tommy said, shifting the blank paper over so she could reach it.

Sabrina opened the binder and took out the witness testimonies. "I'll let you know if we come across any other times."

"The toxicology seems off," Bryan said with a frown.

"I think I saw that there are drug analysis breakdowns at the back of the binder," Sabrina said, flipping through the tabs. "Yeah, here, you can look at these more closely."

They continued scanning the files, occasionally giving Faith a time to mark down on her timeline.

"I think I can eliminate the fifth witness," Faith said, frowning. "He says he didn't get to the club until just before midnight, but the last use of the victim's credit card was at ten thirty, according to the credit card statement. The alcohol should have been out of her system by midnight."

"Other people could have been buying her drinks," Bryan commented. "Make a note of your suspicions, but don't eliminate him yet."

"Good call," said Tommy.

"This looks like partial DNA evidence," Sabrina said as she flipped to the next page.

"Whoa, that's cool." Tommy glanced at the series of letters. "I can try to match some."

"I've figured out what's odd about these drug tests," Bryan said. Everyone looked at his papers. He cleared his throat. "The victim had no drugs in her system."

"What?" Sabrina said. "But I'm sure I saw..." She started flipping back through the book until she got to the pictures of the victim. She turned the book so that they could see it. "Look, there are needle marks."

Bryan shrugged. "You can double-check the drug tests. There's nothing in there."

"Weird. I'll make a note of that," Sabrina said. She took out another set of papers. "Here's the victim's virology. See if you can make sense of that."

Bryan grumbled a bit but bent over the data tables.

"Can I get the suspect timelines please?" Faith asked, and then proceeded to continue her work.

Sabrina kept looking at the images of the victim. "There are tiny fractures on the base of her skull. Not enough to be from a blow to the head or a fall, I would think. I wonder what they're from."

"Maybe it's an old injury," Bryan suggested. "Can I look at the tox again?"

"Could be." Sabrina handed back the toxicology report.

"DNA matching is very painstaking work," said Tommy after a while. "I'm not even sure what I'm looking for. If I find a match, what does that mean? I've got DNA from under her fingernails and in her mouth."

"Are they labelled?" Sabrina asked, leaning over.

"They have names like 'suspect one' and stuff." Tommy closed his eyes and pinched the bridge of his nose. "I'm going to be honest; I feel like this is a waste of time."

Faith patted his arm.

"Toxicology readings have a low blood-alcohol level!" Bryan said triumphantly.

"But she was acting drunk," Faith said, confused. "I don't understand."

"I feel like we're missing something super obvious," Tommy said. "Faith, run us through the timeline?"

"Victim arrived at the club with suspect number one and witnesses three and four at seven o'clock. She ordered a vodka and water at eight and her second at ten thirty. She was falling over drunk at midnight when she was slurring her words, telling people she wanted to leave. Suspect number one agreed to take her home and they left together.

"When police questioned suspect one, he said that once they were outside, they argued. She was refusing to go with him and wanted to lie down and sleep. He left her to go cool off, but by the time he'd returned at twelve ten, she was dead. He panicked and left. Witness one spotted the body of the victim in the alley beside the club at twelve thirty."

"Only two drinks and she was falling over drunk?" Bryan shook his head. "That doesn't make sense, especially with the tox report. Did any of the witnesses see her drink anything else?"

Faith shook her head. "Witness two was the bartender. He's trained to notice things like that. She only had two."

"What about witnesses three and four? Were they on a double date?"

"They left earlier, around eight, because they had wanted to get food before dancing, but suspect one didn't want to. They returned to the club at around ten and danced until the police arrived."

"Okay, where does suspect two come in?" Sabrina asked.

"Apparently, the recent ex-girlfriend of suspect one was in the club that night." Faith smirked. "The girls got in quite the argument around nine."

"They think she killed the victim out of jealousy?" Tommy shook his head. "That would be sad."

"Hang on, the victim didn't eat?" Sabrina said suddenly. "Hand me those toxicology reports!" She scanned them quickly. "Look at her blood sugar! It's ridiculously low!"

Faith gasped. "You think she was diabetic?"

"It would make sense, wouldn't it?" Sabrina started listing off points on her fingers. "Didn't eat dinner, high levels of activity, her blood alcohol was low, but she was falling over and slurring her words? That's from the low blood sugar. We need proof..."

"The needle marks!" Tommy exclaimed. "From her insulin jabs! That picture must be a close-up of her belly, not her arm!"

"Who's the witness that said she was slurring? That's the one we want."

"Witness three is the one who described it in those words and was able to give a time."

"Okay, she wasn't murdered, and our three pieces of evidence are the image of needle marks for insulin, the toxicology showing the negative drug test and alcohol levels, and the biochemical report with the low blood sugar. The witness is number three."

Sabrina compiled the data sheets. "Are we missing anything?"

"But what killed her?" Bryan asked.

"The skull fractures," Sabrina said. "They must have been caused by a seizure. That's what must have killed her."

"Damn, you really know a lot about diabetes," Faith said admiringly.

"My mother is diabetic," Sabrina whispered. "My brothers and I are all trained to keep an eye out for symptoms. I'm sorry I didn't recognize it sooner in this case."

"No worries. We're done in under an hour, and I'm confident we got the right answer, thanks to you. Shall we raise our hands?" Tommy asked.

Sabrina squared her shoulders. "Yes, let's do this."

They called the judge over and presented their evidence and witness. Captain Herrington smiled, made some notes on her file, and dismissed them.

As they left, Tommy noticed that Oldtown's area was empty and nudged Faith and Sabrina. They all quickened their pace.

Chapter 18

♥

SUNDAY THE 11TH OF MAY, 2003 -
TORONTO, ONTARIO (MORNING)

The Oldtown group was waiting for them in the conference centre lobby, sitting against the large windows.

"How'd it go?" Carter asked, getting to his feet.

"We figured it out in the end," Tommy said. "Thanks to Sabrina."

George pulled her into a hug. "I'm so proud of you," he said.

"How about you?" Tommy asked.

Alicia started to laugh. "We hadn't even opened the binder yet when Carter said, 'Wouldn't it be cool if it wasn't a murder at all, but a drug interaction or something that killed the victim by accident?'"

"In other words, we spotted the inconsistencies right away," said George. "We were out in twenty minutes."

"Holy shit!" exclaimed Bryan.

Carter looked sheepish. "I just thought it would be a cool twist," he mumbled.

"Didn't I say that you think differently?" Tommy said, practically bursting with pride. "Have you seen many other teams leave?"

"That Baker school and two others that I don't know came down about ten minutes after us," George said.

"The rankings will be very interesting to see," Tommy said.

"And it shows just how much having a high score on the test matters in the rankings," Alicia pointed out. "Our teams have consistently performed better and faster than most of the others, seeing as how we keep moving up the board, but Baker, for one, hasn't dropped at all, even though their times haven't been as good as ours."

"But high scores don't necessarily mean that the team has the smartest people on it," Elyse pointed out. "Lauryn—"

"Stop," Carter ordered. "We don't know what Lauryn would have done if she'd been here instead of me. Let's not make assumptions that aren't testable. She's highly capable, and our team would have done well no matter what."

Tommy squeezed Carter's hand.

"You're right." Elyse ducked her head. "I'm sorry. I didn't mean to imply that Lauryn, or anyone else for that matter, wasn't worthy of being on the team."

"It all turned out," George said. "All the replacements had a chance to participate, something that other teams don't get to say." He grimaced. "I hope the others are feeling better when they wake up."

"Oh, rats," Carter said suddenly. "I'd forgotten that our make-out spot is now a sick room."

The group groaned and laughed.

"How was your date last night?" Tommy asked Sabrina. "Sorry, I meant to ask first thing, but..."

"Oh!" Sabrina smiled shyly at George. "It was nice. I had a great time."

"And bonus! We didn't get sick!" George said with a chuckle.

"Definitely a bonus," Sabrina agreed with a shudder.

"What should we do in the two hours before lunch?" Faith asked. "Explore Toronto a bit?"

"Maybe go shopping?" Elyse suggested. "I don't have any souvenirs for my family."

Neither did anyone else, so they headed out onto King Street to look for the quirkiest souvenir shop they could find.

By the time they returned for lunch, the others had left their rooms and were looking pale, but better.

The seating chart at the back of the room had been removed, so they all sat together near the exit, in case anyone had to make an emergency run.

"I'm glad the event went well this morning," Chris said. "I'm proud of you. All of you."

Adrien nodded his agreement. "Our teams were in good hands."

"Can we announce the surprise now?" Alicia asked, looking around the table.

"Surprise?" Tommy asked, confused.

Carter grinned. "You didn't think we'd forgotten your birthday, did you?"

"You planned something for my birthday?" Tommy blushed. "You didn't have to do that."

"Oh, we definitely did. Anything that means we get to embarrass our new friend," George said, a twinkle in his eye.

Alarmed, Tommy glanced at Carter, who smirked back at him. "It's not so bad. I talked them out of the birthday bumps."

"Thanks for that," Tommy said wryly.

"Up you get!" Alicia said, pulling a birthday hat and purple Mardi Gras mask from her large purse.

Naomi pulled a bright, fluffy pink feather boa from hers.

"Where did you get these?" Tommy asked as they bedecked him.

"We bought them from the dollar store last night." Alicia pulled his chair out and motioned for him to get up on it.

"Do I have to?" Tommy almost whined.

"Yup." Carter held out his hand. "I'll be right here in case you feel wobbly."

"Hey, Naomi!" shouted Alicia. "Did I hear that someone is having a birthday?"

Everyone in the hall stopped eating and looked back at their table.

Tommy moved to get down, but Carter squeezed his hand. "Hey, you don't know any of these people. It's okay."

When Tommy nodded, Carter smiled at him.

"I did hear that!" Naomi shouted back. "Who do you suppose it could be?" She put her hands up to shade her eyes as she looked around the room, making people laugh.

"I know!" shouted George, leaping to his feet. "It's Tommy's fifteenth birthday!"

"And here he is!" Chris joined in, making a dramatic gesture with his arms.

"Happy birthday, Tommy!" the entire table shouted before bursting into song, the rest of the hall joining in.

Feeling overwhelmed, Tommy almost didn't notice Faith taking his camera and handing it to Mr. Travese so he could get a picture of their table, Tommy standing above the rest of them.

When the song was over, Alicia shouted, "Speech!" The cry was picked up by a few others until Tommy raised his hands.

"Thank you," he said. "This will be a birthday I will never forget. Or live down." He stepped down off the chair into Carter's arms to a round of applause and laughter from the hall.

"You are all terrible," Tommy said, shaking his head as he took off the extra items. Then he smiled. "You're the best friends ever."

They all joined in on a group hug, Tommy at the centre.

MONDAY THE 12TH OF MAY, 2003 -
ON HIGHWAY 400, ONTARIO (MIDNIGHT)

The silence inside the bus at midnight is mildly spooky, Tommy thought.

It felt like everyone had dropped off to sleep at the same time. The supervisors were still talking quietly at the front of the bus.

Faith let out a soft snore and nuzzled deeper into his chest. Tommy smiled down at her fondly.

He sighed. *My birthday's over. And what a birthday!*

After lunch, Carter had suggested they hide away in their room for a while. Tommy's lips curved up in a smile, remembering the fifteen kisses that had been pressed to them during that time. *I'm sure we lost track a couple times, so it was easily more than fifteen,* he thought.

When they'd needed a break, Carter had pulled out a little pouch from his suitcase. "I didn't know what to get you, so I thought I'd go for something silly but meaningful," he'd said. "It's a piece of rock from Oldtown High's parking lot. So, I'll be with you even when I'm at school."

Tommy had laughed and kissed him again, but looking back on it now, he felt like he wanted to cry. It was a thoughtful gift, and he would treasure it.

To stave off tears, he instead thought about the closing ceremonies. They had placed fifth, their table almost at the front of the room, and they shared with Oldtown, who had placed fourth. The pride on his sister's face when she'd beamed at him from the judge's table would have been surprising if he hadn't had the chance to get to know her better over the weekend. He had grinned back at her, his hand firmly held by Carter. Neither of them had wanted to let go, even while they'd been eating.

Stop thinking about Carter, Tommy told himself fiercely. *You don't want to wake Faith with your crying.*

He stared out the bus window at the dark trees zipping by and let his mind wander back to the ceremony again.

There had been some smaller awards as well as the main one. Oldtown had won a trophy for finishing the fastest with the correct information for the murder mystery that morning. The trophy looked like a golden DNA strand upright on a black pedestal and it was engraved on a little golden plaque with the event name and the year.

Parry Sound hadn't won anything, but they didn't mind. As Mr. Travese had told them, they had done amazingly well placing fifth in a competition that had the top fifty schools in Ontario, especially since they'd only been training for a little over a month. He'd promised that they would start training in September next year.

Tommy's heart squeezed.

Next year, he thought. *I won't see Carter in person for six months, and that's if I'm lucky enough to go to Door Tech's summer camp* and *grade ten March Break camp.*

He felt a tear trickle down his cheek and blinked back more.

The dance after the ceremony had been fun. Hotel staff had cleared away the tables and set up a DJ station with lights while the students had packed up their belongings. Tommy had changed into his black dress shirt, and Carter had worn his red one.

"You look really good in red," Tommy had said to him.

"Oh yeah? How good?" Carter had replied teasingly. Only the presence of the two older boys had kept them from falling onto the bed together again. They had danced for hours.

Ten o'clock had come, the time that Tommy had been dreading. The supervisors had collected their charges, who picked up their suitcases that had been tagged and put in storage by the hotel staff, and led them to the waiting buses.

By chance, the one heading to Parry Sound had been directly in front of the one heading to Oldtown High.

Tommy and Carter had clung to each other until Mr. Coolidge had tapped Carter on the shoulder. Tommy had stood beside his bus, watching Carter wait in line until he couldn't take it anymore.

Tommy smiled through his tears, thinking about how he had jumped on Carter, who had caught him by the thighs and held him while they kissed goodbye one last time. *"Je t'aime,"* they had whispered to each other desperately, and then Carter had to get on the bus, and so had Tommy.

He had mostly held it together while his friends had cheered him up by singing songs at the top of their lungs until he had no choice but to join in.

Bryan had switched seats with Sabrina so he could be behind Tommy for a little while. He had apologized for the alcohol thing and promised he wouldn't say anything to anyone at school, not even his sister, about Carter.

Tommy believed him. It had been a weight on his mind, but

now, with no worries, he only felt the loneliness. He sniffled and felt more tears escape.

"Hey," Faith said sleepily, sitting up. "You've got a virtual date set up for Tuesday night. You'll see him soon."

"I know." Tommy gulped back a sob, chest heaving. "It's not the same."

"I know." Faith took his hand and squeezed it. "You'll manage. We're here for you."

Tommy buried his face in her neck and breathed in shakily. Faith ran her fingers through his hair, and he shuddered. "I'm so glad I've got you as a friend."

Faith tightened her grip. "Back at you."

They fell asleep like that and didn't wake up until they pulled up to their high school just before one in the morning.

The Parry Sound group disembarked into the arms of their parents. Tommy hugged his mother tightly.

"Missed you," he whispered.

"Oh, my baby," his mother said, a catch in her throat. "I'm so proud of you. You did so well."

"It was a true team effort," Tommy said. "You need to meet the others. They're all amazing."

He exchanged smiles with his teammates. This was a long weekend that they'd never forget.

Epilogue - Carter's Letter

Dear Tommy,

I know we usually talk online, but I overheard some grade ten girls in the cafeteria talking about this project that they have to do for history class. They have to write letters between a soldier of World War II and his sweetheart at home. They used a fancy word: 'correspondence.'

Anyways, they said that it was super romantic, and they wished that their boyfriends would write them love letters like the real ones that they got to read in class.

I thought I'd try it out. Maybe you'd think it was romantic, maybe you'd think it was funny, but either way, I figured you'd enjoy it.

Here goes.

I am very much looking forward to you coming back to Westmeath in a little over a week. It feels like it's been *forever* since I saw you in person. Seeing you a couple of weeks ago in Toronto only made me miss you more. I didn't think that was possible. Thank goodness for the program Veronica put on our laptops that allows us to video call. But that's no substitute for the feeling of your arms wrapping around me, our bodies pressed against one another as we snuggle in bed.

In our pyjamas, of course. Whoo, that got heated quickly. Sorry. Guess you know where my mind is at.

But while we're on the subject, I'm really glad that you're staying with Kennedy and Jason again while you're in town. I know I won't be able to stay over on school nights, but we'll get a couple nights together before you head home again.

How often do you think you'll come to Westmeath after the wedding? I know you're going to try out for Door Tech's summer camp. Do you think your parents will let you come? A whole month of science and being together. Fingers crossed that we both get in.

But after the summer, how often will you come visit? Or maybe I'd be able to drive to Parry Sound with Kennedy and Jason for holidays, although I'm not sure how my dads would like that.

Okay, sorry, this letter got a little depressing there. I just miss you.

I want to kiss you. All over your face, but mostly your mouth. I've had dreams about kissing your lips.

Better bring Chapstick. Maybe water. Because I'm not going to let you go for hours once you get here.

Well, maybe I'll say hi to your parents before we hide away in your bedroom.

I'm glad you're looking forward to telling them about us when you get here.

We are going to have so much fun while you're here! All the parties and dinners, the ball, the wedding itself! I can't wait to spend all night dancing with you, staring into your beautiful, mesmerizing green eyes.

Maybe even sneaking off to make out in the coat check or under the stars.

Only ten days left until I see you again (as of the writing of this letter). I've been counting down for months, but these last few days feel like an eternity. On June 6th, the hours will feel like infinity.

Yours,

Carter

P.S. For my first attempt at a love letter, I think that was pretty good!

Novelette -
Knight of Everdome

♥

Carter couldn't decide where to focus his attention, the large arena where the show *Knights of Everdome* was going to take place, or Tommy, whose rapt expression made him look even more adorable than usual.

The arena won, barely, and Carter pulled out his phone to take a video so he could show Jason, his friend and self-proclaimed Everdome fanatic, when he got home. *He's going to flip!* he thought, giddy with excitement.

"Hey, everyone, let's get a picture with the arena in the background," he said, and everyone gathered behind him. Carter snapped the picture and checked to make sure he could see everyone.

Tommy, his blond hair shining in the arena's lights, was beside him. Just behind them were their friends, Elyse and Faith, their dark hair mingling as they tilted their heads together. Beyond them were the twins, Tommy's older sisters, MacKenzie and Eliza. Carter could see what Kennedy had meant about the younger siblings having similar features as the twins.

They were seated in the middle of the arena, one table back from being right up against the partition. "I think we'll have an even better view than the people in front," Carter mused. "Slightly higher up, so we won't be staring directly at a horse's ass."

Tommy chuckled, and the girls made faces. "Gross," Elyse said.

"At least *someone* appreciates my humour," Carter said, his nose in the air. He squeezed his boyfriend's hand and got one back in response. They smiled at each other.

"I'm going to guess that Pakaha Castle's colour is burgundy?" Tommy asked, looking around at the decor and tablecloths.

"You are most correct, my lord," said a young blonde woman. She was holding menus and had an apron over her burgundy dress. "Burgundy with a silver and gold crown emblem is the symbol of the central castle of Pakaha, the High-King's residence. Burgundy with a white tower emblem belongs to the Dome of Pakaha." She lifted the menus in her arms. "My name is Daria and I'm your server for tonight." She handed out the menus to each member of the group. "If you have any questions, please don't hesitate to raise your hand to call for me."

"Thank you, Daria," said MacKenzie.

Carter opened his menu, and a piece of paper fluttered to the table. He glanced at the others, who hadn't seemed to notice, and read it quickly.

You have been invited to participate in Knights of Everdome *tonight. Please select your meal and meet your server at the back of the arena for further instructions.*

Carter's jaw dropped. *What?* his brain screamed at him. He closed his mouth, hid the paper in his hand, and glanced quickly through the menu. "I'll be right back," he said, putting his menu down.

"You okay?" Tommy asked, his brow furrowing with concern.

"Yeah, I just want to make a visit. Can you tell Daria what I want to eat, please?" He pointed at each item and then got to his feet. "You won't even notice I'm gone," he teased.

"Sure I will. My hand will get cold," Tommy joked back.

Carter chuckled and quickly exited the arena. He found Daria waiting for him.

"Yes!" he said excitedly.

She smiled. "Follow me, please."

Daria led him through a large wooden door that read *Employees Only* and knocked on the first door in the blank hallway.

"Come in," said a muffled voice.

"You'll be fine from here," Daria said after opening the door and waving to the person inside. "Have fun."

Carter strode confidently into the office. He glanced over the multiple screens behind the desk showing the entryway, training court, and target area before calmly meeting the gaze of the woman in the chair. She was in her early forties, he thought, and was wearing an awful lot of makeup and expensive jewellery for a fantasy-themed dinner theatre.

"Good evening, my lady," he said, bowing low. "I received a letter from your office, I believe."

"You did indeed. After that impressive work with the knives, I would have been foolish not to invite you." The lady frowned. "You're a little younger than I thought, though. How old are you?"

"I'm fifteen. I can call my dads and get parental permission if that's a problem," he rushed to reassure her.

"No, you can sign for yourself." She held out her hand. "Pleased to meet you. I am Ms. Burt."

Carter's eyes widened. "The actual owner?" he said, his hand limp in surprise.

"You are remarkably well-informed for a fifteen-year-old," Ms. Burt replied with amusement.

"I pay attention." Carter shook her hand. "I'd like to ask my dads for permission anyways, if it's alright." At her nod, he pulled out his phone and dialled the number for the back of the store. At this time of day, the front was usually busy with last minute customers.

"Carter? Is everything alright?" the deep rumble of his father's voice greeted him.

"Everything's fine. Father, I'm at *Knights of Everdome*. Please don't tell Jason, I want to see his face when he finds out it exists! I've been chosen to participate on stage. May I? Please?"

"That sounds very exciting!" Carter could hear his father's smile in his tone. "Of course, you may. May I speak to the person in charge for a moment?"

"I'm going to pass you over to Ms. Burt." Carter handed her his phone. "This is my father, William Batudev."

"Thank you. While I've got him on the line, please read this contract and make note of any questions you might have."

Carter took a deep breath to calm his excitement and focus his mind. He didn't want to give Ms. Burt any reason to rescind the invitation.

The contract was full of safety rules and stated that he was to fight cooperatively, not actually try to injure the actor. He'd have a microphone and earpiece put on him before he entered the stage, and he was to follow the instructions exactly. It also laid out that he would not be paid for participating. *I don't care about being paid! This is so cool!* he thought.

By the time he was done, Ms. Burt was smiling and handing him the phone again.

"Yes, Father?"

"Remember to be careful, Son," his father said. "And enjoy yourself. Give our best wishes to Tommy. We look forward to hearing all about your trip when you get home."

"The problem will be to get me to shut up!" Carter said with a laugh. "Love you both!"

"Love you too, Son."

"Any questions?" Ms. Burt asked him after he'd hung up.

"None."

"Do you have any experience with stage fighting?"

"I choreographed the wrestling for my high school play and I'm a first degree black belt in Kung Fu," Carter said. "I can read fighting cues pretty well."

Ms. Burt's eyebrows had risen as he spoke.

"We really did pick well today, didn't we?" she said at last.

"Keep your language clean while on the mic, listen to your cues, and most of all, have fun!"

"I can do all that," Carter replied.

"Sign here, please." She pointed with a pen to the bottom of the page he had read.

While he was signing, a large man entered the room and had a hushed discussion with Ms. Burt. "Roger, this is Carter. He'll be the audience participant today."

Carter stood up and shook the man's hand.

Roger looked him over and grinned. "What's your weapon of choice, kid?"

"Hand to hand, staff, or throwing knives," Carter said.

"I'll let the stunt choreographer know. The important thing for you to do is listen to instructions and trust me not to hurt you." Roger patted his shoulder. "Think you can do that?"

Carter searched his face. He seemed more than competent. "I trust you. Do you trust me?"

The man roared with laughter, throwing his head back and gripping Carter's shoulder to keep his balance. "You're funny. The audience is going to love you. You wouldn't be able to land a blow on me even if you tried."

"That sounds like a challenge." Carter's eyes narrowed and he smirked. "But don't worry, I gave my word to Ms. Burt that I wouldn't hurt the actors, so you're safe. On stage."

Roger laughed again. "I look forward to our fight, my lord. Enjoy the show. I shall see you near the end." He clapped his hand across Carter's back as he left the room.

"Still excited to participate?" Ms. Burt asked.

"More than ever!"

"You should get to your seat. The show's about to begin. Good luck."

Carter returned to his seat just before the show started. "Sorry, my dads called," he said breathlessly. "They're really proud of all of us and want to wish you happy birthday, Tommy."

The lights went out, leaving them in complete darkness.

"Welcome to Castle Pakaha and the *Knights of Everdome!*" boomed the king's voice throughout the arena. "May you enjoy tonight's feasting and revelry!"

A bright flash appeared in the centre of the ring, followed by a billow of smoke, and suddenly three figures were standing in the middle of the arena, lit by spotlights.

"How did they get there?" gasped Tommy as he blinked.

"Magic!" said Carter, waving his hands dramatically. *This is going to be epic!*

The smoke settled around the feet of the figures.

"The Three Sisters," breathed Carter in awe.

The three women clasped their hands in a little circle, facing outward. One looked as if she had never seen the sun, she was so pale, and had white-blonde hair. The second was a complete contrast; Black with dark red hair. The last had no hair at all and her skin gleamed gold in the bright lights.

They started speaking in unison, their voices melding together in an ethereal harmony.

"Welcome, nobility, to an evening full of entertainment. But beware, for tonight there will once more be a betrayal of trust." The women paused and regarded the audience solemnly. "Your assistance in uncovering the traitor will be invaluable. Keep your eyes open. The traitor could be anyone."

The smoke gathered again, whirling around the three women. "Good luck!" they said. There was another brilliant flash of light, and they were gone.

The audience gasped with delight as the wooden doors opened with a bang, revealing two heralds with long trumpet-like instruments. They played a jaunty, magnificent introduction, and a man on horseback, bearing a burgundy flag with a silver and gold crown, entered between them.

"All rise for the High-King Pincas, first of his name, ruler of all Everdome!" a herald proclaimed.

Chairs scraped as the audience got to their feet. In rode the man that they had met earlier that evening. He was wearing the same crown, but he had changed into a formal tunic and had a long cloak draped over the back of the black horse he was riding. Carter let out a cheer that others in the audience echoed before they all sat down again.

King Pincas smiled and waved regally, acknowledging the audience. He rode to the middle of the arena before he addressed them.

"Welcome, my lords and ladies, to tonight's feasting and revelry! Tonight, we will crown a new king or queen of Gaulan. For those of you who have not heard, the royal family of Gaulan were tragically killed in a hunting accident last month. As there is no living heir, the position will be won tonight. Over the last month, many knights have gone through a series of gruelling challenges. The highest-ranked in each of the twelve Domes will be competing here tonight. There will be skills of agility, of precision, and of strength. This will narrow the field to six, who will face off against each other. Would you like to meet the twelve knights of Everdome?"

"YES!" roared the audience.

The king turned his horse so that he was facing the entrance and raised his right hand. "Enter the knights!"

In they rode, each one followed by a squire carrying their flag, and two pages dressed in the same colours as their knight. They were each announced by the herald, but Carter quickly lost track of who was who. He had read the books twice over since Jason had introduced them to him in September, but he hadn't bothered to remember which insignia and colours belonged to which Dome.

There was one knight for each Dome arranged around the edge of the arena. The horses stood calmly, despite the music playing over the speakers and the clapping and cheering from the audience.

Directly in front of them were knights in black and in royal blue.

"The Frozen Wastes and Abrasax," whispered Eliza to the

group as she pointed at each knight. "The horses are trained to hit their marks no matter what the distractions are."

"At this rate, you're going to know more about Everdome than Jason!" Tommy exclaimed.

Eliza chuckled. "I doubt it. I know a lot about the year 1285 Post-Cataclysm and about the colours of each Dome, but that's pretty much it."

King Pincas had walked his horse to the dais opposite the entrance and was now standing on it. "Let the challenges and feasting begin!" he said regally.

Carter could smell the food as it arrived and his stomach rumbled, but before he could look for their server, the knights had started moving again. They split, half moving to each end of the arena, as three long bars lowered from the ceiling with golden rings hanging from ribbons at intervals. Two knights from each side raced across the arena with lances, trying to catch all three rings.

"They're going to crash!" squeaked Faith.

The horses kept to their lanes and didn't crash. Once they had finished their pass, the next four had their turn, and then the last four. The rings were counted, and the totals put up on the large scoreboard that had been moved into place under the dais. Abrasax had three, but the Frozen Wastes only had one.

Their food arrived while they watched the scores go up and they dug into their chicken with gusto.

"Oh, they've dismounted," pouted Faith.

"Don't worry, you'll see the horses again," said Eliza. "It's easier to avoid accidents in archery if the knights aren't mounted."

Two targets were set up at each end and the knights faced off back-to-back. Their pages were with them, handing them arrows. The man in the royal blue of Abrasax was smiling and teasing both the knight beside him and his page, who kept blushing. Every time the page blushed, the knight roared with laughter. Carter smiled to himself; this was Roger, the knight he'd be fighting at the end. He had impressive skills; each of his three arrows were close to or in the centre of the bullseye.

The knight beside him was not faring as well. All of his arrows had hit the target, but only barely. He was wearing emerald green.

I wonder which Dome that is? Carter thought. *He shouldn't be letting the teasing get to him.*

The knights switched out, the emerald green one angrily throwing his bow halfway across the sand for his page to collect as he stalked toward the waiting area.

The orange knight had shot her arrows quickly, a cluster in the centre of her target, and was watching the other knights. Each time one shot, she would make a theatrical arm movement, and Carter could see the target shifting slightly to give the knight a better score.

While he knew that magic existed, it seemed unlikely that it would be used so obviously in a dinner theatre show.

This must be a trick with remote-controlled targets. The spotlights added credence to that theory. *What is she up to? How would helping other knights score better help her?* He decided to keep an eye on her. She didn't seem like a traitor, not if she was helping others to win, but he was curious to know her end goal.

The knights switched out again, all with much higher scores than if the orange knight hadn't been helping them.

The last group had a dark green knight who walked on, practically ignored his page except to grab the arrows, and walked off. He looked like he had better things to do than be there.

I hope that's part of the show, Carter thought.

When the scores were tallied, the orange knight was at the top of the leader board, followed closely by the royal blue knight. She looked focussed and determined, while he grinned and waved at the crowd cheerfully. The emerald green knight was at the bottom of the list, and he was sulking in a corner.

Next was a spear-throwing contest. Two bales of hay were set up at each end of the arena. The knights had one chance each to embed their spear into the hay.

Carter kept a close eye on the orange knight. She was focussing her helpful attention on the knights in silver, red, and purple. Each of their haystacks moved slightly closer to the knight. He was interested to see that her targets didn't shift, so she didn't need any help herself to win.

Only seven knights managed to throw their spears into the hay; royal blue, orange, dark green, cream, and the three that orange had helped.

Maybe she has some sort of alliance with them?

"Thank you to all the knights who have participated in the challenges thus far!" said King Pincas. He was standing on the dais again, his arms outstretched. "We have been well entertained!"

There were cheers from the audience.

"I have the pleasure of announcing the six knights who will be moving forward in the contests." A herald handed him a piece of paper. "When I call your Dome, please step forward. Abrasax!"

The knights had formed a line facing the king in the centre of the arena. The royal blue knight stepped out of the line to smile and wave at the audience.

"Ohana!" The purple knight looked surprised as she took a step forward.

"Raini!" The silver knight calmly stepped out of the line.

"Ruby Isles!" The red knight stumbled a bit as she joined the other knights.

"Sartorna!" The dark green knight robotically stepped forward, his nose in the air.

"And last but not least, Wild Nations!" The orange knight quietly joined the rest of the knights.

"Your scores will be wiped clean for this next portion of the contest. Now, you will face each other in a joust! Please attend to your horses and ready yourselves."

At the clear dismissal, all the knights but one turned to leave. The emerald green knight fell to his knees in supplication. "Please, King Pincas, I must get through! You—"

He was cut off by soldiers in the burgundy of Castle Pakaha

picking him up off the ground. "No! You don't understand! I must compete! Please! Don't do this!" His cries grew louder and more desperate until he was out of sight.

The king cleared his throat. "While we wait for the knights, the horse trainers have informed me that they've been working on a horse ballet. Would you like to see it?"

"Yes!" shouted the audience.

"Very good." The king clapped his hands and the wooden doors opened, admitting six horses ridden by knights wearing Pakaha livery.

"Ooh, they've put in the newbies," Eliza said excitedly. She pointed out the last two horses that had entered. "We just got them a month ago."

The horses pranced around the arena in perfect time, executing little tricks in perfect synchronicity. The audience was riveted.

The second act, and the dessert course, started as soon as the horses left the arena. Pages entered the arena, carrying long barriers that they set up in the centre. The red and dark green knights entered, the red walking her horse slowly to the other side while the dark green knight waited, his horse impatiently stamping at the entrance.

The pages handed their knights their lances; the knights closed their visors and readied their shields. A squire in a different coloured uniform raised a flag in the middle of the arena. It dropped, and the squire booked it for the edge as the knights thundered toward each other.

The resulting crash echoed in the silent arena, and the red knight tumbled off her horse, rolling away from its hooves. The dark green knight rode once around the arena in a victory lap, coming to a stop in front of the king, who nodded in acknowledgment of the win. The knight inclined his head slightly before leaving the arena. The red knight bowed and followed on foot.

"That was exciting!" said Elyse. "I can't believe we're getting to see a real joust!"

Next up were the orange and silver knights. They followed the same routine that the first pair had, except that on the first pass, neither knight was unseated. On the second pass, their lances shattered.

As they readied for a third, Eliza whispered to the group, "The king will have to declare a winner if one of them doesn't fall off their horse."

In the final pass, the silver knight was unseated, and the orange was declared the winner. Both knights bowed deeply to the king before leaving the arena.

Carter noted that the orange knight hadn't used any special trickery, that he could tell, during that round.

The last round of jousts was between the royal blue knight and the purple knight. Despite the friendly banter the blue knight was having with his pages and squire, when it came time for the joust, the knight was all business. Surprisingly, the purple knight managed to stay on her horse after the first pass, although her lance shattered. She flew through the air on the second pass and did not get up. The blue knight rode over to check on her, dismounting once he reached her. After a few seconds, he helped her to her feet to the cheers of the crowd.

The king acknowledged the victory of the blue knight.

King Pincas clapped his hands together. "With the defeat of the red, silver, and purple knights, we have three strong contenders for the throne of Gaulan. Abrasax! Sartorna! And Wild Nations!"

Pages rushed to remove the jousting barriers, while the two horses were led out of the ring. The other two knights returned to the arena on foot. The blue pages and squire assisted their knight to remove the jousting armour and handed him his sword.

"We shall now have the swordsmanship portion of the evening. The three challengers will face off against each other." At his words, the three knights sprang apart, eyeing each other warily. "Once one knight is disarmed, the other two will have the chance to change to their favoured weapon before they face off against one another. You may begin... *Now!*"

The three knights circled the middle of the arena in fighting stances.

"The men are going to attack the woman at the same time!" hissed Tommy, fists clenched tightly on the table.

The dark green knight of Sartorna scoffed at the other two, his voice carrying throughout the arena. "Neither of you stand a chance. I'm the only one who has studied fighting techniques in all the Domes. I have seen what the Wild Nations consider 'civilized' fighting; you're no match for me! And you, Abrasax, your regimented training is stiff and unyielding. I could beat you with one hand tied behind my back!"

The Abrasax knight laughed. "If you're so certain of that, why are you standing all the way over there like a coward?"

The Sartornan yelled and threw himself at the blue knight, sword flashing in the bright lights. The clang of metal on metal rang through the arena as the two knights fought, their swords sparking on every hit.

"Guess you were wrong," Carter whispered, never taking his eyes off the blue knight.

He was analyzing his fighting style the way Judy, his Sifu, had taught him. The knight was highly skilled; he used controlled attacks and parries that left little opening for his opponent. The green knight was starting to make mistakes, swinging wildly at times, and not keeping his guard up.

"The blue is toying with the green!" he gasped in realization. Then he looked around the arena. "Where'd the orange knight go?"

"They said you were a clever one," whispered a female voice in his ear. It also echoed around the arena, as an orange cloak and hood was clasped around his neck. "Keep him occupied for me. I have an errand to run." Then she disappeared.

"Carter?" whispered Tommy, mouth open with shock.

"Don't worry," Carter said. He emptied his pockets. "Keep an eye on my things, please."

On the stage, the blue knight easily disarmed the green with a flick of his wrist. "Come out, come out, wherever you are," the Abrasaxan called cheerfully. "I can't believe you ran away from a fight. What kind of queen would do such a thing? Or is that the Wild Nation's way of fighting? Find her!" he ordered guards in burgundy livery.

Several spotlights swooped over the audience as the guards walked through them. "There!" shouted one, pointing at Carter, and three guards converged on his position.

"Up you get!" said one.

They marched him down the stairs to a door to the arena. One gave him a combination microphone earpiece, which he hooked over his ear.

"Think you can disguise yourself as an audience member with your magical trickery?" said the second.

"We're smarter than you think we are," said the third.

"You're exactly as smart as I think you are," said Carter, his voice amplified by the microphone.

The audience laughed.

"Nice," said a voice in his ear. "Now walk toward the blue knight."

Carter stepped forward obediently. "I seem to have lost my sword." The audience chuckled again. "Where are these weapons we can choose from?"

"Bring forth the weaponry," proclaimed the king.

A wall of weapons on wheels was pushed out into the arena and Carter walked over to it, examining the weapons.

"Halt!" said the blue knight, striding up to Carter and looming over him. "I have watched this upstart closely throughout today's challenges, and I call foul! She's been using magic!"

Carter affected a bored expression. "I can assure you, good sir, *I* have not been using magic to help myself win any of these challenges."

The audience tittered with laughter, as did the voice in his ear.

"I saw you using magic!" the blue knight said. "Even now, you stand before me wearing a different face!"

"I cannot deny the latter," Carter said to the amusement of many. He saw the blue knight's lips twitch. "If it would please you, I shall complete a challenge right here and now to prove I am worthy," he recited after the voice in his ear.

The knight of Abrasax turned to the High-King. "I suggest she complete a knife-throwing challenge, Your Highness. If she is truly not using magic, then this will be of no issue for her."

King Pincas nodded.

Carter yawned. "If I must," he drawled.

He noticed the pages setting up a target like those they used for archery in the centre of the arena.

"How many knives would you like me to throw?"

"Five," said the blue knight. "One for each challenge."

Carter nodded. He selected the knives from the base of the wall of weapons, noting that they were like those he had seen and used in the souvenir shop. He weighed them in his hand, balanced them on a finger, and then nodded. He turned to the High-King. "With your permission, Your Highness?"

King Pincas looked surprised but smiled and gave a wave of his hand.

Carter bowed a little clumsily before turning to face the target. He took a deep breath to centre himself, tuning out all distractions. Raising his right arm, he drew back and threw the blade. It hit perfectly in the centre of the target. He smiled as the audience roared its appreciation.

"Psh, that's one throw. I doubt you could do it again!" scoffed the knight.

"I notice that there's no target for you to show your own skills," Carter retorted. He threw the second blade, and it hit the target neatly beside the first. The noise level increased.

"She's obviously using magic!" spluttered the knight.

"Alright, I'll do a called shot. You tell me where to throw the knife," Carter said.

The blue knight ordered he hit the outer ring on the right and when he succeeded at that, the outer ring at the bottom. With one knife left in his hand, Carter spun it on the tip of his finger. "Last one. Where do you want me to throw this?"

The blue knight's eyes gleamed. "Right between the first two."

Carter blew out a breath. *That's going to be challenging,* he thought.

"I'm not done," the blue knight said, interrupting his preparations. "While blindfolded!"

Carter's jaw dropped, but he got himself under control quickly. "With such a tricky shot, I don't think it should count, whether or not I manage it."

"That's up to the High-King to decide," said the knight with a smirk. "Prepare yourself to be blindfolded!"

Carter squared off against the target. "I'm ready." His heart thundered in his chest. *Will I be able to do this?* Suddenly, he remembered that this was a show. He wasn't *actually* in Ever-dome, and this wasn't a life-or-death situation. He closed his eyes and relaxed as an orange page tied a scarf over his eyes.

He took a breath, drew back, and let the knife fly. The audience exploded with noise. He opened his eyes to realize that he could see through the scarf and felt a little silly that he hadn't checked that first. He tore it off to see his fifth knife so deeply embedded in the target between the other two that it was up to the hilt.

"Oops," he said. "Want me to get that?"

The knight snapped his jaw shut. "How else could she perform that shot except through trickery?"

"Gee, I don't know, skill?" snarked Carter. "Fight me, knight to knight, and you'll see that I am not using tricks. With your permission, Your Highness," he added quickly, turning to the High-King.

"Roger is going to charge at you now," said a calm voice in his ear.

Carter bowed to the king, one eye on the knight, and saw the large man silently launch toward him.

The audience screamed a warning, but Carter was already

moving, twisting his body to the side, and grabbing the man's arm to allow his momentum to carry him over his shoulder.

The knight tucked and rolled, back up on his feet in seconds.

"Attacking me while my back is turned?" Carter said, backing up toward the weapons wall. "Tsk, tsk. And you call yourself honourable?"

The big man roared with anger, drew his sword, and rushed at Carter. Carter reached out for a weapon and found himself holding a staff, exactly the weapon he had said he was most proficient with. He smiled grimly, ducking under the first swing, and sweeping at the knight's ankles.

The knight jumped over the staff and circled Carter, putting his back to the king.

"He's going to rush you again. Let him move past you to the centre of the arena," said the voice in his ear.

The action proceeded exactly as the voice in his ear had described.

Carter turned with the motion of avoidance he had done and closed in on the knight. "I guess we'll soon see who's worthy of Gaulan's throne!" Out of the corner of his eye, he saw the target he'd thrown the knives into. All but the deeply embedded knife had been removed. *Why didn't they remove the target?*

The knight and Carter circled each other cautiously. Suddenly, the big knight attacked, his sword flashing as he rained down blows on the staff in Carter's hands. He was grateful it had metal around the middle and kept his fingers far away from the centre. One swing went a little too far to the left, and Carter swung the butt of his staff around to lightly smack the knight in the ribs. The knight's eyes widened in surprise, but he reacted as if Carter had struck him with full force. The audience cheered loudly.

"Nice hit!" cheered the voice in his ear. "But you're supposed to lose, remember?"

Carter mentally grimaced at the reminder. "Had enough, big guy? I'm just getting warmed up!"

The knight roared.

"Let him disarm you and run for the knife in the target," the voice told him.

Carter held the staff in one hand and gestured with the other. "Come on then." He lazily spun the staff around. He knew the action would look good to the audience and make him appear overconfident, so the disarm wouldn't be completely unexpected.

The knight charged at him, and Carter grabbed at the staff, but the sword swung down quickly and knocked it from his grasp.

The audience gasped in unison, and a couple people booed.

The knight smirked at him, his sword hovering around Carter's neck. "Not so cocky now, are you?"

Carter looked behind the knight and gasped in shock, making the big man turn around. Taking the chance, Carter ran for the knife in the target and yanked it free.

"Oops," said the voice in his ear. "You weren't supposed to be able to do that."

"Adrenaline can make one stronger than usual," Carter said, hoping that was enough to cover for his unusual feat of strength to the audience and actors.

"Look at the king," the voice urged.

King Pincas was on his feet. "You have been disarmed, knight of Wild Nations. Admit your defeat."

Carter bowed his head and pressed the knife between his palms. "You are correct, Your Highness. I concede defeat." Out of the corner of his eye, he saw the knight of Abrasax creeping toward him.

"Ignore the knight. Continue to bow," said the voice.

Carter kept his form relaxed despite the screams from the audience to look out. A bright flash sparked beside him, and he saw the orange knight appear from a hidden trapdoor to block the blue knight's sword.

The audience gasped and cheered.

"Go to the weapons wall," said the voice in his ear.

Carter gaped dramatically at the fight beside him and ran as the voice had instructed him.

"What is this treachery?" bellowed the blue knight, fighting off the orange knight. "Who are you?"

"I'm the true knight of the Wild Nations and, at risk of being trite, your worst nightmare." The orange knight disarmed the blue with a twist of her sword.

"You're too late. I've already won," smirked the blue knight.

The orange knight bowed to King Pincas. "Before you declare the winner, Your Highness, may I speak?"

The king inclined his head.

"I left the competition, choosing a replacement, to attend to an urgent mission. I rescued a wrongfully imprisoned knight from your dungeon. In fact, I doubt you were even aware that she was in your dungeon."

The orange knight gestured to a woman to join her. "This is a knight of Gaulan and the sole living witness to the royal family's murder."

"What folly!" scoffed the knight of Abrasax. "Why should we believe this trickster or prisoner?"

King Pincas raised his hand with a frown. "You are correct, knight of Wild Nations. I see no reason a knight of Gaulan would be imprisoned here, nor do I recall doing so. Please state your evidence, Gaulan."

"I was the advance guard of the royal family. I heard fighting from behind and rushed back to assist. When I got there..." The knight shook her head sadly. "Everyone was already dead. Then I noticed movement amidst the bodies. I hurried forward, hoping for a survivor, but instead I found a thief, his sword stained with blood of innocents! He had removed the royal ring, the symbol of the throne, from the hand of the king. He didn't notice me, and I hid amongst the bodies of my brethren. Later, when I tried to confront him, he laughed. We fought, but I lost, and he knocked me out. When I came to, I was hidden in Pakaha's dungeon."

"And who might this traitor be?" the king asked gravely.

"The knight of Abrasax," she replied, pointing at the royal blue knight.

The audience gasped as the knight backed away from his accuser.

"She's obviously lying!" the big man blustered.

"This coming from a man who was planning on attacking my replacement while he wasn't looking," scoffed the orange knight. "A lord, not a knight."

King Pincas was solemn. "You stand by these accusations?" he asked the knight of Gaulan.

"I do," she replied.

"Search his belongings!" shouted the High-King. "Search for the ring of Gaulan!"

Several burgundy soldiers appeared and made a show of searching some bags.

"I've found the ring!" shouted one, raising his fist high in the air.

"That... That was obviously planted!" shouted the Abrasax knight. "You... You're all plotting against me!"

"The testimony as well as the discovery of the ring of Gaulan in your belongings provides incontrovertible evidence. Guards, seize him! He shall be stripped of his titles and thrown in the dungeon," King Pincas ordered.

The former knight ran toward the wall of weapons, where Carter was standing.

"A sweep at his feet and a tap to the temple with the hilt of the knife you're holding," said the voice in his ear.

Carter, who had been wondering if he'd been forgotten but was enjoying his arena view immensely, reacted quickly. The big man dropped to the ground like a stone to wild applause.

"Take him away," said King Pincas. "We have a crowning to attend to."

The rest of the knights returned to the arena for the ceremony. There was an emotional moment when the emerald green knight, who had spent most of the competition angry, reunited with his sister, the knight who had been trapped in the dungeon.

The orange knight of Wild Nations was given a formal cloak of emerald green and led before High-King Pincas, who had descended from his dais, and the Three Sisters.

"Do you promise to uphold the law, to renounce any claims in Wild Nations, and to serve Gaulan with justice and righteousness?" the Sisters asked the orange knight in unison.

"I do."

"We crown thee Queen Dani of Gaulan. Long may you reign!"

"Hooray!" shouted all the knights, the audience echoing them.

"Thank you," the new queen said. "My first act as queen shall be to bestow a knighthood unto a young lord. Come forward, please."

Carter, who had been encouraged to stand among the knights, felt his jaw drop as the people in front of him stepped aside to make a pathway to the royalty. He pointed at himself disbelievingly and looked around for the real lord.

"Yes, you," Queen Dani said with a smirk. "Who else completed a challenge, who fought against a fully-fledged knight, and who stopped a murderer from getting away? Step forward, young lord."

Carter shakily walked forward, accepting handshakes and claps to his back in a daze. *I know this is just a show, but* holy crap *this is so cool!* He reached Queen Dani and dropped to one knee. "I did the best I could to make you proud, Your Majesty," he said.

"And I am. What is your name?" she asked.

"Carter."

"Very well. I dub thee Sir Carter, Knight of Gaulan and Protector of Everdome." She tapped each shoulder with the flat of her blade. "Rise, Sir Carter, and accept the livery of your office."

His orange cloak was exchanged for an emerald green one and the queen hung a medal on a silken ribbon around his neck. A squire handed her a rose.

"For you to give to a special someone," Queen Dani said with a wink.

"If you don't want to give it to someone you know, give it to someone cute," said the voice in his ear.

Carter grinned and looked into the audience, his eyes meeting Tommy's. "I know exactly who I'm going to give this to. Thank you, Your Majesty."

He bowed twice more, once to Queen Dani and High-King Pincas, and once to the Three Sisters, and was led to the exit of the arena by Dani's pages and squire amidst thunderous applause. They took back the microphone and Carter returned to his table. He presented the rose to Tommy with a bow. "For you, my lord," he whispered and the people around them applauded.

He took his seat again, blushing slightly from the attention, and focussed on the arena. The High-King and new queen were leading a procession around the oval, and the audience was clapping for them. When the last attendant had exited the arena at the end of the line, the king and queen returned.

King Pincas said, "Now we drink and dance, all courtesy of the new queen!"

Everyone in the audience laughed.

"Ah!" said Queen Dani, crossing her arms. "There's the legendary generosity of your hall!"

The king laughed. "The attendants will lead you to the ballroom. Please do not leave anything behind," the king continued. "Make merry and have a wonderful evening!" They waved and exited, the lights going dark in the entire auditorium.

A bright light flashed in the centre of the arena and the Three Sisters returned.

Still speaking in unison, the women said, "The traitor has been uncovered, the new queen of Gaulan crowned, and a lord of Gaulan has been knighted. Many thanks to you, lords and ladies, for bearing witness to this auspicious occasion! May your travels be blessed." They bowed their heads and disappeared in a flash of light and puff of smoke.

After the auditorium had cleared, and Carter had answered altogether too many questions about his brief acting stint, Eliza led the group down the back halls of the facility to the actor's common room. She'd promised to take them to the stables afterward to see the horses. She was the vet for the animals and would need to check them over for any minor injuries.

She pushed open a door. "Hello, everyone, this is the birthday boy. I believe you've already met his boyfriend, the knight who almost bested Roger?"

Loud cheers and catcalls greeted this statement, and the teenagers were pulled into the party.

Carter found himself and Tommy the centre of the crowd, birthday congratulations overlapping with chatter from the actors about how well he had performed.

A man shook his hand. "You did an excellent job of following my directions. I barely needed to speak!"

"You were my guide!" Carter said, grinning broadly. "Thanks for having my back! You gave great directions."

The man shook his head. "I still can't believe you managed to take that knife out of the target! For that matter, you sank it in there so deep that nobody else could get it out! Did you like the trick with the blindfold?"

Carter blushed. "Ah. I had closed my eyes before it was put on, so I didn't notice I could see through it until after."

The stunt coordinator's eyes widened. "You sank that blade while *actually* blindfolded? Do you want a job?"

"I'm in grade nine, and I live in Westmeath," Carter said, blushing further.

"Keep us in mind if you decide to go to post-secondary in Toronto. We have several college students among the cast. I don't think we'll ever get an audience participant like you again!" the man said.

"That's quite a compliment," Tommy said, elbowing Carter in the side when Carter couldn't think of anything to say.

"Thank you," Carter said on autopilot.

"Carter!" boomed a big voice, and suddenly Roger was there, pushing past the stunt coordinator to pick up Carter in a tight hug.

"Can't breathe!" wheezed Carter and he was released.

"He actually landed a blow on me!" Roger declared to the room. "He said he would, and he did! Good thing he knows how to stage fight, or I might have broken ribs right now!" The man laughed a big belly laugh, one hand firmly around the back of Carter's shoulders. "Love this kid!" To Tommy, he added, "You've picked a good one." He winked.

Tommy blushed and squeezed Carter's hand. "I know."

Carter felt like his heart was going to explode, and his cheeks were aching from smiling too hard.

They greeted several more actors before there was a break and he whispered to Tommy, "Want to sneak out?"

Tommy chuckled. "Are you feeling claustrophobic with so many adults fawning over you?"

"Nah, I'm used to that," Carter said with a smirk. "I'm just feeling a lot of emotions about you right now and want to express them."

Tommy ducked his head, bit his lip, and stuck his fingers through Carter's belt loops, swinging his arms a little. "You were so impressive out there. There's some 'expressing' that I'd like to do too."

"Not to interrupt," a voice behind Carter cut into their little bubble, "but they forgot to give you something."

Carter reluctantly turned to face the speaker, an old, dark-skinned man in purple wizard's robes holding a crystal-topped cane. "They've already given me plenty."

The man smiled, his wrinkled face scrunching up. He held out his free hand and opened it. Resting on his palm was a golden ring with a stylized 'G' in a crest. "This is the ring of Gaulan. Only knights bear this ring and you, Carter Batudev, have proven yourself a true knight of Everdome. Truth is never weakened by fiction, but fiction is always strengthened by truth. One truth of Everdome is that she always claims what is hers."

"Wow, thank you." Carter put the ring on his right hand. "I'm honoured." He bowed. "Love your robes, by the way."

"Thank you. They're specially made." The old man gave them a swish as he walked away.

"Now, where were we?" Carter said, turning back to Tommy.

"You know, I don't remember there being a wizard in the show," Tommy said thoughtfully. "Do you?"

"No, I don't." Carter whipped around to look for the old man but couldn't see him anywhere. "That was very odd."

"Would you like to see the horses now?" Eliza asked. "What are you looking for?"

"It's a who, actually. Is there an old man wizard in your show?" Tommy asked.

"A wizard?" Roger exclaimed, overhearing them. "The man's a myth!"

"What?"

"Yeah, on the eve of our first show, a couple people saw an old man in long robes walking around the arena. A couple more saw him with the horses. Nothing was found amiss, and the shows have gone well, so we consider him our friendly wizard Emrys, like in the books. You saw him?"

"I did. He was quite solid," Carter said. He showed the man the ring. "He gave me this. Is it from your props?"

"Let me see." Roger squinted at the inside of the ring. "All our rings have the company name engraved inside. This one is blank. It's as real as a ring from Everdome can get!" He chuckled as he walked away.

"Actors are quite the superstitious bunch, aren't they?" said Eliza. "Come on, the horses need to be checked over." She headed for the door.

"That was... really unusual," said Tommy.

"Unusual doesn't even begin to cover it," Carter agreed, staring down at the ring on his hand.

When they had finished petting each horse, they returned to the main building.

"Ready for some dancing?" MacKenzie asked.

"Definitely!" exclaimed Carter.

"Ah, there you are." All six turned to see Ms. Burt standing near the door. "I thought you might want a copy of the footage from your part in the show." She held out an envelope. "Only your part, I'm afraid. Can't give away all our secrets," she said with a smirk.

"Thank you," Carter managed to say as he took the package from her. "This is more than I thought I would get."

"I thought it would be nice for your parents to see how well you did." Ms. Burt smiled. "I was very impressed."

"Thank you," Carter said again.

"There's a letter for your parents in there as well. As you may not know, we haven't started our advertising push yet. We would like to use some of your footage in our marketing."

Carter's jaw dropped. "Um, wow. Thank you. I'll talk to my dads about it." He bowed. "I had a lot of fun and I hope that the rumours of an Everdome theme park come to fruition."

"As do I." Ms. Burt inclined her head and left.

"Wow, Carter, you're going to be a star!" Elyse teased.

"Will you still talk to us lowly commoners now that you're a knight *and* a celebrity?" Faith said with a smirk.

"Oh, stop it," Carter said, flushing.

Appendices

Door Technology's camp schedule

Monday: ice breakers and tour
Tuesday: engineering and biology
Wednesday: coding and electronics
Thursday: forces and chemistry
Friday: biotechnology and awards

STEM Competition schedule and references

Thursday afternoon: Optics
  Light and its properties (https://letstalkscience.ca/educational-resources/backgrounders/light-and-its-properties)
  Speed of light equation (https://www.chemteam.info/Electrons/LightEquations1.html)

Friday morning: Electronics
  How to build an automatic vacuum (https://www.youtube.com/watch?v=dyiG_MmUXbc)

Friday afternoon: Robotics Part 1
  Building a robot (https://moonpreneur.com/blog/build-your-own-robot/)

Saturday morning: Robotics Part 2

Saturday afternoon: Civil Engineering
  Truss bridges (https://www.instructables.com/Teach-Engineering-Truss-Bridges/)

Sunday morning: Mystery

GET TO KNOW YOU

Capo (3)

```
      Eb(C)
When I first saw you, I was looking through a window,
Eb(C)                                  Abmaj7(Fmaj7)  Eb(C)
Didn't get why I felt the way I did, I didn't              know,
Eb(C)
Then when you touched my hand,
Eb(C)            G(E)
I needed to understand...
```

Chorus:

```
Cm(Am)                Eb(C)
Ooh, I wanna get to know you,
Cm(Am)                   Eb(C)
And, ooh, I maybe want to kiss you,
   Abmaj7(Fmaj7)
I want to hold your hand,
   Abmaj7(Fmaj7)
As beside you I stand,
Cm(Am)                   Eb(C)
Ooh, you know, I think I might be—
```

```
      Eb(C)
Today I saw you moving with such lethal grace,
Eb(C)                       Abmaj7(Fmaj7)      Eb (C)
Carved open my chest just to watch my heart        race,
Eb(C)              Gm(Em)
It's like I was hit by a meteor,
Eb(C)                      G(E)
I think I'm ready to open the door...
```

Chorus

Bridge

```
C(A)                                    Eb(C)
I can almost see the lightbulb when you're learning,
C(A)                             Eb(C)
You're so bright it's almost like you're glowing,
Gm(Em)    Cm(Am)
I can't look away...
```

Chorus:

```
Ooh, I wanna get to know you,
And, ooh, I maybe want to kiss you,
I want to hold your hand,
As beside you I stand,
Ooh, you know, I am—
```

Family Tree

♥

Tommy's Family

André Lake (1920-1992) and Denise Lake, née Lance (1924)
* Lilah Lake (1946)
* Arthur Lake (1977)

André Lake (1920-1992) and Charlotte Lake, née Pelletier (1928-1974)
* William Lake (1954)
* Nancy Lake (1957)

Lilah Fairfield, née Lake (1946) and Gerard Fairfield (1946)
* Phillip Fairfield (1972)
* Eliza Fairfield (1976)
* MacKenzie Fairfield (1976)
* Kennedy Fairfield (1980)
* Thomas "Tommy" Fairfield (May 11, 1988)

Phillip Fairfield (1972) and Sarah Fairfield, née Weber (1972)
* Arthur Fairfield (2001)

Arthur Lake (1977) and Mary Lake, née Landry (1978)
* Randal Lake (1998)

Carter's Family

William Batudev (1940) and Sam Batudev (1940)
* Carter Batudev (Mar 5, 1988)

Songs in order of appearance

"I Want You" by Savage Garden
"Get To Know You" by Tommy Fairfield*
"Clocks" by Coldplay
"Survivor" by Destiny's Child
"Twinkle, Twinkle, Little Star" by Jane Taylor (nursery rhyme)
"Old MacDonald Had A Farm" by Thomas d'Urfey (nursery rhyme)
"Puff, The Magic Dragon" by Peter, Paul, and Mary
"Cartoon Heroes (Speedy Mix)" by Barbie Young
"In The Navy '99 (XXL Disaster Remix)" by CAPTAIN JACK
"Sexy Planet" by Crystal Aliens
"Circle of Life" by Elton John and Tim Rice
"I Just Can't Wait to be King" by Elton John and Tim Rice
"Hakuna Matata" by Elton John and Tim Rice
"Can You Feel The Love Tonight" by Elton John and Tim Rice
"Be Prepared" by Elton John and Tim Rice
*Artist is fictional

Spotify Playlist
www.jeneric-designs.ca/playlists/#CrushingIt

Acknowledgments

♥

First and foremost, I need to thank my husband, Éric Desmarais. Thank you for your patience and helping me with plot ideas, and especially helping with the science. Allowing me to play in your world of Everdome and essentially writing the dinner theatre plot were going above and beyond.

My sister, Lindsay Coderre, and mother, Anne Coderre, for talking me through robots and programming. It may have only been a chapter or so in the book, but without your help, it would not have been written at all. Thank you.

My music mentors. First, my dad, David Coderre, who encouraged me to try his guitar and brought me to buy my own when his proved to be too large for me to handle. You also provided the spark; I have such fond memories of you playing your guitar for us when we were little, letting us strum while you changed chords and sang. Second, Bruce Gordon, your expertise and assistance were invaluable to me. Not only did you take the song I wrote, "Get to Know You," and put chords to it, but you coached me through the first few months, giving me encouragement and pointers that helped immensely. I appreciate every second that you spent helping me through our virtual calls.

My children. Adrien Desmarais, for humouring me and pronouncing various words so that I could write them down exactly the way an eighteen-month-old would say them, and just being yourself that I could translate to the page. Arthur Fairfield is based mostly off of you. Keladry Desmarais, for being my very first fan. You were only four years old when I wrote this book, but you were an eager and attentive listener, following along and asking questions about the characters. You love them as much as I do, and that makes my heart so happy.

Tommy Liu, who let me use his name to be Kennedy's brother, and then he unexpectedly got a full book.

Tasha Kalbfleisch, for answering my million and one questions about what teenage boys were like, and LGBTQ+ experiences, and just generally reliving high school with me. I can't think of anyone else that I could ask about this stuff without being even more awkward than I already am.

My beta readers (alphabetical by first name). Daniela Neri Barberena, your science background gave you a unique perspective. I appreciate all the time you spent talking with me about this book. Fadhili Samba, your comments were super helpful and I appreciate your insight. Jamieson Wolf, I appreciate how thorough you were with your comments and didn't shy away from pointing out when things didn't work for you, and you loved it despite those flaws. Jasmine Murray-Bergquist, your enthusiasm and excitement over my book brings me such joy and is much appreciated. Sonia Carrière, you pointed out problems I didn't even know were there, which is much appreciated.

The Inkonceivables, my writer's group, to whom I read the entire book over the course of a year. Your comments, encouragement, and eagerness to hear more was good for my ego (and really helpful when it came to pointing out repetitive words and ableist terms!).

The cover artist, who wishes to go by pinkpiggy93, who took my cover idea and made it reality. To see this cover, which had lived inside my head for over a year, become reality is such a dream come true. I can't wait to hold it in my hands.

I would like to acknowledge that this book was written on the unceded, unsurrendered Territory of the Anishinaabe Algonquin Nation, and I pay my respects to elders both past and present.

Last but certainly not least, the entire team at Renaissance Press, from the acquisitions committee who approved the acceptance of my book, the editors who polished it up, and to most especially Nathan Fréchette who was there for me every step of the way. Thank you for taking a chance on my first solo novel. I am so honoured that you are publishing it.

About the Author

Jen Desmarais is the creator of the sex education game Blush and co-author of *Assassins! Accidental Matchmakers*. *Crushing It* is her first solo novel, and she's not entirely sure how it happened; she had a novella and a couple short story ideas and then all of a sudden it was a full-length book. Jen started learning guitar because of this book so that she could write her own music to go along with her lyrics.

Co-founder of JenEric Designs, she creates unique geeky crocheted items. Her blogs *The Travelling TARDIS* and *How I Taught My Dragon* have been nominated for the Prix Aurora Awards over 2018-2023.

She lives in Ottawa with her author husband, daughter, son, and their library of over 3000 books.

Other Works

The Gates of Westmeath
1. *Assassins! Accidental Matchmakers*

Lucky in Love
1. *Crushing It*

Short Stories
"The Summer of '95" in *The Mystery of the Dancing Lights*
"Semper Ubi Sub Ubi" in *Nothing Without Us Too*

About Renaissance

Renaissance was founded in May 2013 by a group of authors and designers who wanted to publish and market those stories which don't always fit neatly in a genre, or a niche, or a demographic. Like the happy panbibliophiles we are, we opened our submissions, with no other guideline than finding a Canadian book we would fall in love with.

Today, this is still very true; however, we've also noticed an interesting trend in what we like to publish. It turns out that we are naturally drawn to the voices of those who are members of a marginalized group, and these are the voices we want to continue to uplift.

At Renaissance, we do things differently. We are passionate about books, and we care as much about our authors enjoying the publishing process as we do about our readers enjoying a great Canadian read on the platform they prefer.

pressesrenaissancepress.ca

pressesrenaissancepress@gmail.com

Assassins! Accidental Matchmakers

Kennedy Fairfield just graduated in the class of 2002, and is now trying to find her purpose in life, or at least a job in her field. When she saves Jason Johnson, the leader of a secret Community of supernatural people called Aetherborn, from an attempted assassination, they embark on a whirlwind epic romance and adventure.

For Kennedy and Jason to discover why people are disappearing in time to save her friends, they'll have to face teleporting assassins, grumpy wizards, gossiping hags, mafia robots, and secret military groups, all in the city of Westmeath, Ontario, which has more secrets than residents.

The first book of four in The Gates of Westmeath series.

The Baker City Mysteries

A Study in Aether

Elizabeth Coderre has always known that there was something strange about her home town, Baker Ontario, but it isn't until her English teacher disappears that she starts to find out how strange. Getting through classes, killer kitten swarms, and bullies are going to be the easy parts of surviving at Sir Arthur Conan Doyle High. Elizabeth and her best friends, Jackie and Angela, are up to the challenge... they hope.

The Sign of Faust

Elizabeth Coderre solves mysteries. Magic, wizards, and killer kittens didn't stop her last semester. Now someone is trying to kill her in absurdly complicated ways, she's hearing voices, her best friends are constantly fighting despite being madly in love, and the desires of Baker City's residents are becoming reality. Can she find out who's trying to kill her and discover the source of everyone's luck, while navigating dating, concerts, school, and competing in the science Olympics? She can only wish... and you know what they say about wishes!

A Case of Synchronicity

Elizabeth Coderre loves mysteries. She's faced down deranged Hags, killer kittens, wiley Artificers, and evil Genies, all with the help of her two best friends. Now she's stuck in summer 1985, Jackie is in a coma, and Angela is quarantined. Can Elizabeth cope with her inner demons, the 80's, and a new voice in her head? Can Angela save Jackie and the entire Bytown Memorial Hospital? This is going to be the least relaxing March break, but can they solve the mystery... in time?

The Mystery of the Dancing Lights

Mysteries are Elizabeth Coderre's life, and after wizards, hags, artificers, vampires, kobolds, genies, and killer kittens, she thinks she's seen everything.

She's wrong!

And when she goes to Riding Thorpe summer camp, which is built on an old government experimental facility, she discovers that there's a lot she doesn't know.

Can she solve the mystery of the dancing lights, save her friends, and escape a time loop? Or is she cursed to relive her friends' deaths forever?

Includes a brand-new murder mystery novella by Jen Desmarais starring Kennedy Fairfield (from *Assassins! Accidental Matchmakers*) about her 1995 summer vacation in Baker.

Everdome

S.M. Ardwur's epic ten novel series and the world's biggest MMORPG is a world fractured by a magical disaster and saved from destruction by a brave king and mad wizard. It is now formed of twelve floating continents with magical domes protecting them.

For thirteen lucky contestants, when a man dressed as a knight offers them the opportunity to visit their favourite fantasy world as an immersive reality show, there's only one answer they can give: YES!

The level of impressiveness is beyond anything they can believe and some of them start to wonder why.

Abigail, James, Krista, Nicole, Richard, and Megan have to learn how to play the game and win; the fate of Everdome depends on it.

Nothing Without Us Too

ulti-genre fiction where once again, we are the stars.
Nothing Without Us Too follows the theme of *Nothing Without Us* (a 2020 Prix Aurora Award finalist), featuring more stories by authors who are disabled, d/Deaf or hard-of-hearing, Blind or visually impaired, neurodivergent, Spoonie, and/or who manage mental illness. The lived experiences of their protagonists are found across many demographics—such as race, culture, financial status, religion, gender, age, and/or sexual orientation. We want to present these stories because diversity is reality, and it belongs in literary and genre fiction.

So, whether we're being welcomed to Sensory Hell by hotel staff, witnessing a stare-down between a convenience store worker and an arrogant vampire, or unsure if our social media account is magic, these tales can teleport us elsewhere yet resonate deep within.

Murder at the World's Fair

The year is 1893, and airships cloud the skies over the bustling metropolis of Toronto. The city is set to host the world's fair thanks in no small part to the work of two fantastical inventors. The New World Exhibition is to be a celebration of cultural and technological marvels; roving automatons, clockwork contraptions, the world's biggest steam-powered paddle boat, all to be fully lit by the wonder of electricity!

On the day of the grand opening, young Norwood Quigley, aspiring journalist, photographer and scion of a world-famous airship magnate, stumbles onto the scene of a murder; the victim: a Prussian Ambassador; the perpetrator: a Chinese assassin, or so the powers-that-be say. In truth, the suspect is Jing, a roguish but amiable youthful delinquent.

Concerned by Jing's claim of innocence and his assumed guilt by higher powers, including the British Empire's military, Norwood is thrown into a grand intrigue that hinges on Toronto's world fair. As chaos consumes the celebrations, he fears that his influential family is being manipulated in a plot to create an international incident that will lead to a war that spans the world.

Mighty:
An Anthology of Disabled Superheroes

With great powerchair comes great responsibility…
It's a bird, it's a plane, it's… accessibility!
You wouldn't like me when I'm out of spoons…

All too often, superhero media depicts disability as something to overcome on the journey to becoming a hero, or as a sign of villainy. It's time to make heroism accessible for everyone.

In these 15 stories, you'll meet winged wheelchair users, supernatural spoonies, guardians with glaucoma, and many more. These disabled superheroes fight villains as well as outdated ableist stereotypes, and show that anyone can be Mighty.

www.ingramcontent.com/pod-product-compliance
Lightning Source LLC
Chambersburg PA
CBHW061144210726
48294CB00006B/1569